The
Dancing Willow Tree

Anita Ballard-Jones

BLACK DEER BOOKS
http://www.BlackDeerBooks.com
BlackDeerBooks@aol.com

Mailing address

Black Deer Books
P. O. Box 841
Henderson, N C 27536

First Edition

ISBN 10: 0-9729455-2-0
ISBN 13: 978-0-9729455-2-3

Library of Congress Control Number: 2007907021

Printed in the USA

DEDICATION

To my mother, Alice Idell Parker

ACKNOWLEDGMENTS

First and foremost, I would like to thank my Lord and Savior for his gift of creativity that allows me to write. Thanks to, Joseph Jones, my loving and supportive husband, and to our children Clarisa Jones, Steven Jones, Darlene Jones, Thomasina Hurtt, Carmena Murphy, and Michael Jones.

A special thanks to my sister and best friend Anna Jackson, without her I would be a very lonely person and to my favorite uncle and aunt, Mr. & Mrs. Leroy and Shula Davis—two people other than my parents who made the most difference in my life. I cannot forget my two loving brothers, Robert L. Parker Jr. and Leon H. Parker, who have made my life interesting.

To Adele Philips, Shardel Collins, Bedelia Hall, Kristi Williams, Annette Jamison and Joann Smith—thanks for your continued support and encouragement.

I will never forget my fans. Thank you for your letters of support and words of encouragement. Thank you for asking to revisit *Rehoboth Road*. You are my inspiration. I am praying you enjoy *The Dancing Willow Tree* and my future novels. Please continue to write me with your comments.

Also by Anita Ballard-Jones

The
Dancing Willow Tree

Chapter 1

Johnny stood at the window, placed his hands in his pockets and watched Malcolm help his father into his car. He wanted to go to Reverend Oliver; after all he was his father too. He wanted to tell him how much he loved him.

The Oliver family had attended a meeting at the home of Reverend Turner. Everyone present had listened to Reverend Oliver's confession. He had apologized to Johnny's mother, Elizabeth and admitted to Johnny that he was his father. While the other members of the Turner family had their own positions to stand behind, Johnny was torn between his love for his mother and his love for Reverend Oliver. He hated that his mother was raped and forced to wear scars that lasted most of her life, but it was this rape that resulted in his being.

Elizabeth was a wonderful mother for keeping him safe and shielding him from the harm of the evil words and deeds of others. She even switched her membership from the Concord Baptist Church to the Bethlehem Baptist Church to keep Reverend Oliver away from him. She did everything she could to keep Reverend Oliver out of his life, but then there came a time when she was simply powerless to prevent their meeting. Johnny didn't know this man until he went to school. It was there that his mother lost her power.

Reverend Oliver was a third grade teacher, but Johnny remembered when he visited his first grade classroom to see Malcolm. It was their first day at school. That day became vivid in his mind, and Johnny lifted his head and allowed his memories to flow. *Mama had just left my classroom to go to the school's cafeteria where she worked. I was a little afraid. I didn't know anyone, but I did know she would come back for me. There was a man leaning over and talking to the boy in the seat in front of me. I guess I was looking a little afraid and he asked me my name. I answered him in a voice just above a whisper.*

"Johnny Turner?" he repeated. "So yuh must be Elizabeth Turner's boy?"

"Yes sir," I whined and nodded my head.

Reverend Oliver's eyes locked on me with such a force, I felt like I was being pulled into his arms. When the hold was finally broken I turned to Malcolm and his eyes were shifting between the two of us. I dropped my head and wanted to cry.

"Johnny, the last time Ah saw yuh, you were six weeks old. Yuh don't know how good it makes me feel tuh see yuh again." He put his hand on Malcolm's shoulder. "This is my son, Malcolm. Ah hope you two will become the best of friends."

I looked at Malcolm and smiled and he turned away. Reverend Oliver turned to me and mouthed, "It's okay."

When I turned around Mama was standing at the classroom door and until this week I never understood the angry look she had on her face.

Johnny continued to stand at the window and watch as the Olivers drove away from his grandparents' home. Malcolm gave the engine more gas than the car required and the rear wheels spun wildly, kicking up dirt and gravel before snatching enough traction to grip the road's surface. He kept a somber face as he watched the car go around the bend in the road and then it was out of his sight.

All of those years Mama allowed Reverend Oliver to be close to me and in turn I grew to love him. Johnny's thoughts shut out the chatter in the room. He took a deep breath and continued to stare out the window, but his eyes were focused on the pictures his mind was painting for him. *It started that day in school and for years he was the only man in my life. All those years I didn't know Mama didn't want me to have a relationship with him. Back then, and at school, she was powerless to stop him from being with me. She could have gone to him and asked him to stay away from me, but she was a cafeteria worker and he was a teacher, and on the school grounds, and without being willing to state her reason, his position carried more weight, even more than that of a parent. I was happy, so Mama just let me be. She took her revenge in knowing she had me, the son he could never have.*

Now, how am I supposed to just stop loving this man? What he did was terrible and unforgivable, but what my grandfather did was worse. He knew Reverend Oliver was my father. Mama told him he had raped her right after I was born. He told Mama she was no longer his daughter and she and her bastard child could never come home again. Grandfather was a coward; it was easier to throw his child away than to confront the man who violated her.

Johnny turned away from the window and his grandfather was walking in his direction.

"Johnny, may Ah speak with yuh privately?" Reverend Turner spoke softly, but not as a humble man. He stood tall and waited for Johnny's eyes to meet with his.

Johnny's thoughts had made him feel edgy. His grandfather was the last person he wanted to speak with. Johnny cut his eyes at him from a slightly turned head and Reverend Turner cowed down. "Yes . . . I'll hear you," Johnny said in a strong definite tone. He followed his grandfather toward the living room, and he could see his mother, grandmother, and Aunt Sarah watching the two of them as they left the room.

Reverend Turner held the door for Johnny and as soon as he entered the room, he eased it shut until it latched. He sat in one of the lounge chairs and Johnny sat across from him in the other. Johnny knew what his grandfather wanted to say and he held his head down refusing to give him the satisfaction and respect he sought. He rested his elbows on his knees and clasped his hands in front of him.

"Johnny," Reverend Turner spoke softly. He waited for him to raise his head. He clenched his teeth and took a deep breath. Humility wasn't something he was used to experiencing. "Johnny, Ah'm seventy-two years old," he continued. "Ah can't begin tuh tell yuh how sorry Ah am. Can yuh ever forgive me?"

"Forgive you?" Johnny leaned back in his chair and crossed his leg. "Do I have a choice? I'll forgive you, because I don't want to be like you." The irony of his grandfather's request caused him to faintly chuckle; he dipped his head and shook it slightly before he continued. "You ripped this family apart. If I don't forgive you, then I'll be the one causing the rift, and I won't have that on my conscience." Johnny placed his hands on the arms of the chair and made a special attempt to remain calm and speak in a soft tone. "For years you knew the truth, but you kept hurting my mother. A long time ago she didn't care if you believed her or not. All she wanted was for you to love her, but you threw her away when I was born."

"But . . . Johnny, please." Reverend Turner sat forward and raised his hand like a child wanting to be recognized.

"No, sir, it's my turn to speak. You had your way for years. Everything had to be on your terms. Even now, you believe you can set things right before your number is up."

Johnny stood and walked to the window. He was quiet for a moment and Reverend Turner had an opportunity to squeeze a few words in, but he appeared to be afraid to speak, afraid he would be silenced again. Johnny turned and stood near the edge of the window with his back propped against the wall.

"Even before I found out about Reverend Oliver, I've wondered if you ever thought about how evil you are. You knew your daughter was raped and you threw her away. My mother was raped on Sunday, May 14, 1950, and I was born prematurely, seven months later, on December 17th; she almost died that day, and all you thought about was your image in the community."

"But … Johnny . . . yuh don't know how it was," Reverend Turner whined. He was sitting so far to the edge of his seat he could have slid to the floor.

Johnny stretched out his arm and positioned his palm outward; he frowned and cut his eyes at his grandfather. Reverend Turner pushed himself back onto his chair.

"My Lord, Grandfather, you've raped our family every day since then. You've caused more pain to this family than that single act of rape. All you had to do was share your love, but you chose to be the devil's disciple instead. You're the one who needs to confess and ask for forgiveness."

"But, I do love yuh Johnny."

"I don't love you grandfather. I don't even like you. I don't hate you either, that would've taken too much of my energy, and you don't deserve my energy. I only tolerate you for Mama and Gram'ma's sake. I can count on one hand the number of times I've been in this house. I was a man before you stopped calling me 'the boy', and I was named after you. I will respect and attend to you for the sake of the others and I hope you will understand that's all I can give you. You and I must pull our family together, so let's just say we'll have a 'harmonious relationship' when we're in their presence."

Reverend Turner stood, walked across the room and placed his hand on Johnny's shoulder. "Ah understand." His extended hand was met by a detestable glance from Johnny.

"Not yet Grandfather. We're not in the presence of others." Johnny walked across the room, opened the door as quietly as his grandfather had latched it and left the room.

Loretha hurried over to him as soon as he returned to the den. "How'd it go with yuh grandfather?" she placed her hands on his arm and looked up at him hoping for the right answer.

"I need time Gram'ma.

"He ain't got much time, Johnny."

Johnny smiled and kissed her on her head. "I'll try harder."

"Somehow Ah know yuh will," Loretha whispered as she placed her praying hands gently against her lips.

* * *

Thea only looked back at Owen one time when she climbed in the back seat of Malcolm's car. "Are yuh leavin' me?" His words played over and over in her mind. She rested her head on the back of the seat and closed her eyes as Malcolm drove from the driveway. The humming of the car was soothing enough to allow her to relax after a day that had not begun with her usual morning smile. On that Sunday morning she awoke with the ray of sunlight that made her believe it was going to be a wonderful day. Just as wonderful as the Saturday before, or the Friday, or any other day in her life with Reverend Owen Oliver. Thirty-seven years of marriage, a beautiful marriage, but one that coincided with a criminal act, the theft of a child's innocence, and later, eventually leading to the corrosion of the soul of a family.

Malcolm and his wife, Theresa spoke quietly, their voices harmonized with the monotone sounds of the engine. Thea believed herself to be fortunate because they were engaged in a pastime chit-chat other than attending to her. She kept her eyes closed, and pushed her tears inward to be reabsorbed by her system. Her chest ached as she took shallow breaths of air, because deep breaths might cause her to quiver when she inhaled and that would make a frightening sound.

Thea didn't think of what she would do about Owen, her immediate fear was the shock to her way of life. She knew time and prayer would ease her suffering and give her guidance. She didn't want to think about her husband, she was too hurt and angry to even pray for him. *Later,* she thought. *Later . . . I'll pray for him later, but not now. He doesn't deserve my attention . . . not even in prayer . . . not yet . . . not at this time.* But thoughts of him were all around her, invading her, haunting her. She wanted to scream and blast them away. Make him a blank slate in her mind. Erase him from any and all things associated with her. All the good and loving qualities she believed Owen possessed were painfully questionable. He was no longer the man she knew.

Her thoughts were continuously invaded by the events of that one day. She thought back to early that morning. *The brightness of the new day's sun had shone through my bedroom window, welcoming me tuh another one of God's gifts. Ah stretched and began tuh smile before noticing Owen sittin' in my bedside chair waitin' for me tuh awake. He looked so frightened and that concerned me. He stole my mornin' smile and didn't give me an opportunity tuh say my sunrise prayer. He told me he was the man that raped Elizabeth Turner. A bolt of pain shot through me and made my heart pound like it was going tuh leave my chest. Tears poured from my eyes and painful screams escaped my lips. "Get out! Get out! Get out of the room!" Ah yelled and slammed my fist against my bed covers before easing back and crying a jerking, pillow soaking cry.* Thea rocked her head on the back seat of Malcolm's car and when tears rolled down her cheek she quickly captured them in her handkerchief.

* * *

"Okay Mama. We're home." Malcolm opened the car door and assisted her out before opening the trunk to get her suitcase. His voice and actions were a welcome pull from her plaguing thoughts

"Come Mother. Ah'll take yuh tuh yuh room. Yuh must be tired." Theresa spoke softly because she was just as weary.

Thea turned away from the sadness in her daughter-in-law's eyes. She didn't want Theresa to be sad. It was okay if she was tired, but not sad. Her beautiful bright eyes and brown complexion could not cover the fatigue and dismay she was experiencing.

It was 9:15, almost her bedtime, and Thea was happy to seclude herself in the bedroom. She couldn't bear Theresa's sympathetic glances anymore than she wanted the confusion of Owen's presence in her mind. She believed a shower and a good cry would help silence his words and pleas for forgiveness.

"Unthinkable," she whispered, just as she sat at the vanity table and closed her eyes. Impulsively, her fingertips began to massage her forehead and temples. Her thoughts were so noisy she almost believed she was speaking aloud. *How could Owen ask for my forgiveness? Oh Lord, help me find peace. Take Owen from my mind. Remove my confusion. Ah have tuh pray on this and maybe time will soften the sharp, jagged edges, but it's unthinkable for him tuh believe Ah could forgive him so effortlessly. Lord, please give me a sign to guide me.*

She glanced at herself in the mirror and was startled. Her fifty-nine year old caramel colored skin seemed pale and droopy, making her look like a walnut. Her lips held a tight frown and raccoon rings circled her reddened eyes. Disappointment and betrayal had begun to take its toll in just one day. She threw her towel over the mirror, brushed and braided her long, gray streaked hair from habit, before walking toward the bed and kneeling to say her prayers. She asked the Lord for strength, understanding, and guidance. Her emotions swelled again. Tears flooded her closed eyes, and rolled down her cheeks. Her heart ached and her lips pinched into a tight knot. She labored as she tried to hold back breaths of air necessary to subdue the agonizing sounds of her response to betrayal. She cried a whisper of sobs, quiet sobs so as not to summon Malcolm and Theresa. She wanted to pray but her rambling thoughts of Owen pushed her praying aside, only allowing her to call on the Lord. Her comfort coming from knowing He knew her misery and would soothe her pain and allow her the comfort of peace.

* * *

Johnny could return his rental car in Macon. He had an 8:00 a.m. flight out of Atlanta and instead of leaving early the next morning, he decided to ride back with Sarah and stay overnight at a motel near the airport. He knew he and Sarah could never make up for lost time, but they had to start somewhere.

Sarah suggested they leave for Atlanta around 9:00 p.m. and that was a perfect time. He was tired and wanted to spend time at MaDear's cottage. It was 5:00 p.m. and Nat and his mother were ready to return home. Johnny's car was parked in their driveway and he planned to take the ride up Rehoboth Road with them.

Nathaniel and Johnny stood close and watched Reverend Turner hug Elizabeth again, for the second time that day, but those two hugs could never make up for the lifetime of emptiness she had experienced

Loretha went to Nat. "Thank you for being a wonderful husband to my daughter." She held to his shoulders, stood on her tip toes and kissed his right cheek. "Ah love yuh as much as 'Lizabeth."

"Ah love yuh too Mother," Nat replied. He bent forward and gave her a gentle hug.

Loretha turned to Johnny, and he bent down to keep her from stretching to wrap her arms around him. They embraced. "Ah miss yuh so much when yuh not here," she whined. "When yuh coming home again?"

"As soon as I can Gram'ma, and the next time I come, I hope Julia can come with me."

"Ah'd like that."

Johnny kissed his grandmother and looked up and saw his mother standing beside Nat. He shifted his eyes and his grandfather was standing back watching him. He kissed his grandmother again. "Now don't forget, I'll see you later Gram'ma. Sarah and I are leaving together later this evening."

"Oh thank yuh Johnny," Loretha said. "Ah always worry about Sarah driving those dark roads at night."

* * *

It was only a mile between Johnny's parents and his grandparents' home, but in that time Nathaniel and Elizabeth understood his need to continue his relationship with Reverend Oliver. Elizabeth explained that she no longer hated Reverend Oliver, but she didn't care how much he was hurting. "Johnny . . . Nat and I understand if yuh want tuh continue yuh relationship with him. All we ask is that yuh keep him separated from us."

"Thank you for understanding. Now let me get my hugs," Johnny said. "Ya know I'll be leaving this evening when Sarah calls. I'll call you tomorrow."

Elizabeth kissed Johnny. "Ah worry about yuh every time yuh out on that road."

"Mama, you sound just like Gram'ma. If you only knew how much I travel."

"Man, yuh always gonna be a little boy tuh yuh mama. Just have a safe trip," Nat said as he shook Johnny's hand.

They both watched Johnny walk to his car and start the engine before entering their house. Johnny drove to the end of the driveway and stopped. He turned his head slightly to the right and glanced down Collin's road toward MaDear's cottage. The headrest supported his head and he closed his eyes, *help me Lord,* he thought. He turned, glancing left toward Rehoboth Road and he thought about Reverend Oliver and his mother; *I've absorbed Reverend Oliver's pain and misery, and it drained me. I want to go to him; be there with him because I believe he's alone when he needs someone.* He lowered his head and massaged his brows with his fingertips. *He's my father. Oh Lord, how can I be ungrateful for being in the world you created? I am forever thankful. Had that event never happened, I wouldn't have existed.*

But, no one was with my mother when she was suffering. He lifted his head, turned right and drove down the road toward MaDear's cottage.

Johnny pulled up into the circular driveway and watched the sun drift behind his magic cottage. It took him back to his early years. He shut off the engine and before he knew it, he was resting against the front grill. It was amazing that during that special moment his boyhood home appeared as if it wore a halo at sundown. He remembered MaDear standing behind the screen door ready to greet him when he returned from school and his mind placed him in that moment in time, where he wanted to be.

I jumped off my bike and snatched up my books from the basket in the front. "MaDear, Ah'm home!"

MaDear opened the screen door and walked out on the porch and greeted me with a smile. "How's my boy?"

I hurried up the porch steps and wrapped my arms around her; she'd give me a hug and we'd sit on the porch swing.

"Ah love yuh Boy. Ah love yuh mama too. The Lord knew my heart was aching with loneliness when he brought yuh mama tuh me, and when she put yuh in my arms, Ah felt weak all over. Boy . . . yuh were only a week old. Yuh are my purpose for livin'."

I rested my head against MaDear's shoulder and gently pushed the swing with my feet.

"Boy . . . Ah'm near ninety years old. My time be near."

MaDear died when I was thirteen years old. I believe the Lord said, "Come on home, your work is done."

Johnny blinked, took a deep breath and smiled. He walked up the steps and into the cottage where he knew he would find peace and contentment.

A large portrait of MaDear hung on the wall opposite her favorite reupholstered chair. Johnny had it placed there as soon as he had the cottage renovated. He needed rest, but he always believed he was closer to MaDear's spirit when he sat in her chair. He didn't just see a portrait hanging on the wall, he saw MaDear, a meaty full-figured woman, with a beautiful brown complexion that never gave away her age, except for her long snow-white hair.

MaDear's chair was as soft and spongy as when she would hold him in her arms. Johnny sat back, relaxed and thought about Sarah. *I've known Aunt Sarah all of my life. She has always been around for the important events of the family, but she'd never been a real sister to my mother or a real* aunt to me. She would hug or kiss me whenever she pleased, but turned away if I attempted to approach her. Her door of affection only opened from her side.

Just four days ago Aunt Sarah insisted on meeting me at Dulles International Airport in Northern Virginia. I knew she was lying when she said she had an appointment in Washington. I also knew she thrived on controversy. My mother and grandparents held a secret for thirty-six years. My grandfather had forced this silence on them, but he was an aging man and had suffered a major heart attack. He needed to free himself of this burden before he came that close to death again. He knew if he told Aunt Sarah it wouldn't be a secret for long. I had stopped wondering who my father was, but when Aunt Sarah told me it was Reverend Oliver, the shock was overpowering. The next day I left for Rehoboth, Georgia, in search of the truth.

* * *

The phone rang, pulling Johnny away from his dreams. It was Sarah and she was ready to leave. He arrived at his grandparents' home at the agreed time. Loretha and Reverend Turner stood on the front porch with their arms around each other. Johnny got out of the car, hugged and kissed his grandmother, then turned and extended his hand to his grandfather. They smiled at each other as they shook hands. "I'll see you the next time I'm in Rehoboth, sir."

"Thank you Johnny. Now y'all have a safe trip," Reverend Turner said.

"Ah love yuh Johnny," Loretha said. She pulled him into her embrace and whispered in his ear. "Thank you."

"I love you too, Gram'ma."

Sarah and Johnny hurried to their separate cars; they waved and drove from the circular driveway.

Chapter 2

Reverend Oliver prayed until he began to repeat himself. He tried to rest on his sofa, but his physical and emotional pain continued to punish him. He could still see Nathaniel Baker's fist coming at him like a projectile and believing because he was Elizabeth's husband, it was his duty to defend her even years later. Reverend Oliver remembered how he froze while the punches smashed into the left side of his face. He knew he could have moved, he could have ducked, he could have tried to defend himself, but he didn't. He wanted to be punished, even murdered. The fear of what his life would be like was more terrifying than he could imagine. He remembered trying to speak and the sound of his voice failed to pass his lips. Nat was enraged, his eyes were fixed and his breathing was hard. Reverend Oliver remembered how Nat pulled back his arms and threw him to the ground, cursing and screaming at him until finally releasing all of his suppressed anger. Nat didn't ask why he raped Elizabeth. He didn't ask why he intimidated her, or why he told her she could tell her father he raped her and no one would believe her. But he did remember Nat asking why he didn't leave town.

Reverend Oliver remembered thinking there was no reason to leave Rehoboth. Elizabeth was no threat to him. Even if she told her father, the good Reverend Turner would never believe he could ever do such a thing.

Reverend Oliver heard Nat say, "Hell man! This ain't even yuh home town." Nat was right, he could've taken Thea and left town. They could've returned to Columbia, South Carolina. He was cunning and capable of convincing Thea to follow him anywhere.

For the past two days Nat's words plagued him. "Ah know yuh greatest fear," Nat had said. "How could yuh do what yuh did, and stay around tuh torment Elizabeth with yuh presence all these years?"

Reverend Oliver sobbed and bellowed, "Oh Lord! Ah don't know why Ah did it. Will yuh ever forgive me? Nat gave me one week tuh leave town. Thea has left me. Ah've lost everything; Ah gotta sell the house. If Ah have tuh leave town this week Ah'm gonna lose my job and my pension. Ah have tuh give the school administration a two week notice so Ah don't lose my pension. Oh God, Ah have tuh leave the church. And Johnny . . . Lord, Johnny wouldn't even look at me. Did Ah lose him too?"

As Reverend Oliver quieted his sobbing and tried to relax, his mind took him back to Columbia, to the last Saturday in July, 1949, when he and Thea were married. She was only twenty-one years old and he twenty-three. They were married in a simple wedding at his father's church. There wasn't time for a honeymoon. He had to be in Bibb County, Georgia, to begin working as an elementary school teacher at the Booker T Washington School for Colored Children in a rural area south of Macon, Georgia. They had a week to find a place to live, but in the meantime they found shelter at a rooming house. Reverend Oliver had finished college and seminary school and he and his wife were also looking for a new church home.

Thea Oliver didn't want to leave her home and family, but she was married and her husband's wishes were more important to her than her own. The three bedroom ranch style home they rented with an option to buy was located on Rehoboth Road, in the small community of Rehoboth. Reverend and Mrs. Oliver chose the house for it's charm and because it was just two miles up the road from the Concord Baptist Church. They heard the pastor, Reverend John Turner had the ability to speak words that spiritually moved his congregation and Reverend Oliver wanted to develop his pastoral abilities under his tutelage.

A week after moving to Rehoboth, Reverend Oliver and Thea visited the Concord Baptist Church and the following week they joined. He remembered seeing Elizabeth Turner at the church. She was just fourteen years old and in her first year of high school. Her innocence and beauty had captivated him. But it wasn't just her beauty, it was her smile, and the gracious way she carried herself, he was charmed. Her smooth brown complexion, her shapely, youthful, pre-womanly curves, and clear bright innocent eyes caused him to freeze in place and he realized it was at that moment, his obsession with her began. Strange, unfamiliar emotions filled his mind and frightened him. He slammed the craziness out of his head, but he was still frozen in place. Thea took hold of his arm while she spoke with Elizabeth's mother, Loretha Turner, and it was her touch that pulled him back to reality.

Reverend Oliver remembered how he tried to attend to Thea and Mrs. Turner's conversation, but he could see the image of the beautiful child in his mind's eye. He blinked and added comments to their conversation, but her image continued to infatuate him. Finally, he had to excuse himself from the room, fearing they would discover what he was trying to hide. He was frightened by his crazy thoughts; he was an adult, and a married man, obsessed with a child. He was afraid to sit in the pulpit because he knew her beauty and charm would pull his eyes to her. He remembered hearing his inner voice telling him to leave and return to Columbia. He was a teacher and a minister of the gospel. He could teach anywhere, but a stronger voice told him to stay, that he was a man with a fervent belief in the Lord and he should pray for strength, that he should not, and would not yield to temptation.

* * *

Sarah stayed three car lengths behind Johnny's rental car. They would arrive in Macon in twenty minutes and she was so excited to have him all to herself for the drive to Atlanta. It would be the longest amount of time she spent with him in her entire life and she had no one to blame for that but herself.

There was so much pain. Her mind drifted back to the early days of her life; to a time when her logic was infiltrated with selfishness and insensitivity. *Mrs. Mitchell, the school nurse and Mr. Lacy, the high school principal, removed me from my classroom and told me my sister was sick. Ah thought she was going tuh die. It seemed like half the high school students and teachers were outside of their classrooms whispering and pointing at me. Ah was hurried intuh the back seat of Mr. Lacy's car. Ah hugged my books and neither Mrs. Mitchell nor Mr. Lacy spoke another word as they raced over tuh the hospital in Macon. Ah was terrified. Ah was too afraid tuh question or speak. By the time Mama and Daddy arrived at the hospital, Mrs. Mitchell noticed my fear and began tuh comfort me, but she never told me what was wrong with my sister. Ah had tuh hear that at the same time my parents heard it. Ah almost felt sorry for that Mr. Lacy with his switchy-britches, chicken-little-self; that feminine little man who had tuh stand up tuh my father.*

Sarah burst out laughing and shook her head. "What a trying time, but Johnny, yuh were worth all of it." She continued smiling as she kept her eyes on the car Johnny was driving. *Ah thought Daddy was going tuh hit Mr. Lacy for telling him 'Lizabeth had a baby in the girl's room at the high school. The air seemed tuh suck right out of me that day. Mrs. Mitchell held me; Ah felt dizzy and almost slid off the chair.*

"My daughter wasn't pregnant. How dare you say such a thing," Daddy yelled.

The small framed Mr. Lacy tried not tuh cower, but his eyes fluttered nervously every time my father made a sudden move. Still, he stood up tuh Daddy. "Ah resent yuh tone. Ah'm here tuh help. Ah didn't cause this problem."

"Well Ah'm here now, so you can leave." Daddy almost pushed him out of the emergency room.

Meanwhile, Mama was so emotionally weak she had to prop herself against the wall. As soon as she regained her strength she asked the hospital nurse about 'Lizabeth's condition. Finding out that she was having emergency surgery didn't help. Before Mrs. Mitchell left the hospital with Mr. Lacy, she tried to give the both of us some hope for 'Lizabeth's recovery.

Mama and I held each other, but before we could begin to pray, Daddy was glaring at me. "Who's the father?"

Ah told him Ah didn't know anything; Ah said she didn't have a boyfriend, but Daddy said Ah was her sister and Ah was supposed tuh know. He rushed up on me with his hand positioned tuh slap me, but Mama stopped him. He needed tuh slap 'Lizabeth, but she wasn't there, and Ah was. Someone had tuh be slapped.

There was so much pain and confusion from that day on. Mama was spending all her time with 'Lizabeth, but Daddy didn't have anyone. "'Lizabeth was always his favorite. Ah know things might have been different if Ah stayed closer tuh Mama. But, Ah was twelve or thirteen years old, and Ah was hurting too. Ah wanted attention and Daddy needed attention, so we clung tuh each other. Everything about 'Lizabeth was painful or associated with a painful memory. It was easier to pretend she and Johnny just didn't exist. After a while Ah felt like Ah didn't belong in their lives.

'Lizabeth almost died when Johnny was born, then she tried to commit suicide a couple of days later. It was years later before Ah found out it was because Daddy refused tuh believe she was raped. And just last week, Ah found out Daddy always knew who raped her. There was so much pain, and so many lies, Ah was afraid to love and live my own life.

A blink and a deep breath drew Sarah's fullest attention to following the rental car Johnny was driving. He turned north-east off the highway and headed toward The Master's strip mall. It was Sunday evening and every store was closed, but there were several cars parked in numbered spaces near the

Associated Rental Car Mart. Johnny followed the required procedure before dropping the car keys in the overnight drop box and then he and Sarah were together and on their way to Atlanta in her car.

* * *

It wasn't unusual for the telephone to ring at 11:00 p.m., so Loretha wasn't startled when she heard John pick up the receiver. She had just convinced herself it was all right to quiet down after an exciting day. She opened her eyes and watched John pull his legs from beneath the covers and sit up listening and questioning the caller.

"Yes, hello Reverend Lipton. Yes, we had quite a day and Ah'm happy he got yuh tuh pray with him." Reverend Turner stood and walked to the window. He turned in the direction of Reverend Oliver's home as though he could see what was going on three miles away. He heard Reverend Lipton's laden and alarming voice and he continued to stare up the dark road. "Ah don't have his son's telephone number, Ah only know they live in Jonesboro," Reverend Turner replied.

Reverend Turner listened as Reverend Lipton continued speaking.

"What is it John?" Loretha said as she sat up in bed.

Reverend Turner continued listening and he held up his hand signaling Loretha that he would tell her everything.

"Don't worry Reverend Lipton Ah'll be right there." He hung up the phone and walked over to Loretha's side of the bed. "Reverend Lipton said he was praying with Owen when he suddenly passed out. He said he called for an ambulance and they have arrived. They're going to take him tuh the hospital. He said Owen is alone and unconscious and he doesn't know how tuh get in touch with his family."

Loretha insisted he hurry and Reverend Turner was completely dressed in less than three minutes. He thought about Reverend Oliver's confession earlier that day, but put his anger and disappointment aside.

Within minutes of passing the church, Reverend Turner saw the flashing lights of the ambulance. When he pulled up in the yard he noticed the front door was open. He slammed on the brakes, shifted the car out of gear and began to hurry to the house. He was an aging man in his mid-seventies, who had suffered a major heart attack earlier that year. The excitement and activity during that moment was stressing him beyond his limits. He slowed down, took several deep breaths and rested against the trunk of the large weeping willow tree in Reverend Oliver's front yard. He remained still for several moments longer until his racing, forceful heartbeat slowed down. He could see Reverend Oliver laying on the gurney in the hall near the front door, apparently unconscious. The paramedics secured a safety belt around him and began wheeling the gurney from the house to the back of the ambulance. Reverend Lipton walked from the house behind the paramedics and turned to search for Reverend Turner after seeing his car in the driveway.

"Reverend Lipton!" Reverend Turner called out while he continued to rest under the swaying branches of the weeping willow tree. "Ah'm over here under the tree." He was still short winded and his voice was weak and choppy.

Reverend Lipton hurried over to him and placed his hand on his shoulder. "Are yuh all right John?"

"Ah'm fine," Reverend Turner took a deep breath. "Ah forgot Ah'm not a young man and Ah had tuh stop and rest." He took another deep breath and walked to the driver's side of the ambulance. Reverend Lipton was at his side. "How is he?" he asked the paramedic.

"We're not at liberty to say. We're taking him tuh the clinic first so the doctors can clear him for the trip tuh Macon. Are yuh Reverend Turner?" one of the paramedic asked.

"Ah told them you were comin'," Reverend Lipton explained. "Maybe yuh know how tuh reach his wife?"

"Ah'll do what Ah can," Reverend Turner said. "Ah believe she's visiting their son. Ah'll look for the number."

"It would be very helpful if yuh could get in touch with her. You can catch up with us at the clinic," the paramedic said as he put the ambulance in gear to pull out of the driveway.

Reverend Turner turned to Reverend Lipton and extended his hand. "Thank yuh for being here with him. Ah'll keep yuh informed, but right now Ah'm gonna try tuh find some numbers. Ah'll take it from here."

"Are yuh sure? Ah'll stay with yuh if yuh need me."

"Ah believe Ah can handle it. As soon as Ah reach his wife and son. It'll be awhile before they can get back to Macon. Ah'll wait for his family at the hospital. Thank yuh again."

Reverend Turner walked him toward his car and waved as he left the driveway. He took his time walking back toward Reverend Oliver's house. It was almost midnight and physical and emotional fatigue had taken its toll. He knew time was limited, but his whole day had been overwhelming. He took a moment, sat back in Owen's high back office chair, closed his eyes, and relaxed. The painful events of the day remained with him and were ever present in his mind. He took another deep breath and thought, *the Lord wants me to be here or he wouldn't have called me.* One more deep breath and he was ready to begin. As he searched Reverend Oliver's desk, he couldn't help thinking about when Johnny was born, a time when he didn't believe the truth, a time when his daughter needed him and he wasn't there for her. Now, he was rummaging through a desk searching for Owen's son's address or telephone number, only to find nothing.

Reverend Turner rested his head in the palms of his hands. "Oh Lord!" he cried, "Ah have sinned too. What will my penance be? Ah turned my back on Elizabeth. Whose worse, Lord? Will yuh judge my sin tuh be greater than Owen's? How am Ah gonna make it up tuh 'Lizabeth and Johnny?" His age was apparent as he stood from the chair. His body was bent at his knees, his hip joints, and his shoulders. Fatigue had done that to him; he pulled himself up and his body snapped into alignment. After testing his first steps to make sure his footing was secure, he walked from the house, then drove over to The Collins' Clinic.

Chapter 3

Sarah pulled into the parking lot of the Lexington Airport Motel and waited in the car for Johnny to check in. She watched the way he walked, the way his broad shoulders and chest filled out his tailored shirt. He was a tall man with moderate features, one of the most handsome black men she had ever seen. He possessed all of the attributes most women wanted. He was strong, intelligent, successful and independently wealthy. His sandy colored skin was smooth and free of blemishes and his neatly trimmed hair and mustache were barbershop perfect. *Johnny is a blessing. How could someone so special be the product of such a terrible crime? God . . . look at him,* she thought. *Ah wish Ah could take some of the credit for how he turned out; just turn back the years and spend more time with him. A vice president of The Legend Bank, it seems like he didn't need me. He turned out all right without my help.*

All those years ago, back then when Johnny was born, Ah was afraid of Daddy, but then Ah saw 'Lizabeth's troubles as a way of being Daddy's favorite child. While Ah was running away from 'Lizabeth's pain, Ah lost her, Johnny and myself.

Johnny returned to the car and reached in the back seat for his garment bag. "Thanks for the ride Aunt Sarah." He closed the car door and stepped forward to the driver's side window. "Thanks again for the answers. If you hadn't told me about Reverend Oliver, I guess I would've never known."

"No," Sarah said. "Thank you Johnny. Thanks for calling me 'Aunt Sarah'. Ah never thought Ah'd hear yuh call me 'Aunt'. Thank yuh for being you. Please allow me tuh be a part of yuh life, and please forgive the distance Ah put between myself, you and yuh mother."

"Aunt Sarah, you were only twelve years old when I was born."

"Yeah, but Ah wasn't always twelve years old. Ah denied myself a closeness with my only nephew and sister. Ah lost a lifetime of love and all that lost time can never be recovered."

"You're right, but we've got time. I don't believe God brought us together to pull us away from each other. We have the rest of our lives to make up for the lost time.

"Ah hope yuh right. Now, do yuh have yuh room? Do yuh need a ride tuh the airport in the mornin'?"

Johnny nodded, smiled and held up the room key. "I'm okay Aunt Sarah. Now don't you start worrying about me. I've already arranged for a car to take me to the airport. You just get home safe."

Sarah smiled, knowing she needed time to get use to the 'aunt' word. She motioned a kiss at Johnny, waved and drove off. She looked in her rear view mirror several times trying to keep him in her sight for as long as she could. *My Lord! That terrible day has haunted me during Johnny's entire life . . . during most of my life.* She pinched her fingers over her eyes. *Ah remember wanting Daddy tuh myself. Ah wasn't even sorry tuh see Daddy cry. It seemed each tear pushed 'Lizabeth farther away, and Ah could have him all tuh myself. Ah didn't care how 'Lizabeth got pregnant, even when Ah found out she was raped. Hell . . . Ah didn't even know what 'rape' meant.*

* * *

It was almost midnight when Johnny finally reached his room. He knew his wife would be waiting to hear from him, even if it meant waking her up. The telephone only rang once.

"Hello Johnny?" Julia soft voice rested on his ear like a pinch of cotton.

"Yes, it's me honey." Johnny visualized her resting on her side with the telephone to her ear. Her coal black hair brushed back and a single thick braid laying over her shoulder while she twirled the curl on the end.

"How'd it go?"

"Well, it was difficult, but we seemed to settle everything. I want you to know I didn't say anything to Malcolm. It's still hard to believe he's my brother. And you were right, no matter what happened between us as children, he was still not responsible for what his father did," Johnny said.

"I'm happy to hear you've come to terms with that."

"Reverend Oliver looked terrible, like someone beat him. The left side of his face was bruised and swollen, and his eye was blood-shot. He cried, and I almost cried. I couldn't look at him. I felt so bad for him."

"Beat him? Honey, do you think someone beat him?" Julia said.

"I don't know. I'm sure everyone noticed his face. It looked that bad, but no one asked what happened. I don't think they cared. They just wanted to hear his confession. Looking at his face and hearing his voice crackle was so hard for me."

"I understand honey," Julia whispered softly.

"Anyway . . . I'll be home tomorrow morning, around 10:30. Stan will have the limo at the airport and he'll drive me to my office. What time do you want me to meet you for lunch?"

"I'll call you as soon as the judge calls for a lunch break; probably around 12:00 noon. You know judges, they like long lunches, so we probably won't have to be back in court until 2:00 p.m."

"Okay. I'm gonna let you get some sleep. I know your client will want a well rested attorney." Johnny smiled as though Julia could see him. "Good night honey. I love you."

"I love you more," Julia said before hanging up the telephone.

* * *

At 5:30 a.m. Johnny awoke feeling revived and redirected. His airport transportation arrived an hour later. He planned to be in his Washington, DC office before 11:00 a.m. As soon as he arrived in Northern Virginia, he called his secretary from the limousine and was informed a Mrs. Loretha Turner had been trying to reach him. "She said she was your grandmother," his secretary said. "I told her I would give you the message as soon as I heard from you."

A spike of panic attacked him, but his composure held as he thanked his secretary for the message. His grandmother had never called him at his office. He fumbled with the telephone, misdialing her number twice before reaching her. "Hello Gram'ma. What's the matter? Is Mama all right?"

"Yes Johnny, everyone is all right except for Reverend Oliver. He took ill last night. Reverend Lipton was with him and called the emergency operator, then he called yuh grandfather because he couldn't find Malcolm's telephone number. It seems he fainted while praying with Reverend Lipton. Yuh grandfather has been at the hospital with him since last night. Ah believe he's still unconscious."

"Gram'ma, I was worried about him, do you think I should return to Georgia?" Johnny rested his head on the back of the seat and turned to glance out of the limo window.

"Well, Ah think yuh can wait 'til we get more information. Ah wanted yuh tuh know, but the main reason Ah called was 'cause the hospital needs tuh get in touch with Thea. Ah think she's at Malcolm's house in Jonesboro. John has been with him all night because he couldn't find Malcolm's phone number. Ah thought yuh might know where Malcolm works, and could get his home phone number. Ah need tuh reach Thea."

"I'm still in the limo and on my way to the office. I'll have my secretary look up Malcolm's job and I'll call him. I'll call you back."

"Okay Johnny."

Johnny's racing heartbeat subsided somewhat, but he was still nervous. It seemed he was at the same point on I-495 when Stan, his chauffer had to pull the car off the highway after learning the identity of his father. Stan looked back at him through the rear view mirror and Johnny knew what he was thinking.

"I'm okay Stan. I just found out my father was taken to the hospital." Johnny heard himself say 'father' to someone other than his immediate family and it felt good. While he was trying to reach his secretary, he reminded himself, if he couldn't reach Malcolm, he still couldn't tell the hospital he was available as next of kin. Other than Mrs. Oliver, he believed he was as equal to next of kin as Malcolm. But his parentage was still a secret along the rural and suburban area south of Macon, Georgia, in the small communities of Rehoboth and Victory and the other African American communities that developed with time after the Civil War.

"Yes, Mr. Turner," the secretary answered.

"Would you get me the number for Landers, Landers & Fine?"

"Yes sir, Mr. Turner."

Johnny thought about Landers, Landers & Fine Brokerage, and he remembered the favor he called in and anonymously made arrangements for Malcolm to be hired by the firm. Not to help Malcolm, his dislike for Malcolm had not subsided, but he was Reverend Oliver's son, and he felt obligated to help Reverend Oliver.

"I have the number, Mr. Turner," the secretary responded.

"Great. I'd appreciate it if you'd call the company and try to get in touch with Mr. Malcolm Oliver. He's a broker at the Atlanta branch. If you reach him, have him to call me in the limo. Tell him it's very important."

"Yes sir, Mr. Turner."

Johnny looked at the rear view mirror and met with Stan's eyes. "I'm all right Stan."

"I'm sorry, sir."

"Sorry for what Stan?"

"I wasn't trying to listen to your conversation, but sound does travel."

"I know Stan. Thank you for your concern, but I need to speak with my brother in private." He gave him a pleasant smile and closed the privacy panel.

* * *

"Johnny? It's Malcolm. Your secretary said it's important."

"Malcolm, your father is in the hospital. I need you or your mother to contact Macon General Hospital. He took ill late yesterday evening and my grandfather has been with him at the hospital all night."

There was a long silence before Johnny heard Malcolm speak.

"Is he going tuh be all right?" Malcolm whispered. His voice trembled and was laced with fear.

"I don't know man. I'm scared too. My grandmother said he was unconscious," Johnny said. "I think you should call the hospital to get an update before you call your mother."

"Okay Johnny. Thanks man. Ah'll call yuh after Ah get tuh the hospital."

* * *

Malcolm hung up the telephone and picked it up again. He dialed the number for information for Macon General Hospital and soon after he was able to reach the nurse's station.

A nurse stood at the door and called to Reverend Turner. "There's a phone call for yuh, Reverend Turner. He said he was Reverend Oliver's son."

Reverend Turner hurried to the nurse's station. He turned and watched Owen through the large window as he spoke. "Yes Malcolm. Ah was praying Ah'd hear from yuh soon."

"How's Dad? Ah haven't called Mama yet. We'll be leaving as soon as possible. Ah just got the call from Johnny."

"Listen son, he's been unconscious since late last night. The doctor won't tell me what's wrong with him because Ah'm not kin, but they asked me if Ah knew how he fractured his jawbone." Reverend Turner ran his fingers through his hair and rested his left elbow on the high ledge of the nurse's station. "They're keepin' a real close watch over him. He's in an Intensive Care Unit. There're only two beds in the room and a big window in front of each bed so they can keep a close watch over each patient. They say his condition is guarded, not critical . . . yuh'll see when yuh get here."

"Did my father have a stroke?"

"No son, but Ah think they're watchin' his pressure real close. They check it all the time," Reverend Turner replied.

"Thank yuh for being with him Reverend Turner. We'll be there as soon as possible."

"Okay Malcolm, Ah'll be waiting for yuh." Reverend Turner stretched as he handed the telephone receiver to the nurse.

* * *

Johnny held the telephone while taking time to collect his thoughts before returning his call to his grandmother. "All right Gram'ma, I was able to get Malcolm at work. I'm sure they'll handle it and Grandfather can leave as soon as they arrive."

"Thanks Johnny. Ah haven't heard from your grandfather in a while. Ah'm sure he'll call if there's any change. Ah'm gonna let yuh go. Ah don't wanna tie up the telephone."

"Okay Gram'ma, I'll talk to you later. Tell Mama I've arrived home safely."

"Sure thing Johnny. Bye now."

* * *

Nathaniel glanced at Reverend Oliver's house as he and Elizabeth drove by on their way home from work. Earlier that morning he noticed he wasn't at the teacher's meeting held for the new school year. A feeling of satisfaction stirred him. He smiled and looked down at his note pad, believing it was the first step toward his leaving town. He couldn't help thinking about him, but as the day progressed, the events of the weekend began to take its toll, plaguing him, causing him to doubt his decision, and making it difficult for him to concentrate. He had gone against his nature; he wasn't a violent man, but the state of mind he witnessed Elizabeth experiencing caused him to act contrary to his character. He remembered how Elizabeth experienced a paralyzing fear because she had withheld the truth of her rapist's identity even from him. When he thought of how much pain she had to endure over her lifetime, attacking Reverend Oliver seemed justified. Still, violence of any kind bothered him.

By mid-afternoon, he had begun to experience a mild depressive state. He only punched Reverend Oliver in the jaw twice and even then he knew it was wrong. But, early that Saturday morning his avenging emotion caused him to believe he was doing the right thing.

Nat hardly spoke to Elizabeth during their drive home from work, a drive that was usually filled with non-specific chatter about any and everything. Elizabeth asked him if something was wrong. She turned her back to the door of the car and her eyes were trying to read his expressions.

"Nothing Beth," he said. "Ah just think Ah'm a little tired. Ah feel like Ah may be comin' down with somethin'."

"Well we're almost home, and Ah want yuh tuh just relax. Ah can't have yuh gettin' sick on me."

"Ah believe a little quiet time is all Ah need. Ah'll probably be all right by dinner." He glanced at Elizabeth and gave her a tiny smile just as he turned the car into their driveway. As Nat was getting out of his car, he felt the weight of his weariness, a heaviness that made him believe he was walking toward his front door with a slouched posture even though he was walking tall.

Elizabeth got out of the car and couldn't help staring at him. "Nat, yuh so quiet. Ah really think somethin' is wrong. Ah want yuh tuh relax while Ah fix dinner, and Ah'm gonna fix yuh a glass of sherry tuh help yuh along."

Nat turned the key opening the house door and held it for Elizabeth. He placed his hat and briefcase on the hall table and made his way into the bathroom. He continued trying to convince himself that what he did to Reverend Oliver was necessary, but now he wanted to forget about him.

When he returned to the den Elizabeth was waiting near his favorite chair, with that glass of sherry. "Thanks Beth," he said. "Ah know Ah'm gonna feel better. Ah believe Ah'm just tired."

"Well, yuh need tuh rest awhile. We're gonna have leftovers tuhnight, so dinner will be ready in a few moments."

Nat watched Elizabeth walk from the room and he knew she was different. Just a few days ago he thought of her as happy and complete. He knew of the circumstances of Johnny's conception and birth, of her estrangement from her father, and the coolness of her sister Sarah's relationship toward her. But he never realized how oppressed she had been. Her posture and particulars were familiar to him. Now he sat in his chair and watched her leave the room. She seemed to float like she had a higher level of happiness, happier than he had ever known her to be. He sipped his sherry and immediately the layers of his depression began to flake away. Feeling better and more relaxed, a justification for his violence against Reverend Oliver no longer weighed him down, it happened, and that was that.

* * *

Loretha was standing at her living room window when Nat and Elizabeth drove by. It wasn't a coincidence; she was waiting to see them. Just the day before, her family had finally accepted the truth and severed their relationship with the Oliver family after what seemed like a lifetime. Reverend Oliver had captured her husband's heart the first time he met him, and if it weren't for the injury he caused her daughter, she would have also loved and admired him. Now Nat and Elizabeth were home and Loretha wanted to tell them Reverend Oliver was gravely ill and admitted to the hospital. She wanted to tell them John was called to his aid late the night before and she was worried about him. Before she could dial Elizabeth and Nat's number, her phone rang and she answered it.

"Hi Mama," Elizabeth sang out. "Have yuh heard from Johnny?"

Loretha sank deeper into her chair. She wanted to tell Elizabeth what happened, but the last two days seemed to be so liberating for her, she hated burdening her with another Owen issue. "Yes, he arrived back in DC safely. Ah spoke with him this morning. How was yuh day?"

"Ah'm fine Mama. Ah feel like a new me. Ah wanna thank yuh."

"Thank me for what?"

"For this weekend," Elizabeth said.

"Honey, thank Sarah and Johnny. They got the ball rollin', Ah just tried to include some order."

"Yuh understood what Ah was feelin' Mama."

"Honey, Ah just helped yuh tuh follow yuh heart."

"And yuh don't know how much Ah needed that."

"Okay, Ah'm gonna accept yuh gratitude."

"Mama, yuh sound different. Yuh sound like somethin' is bothering yuh. Is Daddy okay? Is somethin' wrong?"

"Well, Ah'm a little worried about yuh father. Oh, he'll be all right. Ah mean, he's not sick or anything." Loretha sat taller in the chair.

"Then what's wrong?"

Loretha knew she had to tell Elizabeth, and she selected her words carefully. She didn't want her to think her father was finished with Reverend Oliver one day and at his call the next. "Honey . . . Reverend Oliver took sick last night. He was alone. Thea left and went tuh Jonesboro with Malcolm . . ." She continued telling Elizabeth everything she knew, even though she didn't expect her to sympathize with him.

"Okay Mama," Elizabeth answered. "So what's the matter with him?"

"The doctor asked yuh father if he knew how he fractured his jawbone. They wouldn't tell him anything else because he wasn't the next of kin, but Reverend Oliver is still unconscious."

"Is he gonna be all right?"

"Ah don't know. Ah hope so. Ah had Johnny get in touch with Malcolm, so he and his mother could go tuh the hospital. Yuh father doesn't want tuh leave him, yuh know, with him being unconscious, and not able tuh speak for himself. He's waiting for them tuh get there."

"Mama, Daddy's been there since last night?"

"Yes, and Ah know he's tired. He probably got something tuh eat from the hospital's cafeteria. Ah wish he'd call so Ah'd know what's going on. Ah'd like tuh go tuh the hospital and wait for Thea, and let him come home."

"Mama, Ah'd ask Nat tuh relieve Daddy, but he hasn't been feeling well since he left school. He's resting now, Ah hope he's not comin' down with something."

"That's okay honey. Yuh really don't need tuh be worryin' 'bout Reverend Oliver's problems. He's put yuh through enough. Ah'd hope tuh think all this is still part of the bed he made . . . yuh know what Ah mean?"

"Yeah Mama, but Ah don't want yuh tuh be worried like that. Why don't yuh take my car and go tuh the hospital. Yuh might not be able tuh help, but Ah know yuh'll feel better if yuh were with Daddy, and even better, if yuh can convince Daddy tuh come home and get some rest."

"That sounds like a good idea. Yuh father took my car. His needed some work so we ain't been drivin' it much. This waiting around here is gettin' tuh me," Loretha said.

"Okay, yuh get ready and Ah'll be over in a few minutes."

* * *

"Nat!" Elizabeth called out as she returned to the den. "Ah'm going over tuh Mama's for a few minutes.

"Is everything all right?"

"Mama said Reverend Oliver is in the hospital. Daddy is with him because Thea went home with Malcolm last night." Elizabeth spoke quickly while reaching for her pocketbook and keys, and headed toward the door. "Mama wants tuh use one of our cars tuh go tuh the hospital and be with Daddy."

Oh Lord! Nat thought. He cocked his head to one side as though he hadn't heard what Elizabeth said. "What! What did yuh say? Wait . . . wait a minute Beth! Slow down! Tell me what's going on!"

Elizabeth returned to the den and stood at the entrance. She spoke slow and clear and adjusted the strap of her pocketbook over her shoulder. "Ah think Reverend Oliver is still unconscious."

"What's wrong with him?"

"Ah think it has something tuh do with that nasty looking bruise on his face, a fractured jaw or something like that. She gave Nat a smile and a tiny wave before leaving the room.

"Okay Beth," a whisk of a whisper managed to escape Nat's lips. It was like Elizabeth's words had stolen his breath. As soon as she left the house, he knew he needed another drink. The last glass of sherry lifted his depression and now he was angry. *Damn that man. He's pulling us back tuh him. Ah thought he'd leave town and we could just forget about him. He's not gonna talk when he comes around. He still has too much tuh lose. Ah just hope he doesn't die. God! Ah can't bear tuh have that on my conscience. Ah think Ah'll call the hospital and see what Ah can find out.*

"Macon General Hospital," Nat heard the operator say.

"Yes . . . ugh . . . yuh have a patient . . . ugh, Reverend Owen Oliver."

"Yes sir, are yuh kin?"

"Yes ma'am, he's my brother. Ah live in Atlanta. Ah'm comin' tuh the hospital, but Ah'm so worried. Could yuh tell me how he's doing?

"Yes sir, he's stable, and his condition has been up-graded from serious to guarded."

"Thank yuh ma'am." Nat hung up the phone and threw himself back in his chair. He picked up the wine glass, took a gulp, rolled the half filled glass in his hands while he savored the sherry; swishing it slowly around in his mouth.

The telephone rang and Nat reached to answer it. It was Reverend Turner. "Hello, Nat. Ah guess yuh heard about Reverend Oliver."

"Yes sir, Ah just heard the news."

"Ah'm looking for my wife. Have yuh seen her."

"Yes sir, Ah believe she's on her way tuh the hospital. Are yuh still there?"

"Yes, but Thea and Malcolm just came in so Ah'm fixin' tuh leave. How long has it been since Loretha left?"

"Can yuh hold on a second? Ah think Ah hear Beth and Mother pulling intuh the driveway now. Let me try tuh stop her. Ah'll be right back." Nat dropped the receiver on the chair cushion and ran toward the door with his arms waving, and yelling at the top of his voice. Elizabeth had just got out of her car and was perplexed as she watched Nat run pass her. Loretha had her right arm draped over the seat and she was looking through the rear window as she backed the car out of the driveway. The radio was playing and the car windows were up. She didn't see or hear Nat calling her. Nat ran toward Collins Road; the road Loretha would be backing the car onto. "Mother . . . Mother!" he yelled. Just as Loretha put the car in the forward gear, facing Rehoboth Road, he leaped in front of it.

Loretha slammed the brakes and yelled at Nat "What are yuh doing?" The sounds of her voice soaked into the interior upholstery of the car and fright covered her face.

Nat read her lips and vaguely heard her through the rolled-up windows. He noticed her startled appearance and only the Lord helped her slam on the breaks before she hit him. Nat slapped the hood of the car with both hands just as it came to a halt. He was taken back by Loretha's moving lips screaming at him. She paused for a moment before lowering the car window.

"It's Reverend Turner. He's on the phone. He said . . . Malcolm and Miss Thea . . . just arrived at the hospital." Nat could hardly catch his breath from running and then nearly being hit by the car. "Reverend Turner . . . said he's on his way . . . home and wanted me tuh stop yuh from leaving." He placed his hands on his knees, bent over and took a deep breath before standing tall again.

"Thank yuh Nat, but yuh got tuh be careful jumpin' out in front of me like that. Yuh could be the next one in the hospital." She backed the car up and returned to the driveway.

"Beth . . . would . . . yuh get the phone! It's yuh father." Nat still hadn't caught a good breath of air and he hoped Elizabeth could hear his weak voice. "Could yuh tell him Ah stopped yuh mother?"

Elizabeth gave Nat an affirmative wave and ran into the house. She picked up the receiver, "Hello, Daddy?"

" 'Lizabeth, did Nat stop yuh mother?"

"Yes Daddy. She's comin' tuh the phone." Additional words escaped her. She stood in her den holding the telephone and she and her father listened to each other breathing. Years of estrangement had robbed them of the ability to hold a conversation, even a short one. Elizabeth held the receiver with both hands and looked out the window, beckoning her mother to hurry. "Here she is," she said as soon as her mother reached the front door. Her hands were trembling when she handed her the phone.

"Oh John, Ah was so worried about yuh. Are yuh gonna be all right driving home. It's gonna be dark in an hour," Loretha said.

"That's why Ah'm not gonna talk now. Ah'm glad Nat caught yuh before yuh left. Hang up now so Ah can get out of here. Ah'll tell yuh everything when Ah get home," Reverend Turner said.

"All right, take yuh time and get home safe. See yuh soon," Loretha said before she hung up the receiver. She turned and sat on the seat attached to the telephone table. "Ah can't move as fast as Ah use tuh. Ah'm glad yuh stopped me."

"Mama what's going on with Reverend Oliver?"

"Yuh know 'Lizabeth, only a person like you would care. After all that man put yuh through." Loretha took deep breaths, patted Elizabeth's hand and continued, "but anyhow, Ah only know what Ah told yuh. Yuh father will tell us more when he gets home."

"Well Mama, what yuh told us is enough."

Nat was standing near Loretha craning his neck, trying to relax the stress related stiffness that had crept on him again.

Loretha stood and walked to the door. "Okay, if yuh say so," she said. "Now, which one of yuh is gonna drive me home?"

"Ah'll take yuh," Nat said.

"Are yuh all right Nat? 'Lizabeth told me yuh weren't feeling well."

"Ah think it's just the stress of going back tuh work. Summer school was one thing, but another school year tuh look forward tuh is a real stress inducer."

"Yuh shouldn't have worked this summer. Everybody needs some time off tuh rest. Yuh just can't work all the time," Loretha scolded.

"Ah been tryin' tuh tell him that Mama."

"Ah'll see yuh later. Why don't y'all come over later and hear what John can tell us."

"Ah really don't care Mama," Elizabeth said with a touch of sarcasm.

Nat wanted to say he cared, but an explanation would have been required. He just gave Elizabeth an affirmative nod, dug in his pockets for his keys, and headed toward the car.

"Ain't that somethin' 'bout Reverend Oliver? Ah wonder what happened tuh his face," Loretha said as she approached the car. "Ah sure hope he don't die."

Nat opened the car door and held it for Loretha, "Me too, Mother. Ah hope he gets better and just leaves town." He closed the door and walked to the driver's side. Just as he sat behind the wheel, the stiffness in his neck began to radiate to his mid back muscles, and a vibrating spasm grabbed him, causing a breath trapping ache. He couldn't move, couldn't put the key in the ignition, couldn't speak, and he hoped the episode would leave him before Loretha stopped talking. He was already emotionally stressed and the physical exertion from running to stop the car was causing him to experience a back spasm attack. He had experienced it before and knew his next symptoms would be the body shiver, like a person with Parkinson's disease.

"Yes, Ah agree with yuh," Loretha said. She adjusted her position in the seat, and waited for Nat to start the car. "We spent a lifetime livin' in the shadow of the crisis that man put on this family, and when we finally find a way to push him out of our lives, life finds a way tuh pull us back in. Ah'm happy Malcolm and Thea are at the hospital. Maybe we can get away from him now." Loretha was looking out the front window and not at Nat. "Ah understand why 'Lizabeth doesn't want tuh know how he's doin'. Ah guess Ah wouldn't either . . ."

"M o t h e r," Nat manages to squeeze out between the muscle spasms. "Ah'm gonna . . . have tuh . . . have Beth drive . . . yuh home. It's my back . . . it just went out." The aching spasms intensified, as Nat watched his hand show the first sign of a tremor.

Loretha gave him a startled look. "Oh Nat!" she said. "How can Ah help yuh?"

Nat threw his head against the head rack of the seat and braced himself for the full force of tremors his torso was about to experience. "Mother . . . Ah've . . . had this before." He could only watch Loretha run toward the house to get Elizabeth. His body went into a full tremor and all he could do was try to breathe as deeply as he could and hope his stiffened muscles would allow his lungs to expand and break the grip of the spasm.

Elizabeth ran to the car with Loretha close behind. "Mama, Nat's gonna be all right. He's had this before. There's nothing yuh can do. It'll pass. Yuh know 'bout his bad back. It acts up like this from time to time."

"Yuh gonna be all right, Nat?" Elizabeth asked. She squatted down between the door and the driver's seat and waited for him to give her an affirming nod. "Yuh just relax and as soon as it passes Ah'll help yuh intuh the house."

Nat gave Elizabeth a tiny affirming nod. He opened his mouth and tried to take in as much air as possible. A tear rested in the corner of each of his eyes and Elizabeth used a tissue from her pocket to blot them away.

The concern written across Loretha's face was affecting Elizabeth more than Nat's discomfort. "Nat will be okay Mama. Don't worry, he's havin' a muscle spasm. It's very painful, but thank God it'll pass soon. He just needs tuh get intuh the house tuh lay down and relax. Normally, he'd take his Valium, but he'd been drinking sherry. It'll be a few hours before he can take his medicine. An hour or two of bed rest with the heating pad and he'll be fine.

Ten minutes passed before Nat was able to walk to the house. The spasm and throbbing pain had subsided leaving him feeling weak, but he believed he could walk unassisted.

"Ah'm okay," he told Elizabeth when she offered her assistance.

"What happened Nat?" Loretha asked while concern continued to etch her face.

"No, really Mother, Ah'm okay now. Yuh know about my bad back and neck. Well, Ah probably aggravated it when Ah ran tuh the car."

"Mama, Nat was hurt playin' football when he was in college. He's lucky his spasms only last a short while and don't have him laid up for days. He'll be a little sore, but he'll be okay."

"Oh, what a day!" Loretha took a deep breath and exhaled quickly. "Okay, if yuh say he'll be all right, Ah'll believe yuh. Ah don't think Ah can take more troubles tuhday." She rubbed her fingers over her forehead and down the side of her face.

"Mama, Ah'll drive yuh home as soon as Nat makes it tuh bed."

Loretha nodded and watched Elizabeth hurry to catch up with Nat. She rested against the side of the car, and checked the time on her wrist watch. She was concerned about Nat and wanted to be home when John arrived. She wanted to know he was safe and wanted to hear about Reverend Oliver too.

Chapter 4

Thea and Malcolm walked to opposite sides of Reverend Oliver's bed. Clutching her pocketbook close to her chest, Thea's exhaustion pulled her into the chair. The muscles in her forehead pressed her skin into rows and creases that controlled her eye lids, opening them only enough to filter frightening images of Owen's motionless state, while fear stole her words. Owen's face was still swollen and discolored with a deeper, almost majestic blue-black hue. His mouth looked full, as if he were holding a wad of gum in his jaw. A plastic tube had been inserted in his nose and led to a suction bottle hanging on the wall behind his bed. Another tube coming from under the sheet, led to a plastic bag that was attached to the bed frame and was half filled with urine. Thea's hand reached for Owen's arm and her soft touch stimulated the depth of his unconsciousness causing him to lift his fingertips. She rubbed his arm and took another look at the tubes and leads connecting him to the plastic bottles and noisy beeping machines. Tears filled her lower eyelids and she blotted them with her handkerchief.

"Ah love yuh Dad," Malcolm whispered in his father's ear before rubbing his forehead. He turned away from the unbearable pain he saw in his mother's face and reached over the bedrail to gently hold his father's hand. He felt helpless. His mother was weeping and his father lay still. "Mama, Ah'm gonna see if Ah can find someone who can tell me what's wrong with Dad."

Thea nodded and continued rubbing Owen's arm. She watched the jerking movement of his chest as it rose and fell with each breath. She glanced around the room at the other bed, and at the patient who rested quietly across the dimly lit room.

"Mama," Malcolm whispered from the slightly opened door. "Mama, the doctor is here and he would like tuh speak with us. Would yuh come out here in the hall?"

Thea pushed her chair away from the bed and stood looking through the window. Malcolm was speaking with a man that stood equal to his height, at least six feet tall. Malcolm's chocolate skin tone and close cropped hair was a direct contrast to the doctor's youthful honey colored skin and straight, thick, silver gray hair and mustache. She turned and glanced back at Owen and used her handkerchief to dab at her tears as she walked toward the door.

"Hello Mrs. Oliver. I'm Dr. Parks. Your husband is resting comfortably now. Don't be alarmed because he's not conscious. We did have a very serious problem getting his blood pressure under control, but it's stable for now. That doesn't mean he's out of the woods, but his prognosis does seem promising. Now, I do have a few questions. Why don't we come across the hall to the lounge?"

Thea and Malcolm followed the doctor into the small room and sat on the sofa. Dr. Parks waited for them to be seated before he sat on the arm of one of the large chairs. The room was empty and provided the privacy the doctor needed.

"I need to ask you questions about his jaw." He paused a moment and shifted his eyes from Malcolm and Thea. "Do you know how he injured his jaw?"

"Well," Thea was first to speak. She held her pocketbook upright on her lap and rested both hands over the top. "He said he fell on the porch steps and banged his face intuh the banister post. Ah didn't see him fall and didn't notice the swelling in his face until Ah woke up Saturday morning."

"You said he hit his face on the banister post?" Dr. Parks held his head down, looked at the floor, and fumbled with a pen in the breast pocket of his white medical coat.

"Yes." Thea said as her eyes met with Malcolm's.

"What's the matter? That's what he told me too," Malcolm said as he sat at attention on the sofa.

"Well you see Mrs. Oliver. If your husband fell, that would explain one of the fractures, but he has two fractures. Tell me the size of this banister post. Does it have a broad area that's about two or three inches wide? You see, your husband has a fracture in the upper jaw near his eye socket." Dr. Parks touched the area on his own face near his eye socket and close to his nose, before moving his hand. "And he has another fracture about here in the lower side jaw." He touched the side of his face near his chin.

Thea's face frowned with concern. "Well, the ball on the post is about the size of a baseball."

"Well, it's not just the size of the ball, it's the location of the fractures," Dr. Parks said as he slipped his hands in his pockets. "I don't believe Reverend Oliver fell against a banister post. If he did, that may account for one fracture, but it doesn't explain how he received the second one. I believe his injuries are the result of an assault."

"An assault?" Malcolm said. "But who?"

Thea's hand covered her mouth. "Owen said he fell." She pushed her hands up to cover her eyes as if she had a secret to hide.

Malcolm and Thea glanced at each other and back at the doctor without saying anything.

Dr. Parks placed one hand in his pocket leaving his thumbs sticking out and used his other hand to smooth out the mixed gray whiskers of his beard. "Well . . . I just wanted you to know what I believe. You know I'll have to make a police report and there'll be an investigation."

Malcolm and Thea nodded their heads, they understood, but reluctantly agreed with him. They were old school and never would involve the police until they had a chance to speak with Owen.

"Now, let's move on." Dr. Parks continued placing his other hand in his pocket. "Reverend Oliver was unconscious when he came in, but he did come around. As I said, we managed to stabilize his blood pressure, we also decided it was best to sedate him, so we could wire his jaw. His medical records revealed a long history of hypertension. With his history, his injuries didn't have to be the contributing factor for his elevated pressure, but it's my opinion, because he didn't receive medical attention soon after what you said was an accident, his body went into crisis, and as a result his pressure increased."

Thea held tight to Malcolm's hand and gave the doctor her attention. "Will my husband be all right?"

"If he remains stable, I believe so."

Thea didn't want to ask what would happen if he didn't remain stable. Her hand moved up Malcolm's arm and she held him tighter.

"Dr. Parks, how long will he remain asleep?" Malcolm asked. He gave his mother's hand a comforting squeeze, assuring her everything was going to be all right.

"We plan to keep him sedated until tomorrow morning. I suggest you go home and come back then. We'll call you if he takes a turn for the worse."

Thea flinched, her heart raced, and fear registered in her eyes. Malcolm placed his arm around her. "Now Mama, the doctor didn't say Dad would take a turn for the worse. He's just sayin' should it happen, he'll call. Ah really believe he thinks Dad will be okay.

"Yes, Mrs. Oliver, he's doing as well as can be expected. Go home, get some rest and come back in the morning. We're going to take good care of him."

"Thank yuh Dr. Parks." Malcolm stood and shook his hand.

Thea and Malcolm returned to Reverend Oliver's bedside. Thea glanced at the two beds and the large window in front of each that separated them from the nurse's station. It made her feel better knowing Owen would be closely monitored. She kissed his forehead and told him she would return in the morning. She looked up at Malcolm, and he led her from the room.

* * *

Malcolm could feel the rigidity in his mother's body as he assisted her into the car. Her stress was alarming, her emotions were stretched as thin as a veil. He needed to get her home where she could rest in her own bed and hopefully get a good night's sleep. He prayed his father would be awake when they arrived at the hospital in the morning. His mother needed to see his eyes, and then she would know he was okay.

Malcolm wanted to ask Dr. Parks why he would notify the police without first speaking with his father. *I wonder if he thinks Dad won't make it through the night and he doesn't want to tell us. Why else would he call the police?* He quivered when he took in his next breath and immediately turned to look at his mother before exhaling. She had her head back on the seat and her eyes were closed. Slowly he exhaled the air he was holding in his lungs as his cheeks ballooned outward.

The turn off to Rehoboth Road was a welcome sight; it was around 9:30 p.m. and Malcolm and Thea were exhausted. He had promised Johnny he would call him, but he had to wait until he was sure his mother was asleep. He didn't want to upset her with a reminder that Johnny was his brother. His mother always liked Johnny and he wondered if that had changed since she found out he was her husband's other son.

It was so late and he had not spoken with Johnny since early that morning. "Mama, Ah promised Reverend Turner Ah'd keep him informed. While yuh get ready for bed Ah'll call him."

"They've been good tuh us. Yuh know, Ah know they knew what yuh father did all these years. Ah been givin' it a lot of thought, and Ah know they loved yuh father. Ah guess Reverend Turner loved him more than he loved his own daughter. Ah don't know how that was possible," Thea said.

Malcolm was surprised his mother wanted to hold a conversation after the intense conditions she had to endure during the past two days. She hardly said a word during the long drive to the hospital. She was even quiet during the half hour drive back to her home. Now she seemed revitalized, or she simply had time to think and wanted to talk.

"Mama, Reverend Turner knew all along? Ah don't believe he loved Dad more than his own daughter. Ah always respected Reverend Turner, but Mama, Ah believed he did what he did, or didn't do what he should've, because he was a coward."

"A coward? Ah just don't understand none of that kinda stuff," Thea said, her voice trailing off.

"Ah know Mama, but Dad was a thief and a coward too."

"Malcolm!" Thea said. Her tone was harsh and defensive. She stopped and turned around with a jerk of sarcasm. "How can yuh speak of yuh father like that?"

"Mama, it's all right for yuh tuh be angry and hurt, but Ah can't feel that way? Think about it. If yuh think what Dad did was okay, why did yuh leave him? Yuh wouldn't be here now if he wasn't in the hospital. Ah love Dad, but he was wrong, and he's been wrong all these years. He hurt one person and that hurt spread and hurt all of us." Malcolm went to his mother and put his arms around her. "Mama, Ah believe the reason he's in the hospital is a direct result of the years of pain. Pain and hurt never really goes away, scars and old wounds always remain; it festers and it's gonna be there when he's well again. Mama, if yuh only knew how much Ah've been hurt by what Dad did."

"Hurt? Malcolm, how were yuh hurt? Yuh just found out about all this."

"There are things in my life yuh don't know about."

"What things Malcolm?"

"Johnny for one, Mama . . . Ah was drawn tuh Johnny like a magnet is drawn tuh metal. At first Ah was jealous of him. Dad used to like him so much, but then it was more than that . . . he was all Ah could think about and Ah didn't know why. Ah use tuh agitate him. Ah tried tuh make him fight with me, but he pulled away. Maybe if Ah was nice, Ah could've had a friend so close, we would've been like brothers. Ah was so afraid of his pull. Mama, Ah thought Ah was gay. Why else would Ah have such an attraction that lasted my entire life? Even tuhday Ah can't stop thinkin' about him. Ah know if Dad didn't rape Miss Elizabeth, Johnny wouldn't be here and Ah wouldn't have all these mixed up feelings. But Ah'm happy Johnny does exist and all these years of not knowing were worth it, but Ah would've given almost anything tuh know."

"Ah'm sorry Malcolm." Thea closed her eyes, placed her fingertips against her temples and massaged her head in a circular motion. "Ah need rest and Ah need more time tuh pray on all this. Ah left this house with you and Theresa to think. Ah'm angry and hurt. Ah wanted tuh leave yuh father and for my remainin' years, Ah thought Ah'd make a new life for myself. Ah still don't know what Ah'm gonna do. Ah'm here now because Ah need to be, but Ah don't know if I'll be stayin' in Rehoboth. Maybe, Ah'll be going back tuh Columbia." Thea rambled on, her voice quiet and conflicting. One minute she was defending Owen and the next she wanted to be as far away from him as she could. She could speak against him, but no one else had that right, not even Malcolm, at least until her cloudy world regained its clarity.

* * *

Malcolm prepared a glass of warm milk for his mother and kissed her good night before leaving her bedroom. He went into the den and dialed the Turner home. "Good evening Reverend Turner. Dad's condition hasn't changed, but Ah want tuh thank yuh for being with him."

"Thank yuh Malcolm, but the doctor never discussed yuh father's condition with me. Yuh see, Ah wasn't his next of kin."

"Ah see. Well sir, Dad's blood pressure was very high and he has two fractures in his jaw. Mama told the doctor, Dad said he fell on the porch. Ah really think the doctor is more concerned about his blood pressure, because he's keeping Dad sedated at least until tomorrow morning."

"Ah understand," Reverend Turner said.

"Sir . . . Ah promised Johnny Ah'd call with an update. That was this morning. Do yuh think yuh could call and fill him in? Could yuh tell him Ah'll call after we get tuh the hospital tomorrow morning and give him another update?"

* * *

"Okay Malcolm," Reverend Turner said. He used his handkerchief and blotted his forehead just as he placed the receiver in its cradle.

"Loretha!" Reverend Turner called her with a voice so startling she rushed into the den out of breath.

"What is it John? What's the matter? Is Owen all right?"

"Owen's all right!" He waved his hand in a downward motion to calm her. "Owen's all right," he said in a calmer voice. "Ah'm sorry Ah scared yuh. Ah just need yuh tuh do something for me."

"My goodness . . . John, did yuh have tuh yell like that? It's late and Ah'm tuh old for this." She placed her left hand on her hip while her right was busy wavy in the air. "Jeepers, John," she sang out, "don't do that again. Yuh nearly scare me tuh death."

"Ah'm sorry," Reverend Turner apologized again. "Could yuh do me a favor?"

"A favor? After yuh nearly gave me a heart attack . . . yuh need a favor?" She eased herself into a nearby chair and used her hand to fan herself.

Reverend Turner took a minute and explained Reverend Oliver's condition, before he asked her to call Johnny for him. "Malcolm wants me tuh call Johnny for him. He promised he'd keep him informed."

"Well John, yuh need tuh call Johnny and keep him informed."

"Loretha, yuh know this is still hard for me. Can't yuh do this for me?"

"Ah'm gonna do it this time, but yuh got tuh try tuh improve yuh relations with him."

Loretha heard Julia's soft whispering voice answer the telephone. She believed Johnny must have been asleep and Julia didn't want him disturbed; it was after ten o'clock. Julia continued to whisper, assuring Loretha she would wake Johnny if she wanted her too. Loretha apologized for the hour, and only asked Julia to give Johnny the message of Reverend Oliver's condition.

* * *

Malcolm was exhausted, but he had to call his wife and tell her how things were going. It was after 10:00 p.m. and he knew Theresa would be waiting for his call before going to bed. He left so suddenly, calling her away from her teaching duties to tell her he had to return to Rehoboth because of his father's illness. Malcolm kicked off his shoes and propped up the bed pillows. He reached for the telephone and held it against his chest while he stretched out on the bed and dialed his home.

"Hello honey," he said after hearing Theresa's voice. "Ah'm so sorry we had tuh leave like we did. We just returned from the hospital. Ah hope Ah didn't wake yuh."

"No baby. How's yuh father?"

Malcolm gave Theresa the details of his father's conditions with the exception of the doctor's suspicion of an assault. He and Theresa were both tired. All they wanted was to hear each other's voice and that was enough to sustain them until they had the opportunity to speak with each other the next day. The loving words were exchanged as they severed their connection for the night.

Malcolm still had Theresa on his mind when he stood placing his hands on his lower back to stretch and arch his vertebrate backward. "Oh God, Randy," Malcolm called out. He threw himself back on the bed. *Ah haven't spoken to Randy since Saturday morning.* He knew Randy's habit of waiting by the telephone had become a pastime he would camouflage behind his regular routine. He and Randy were friends with double intentions and they hid behind all that was expected of them. Randy was a delight to his wife and two sons. His wife, Gail thought of him as the loving husband, and Randy believed being married and having children legitimized his manhood.

Malcolm sat on the edge of his bed and picked up the telephone while thoughts of Randy continued to race through his mind. *Randy was working at Landers, Landers & Fine Brokerage Firm when we first met.* Malcolm remembered Randy as being the senior agent who was assigned to train him when he was first hired more than ten years ago. *We became instant friends. Coffee breaks, lunch and after work liquid relaxers at the local bar, and as time moved forward our friendship evolved into a relationship.*

Malcolm remembered how still he stood the first time he saw Randy. *He looked like Johnny. He was tall and walked like Johnny, and like Johnny, he had a warm and confident personality. Ah remembered how Randy stood in front of me with a grand smile and eyes so bright they highlighted his light sandy colored complexion. To me, Randy was Johnny.*

Ah loved and admired Johnny so much. My God! Ah didn't know my feelings toward Johnny or Randy were the consequences of my father's behavior.

Malcolm placed the phone back on the table. *I'll call him tomorrow.*

Chapter 5

A warm breeze carried the lacy curtains on a current of air that freshened the stale atmosphere in Thea's bedroom. Daylight was still hidden below the horizon and Thea's sleep was being compromised by restlessness. She dreamed, and then awoke with a startle. She was edgy and troubled, and didn't remember the visions from her dream. Pushing her hair from her face, she remembered her reality and thoughts of Owen entered her mind in jumbled flashes. Wonderful thoughts mixed with the terrible and they all stirred in her mind, blending into confusion and she prayed, asking God when order would be returned to her life.

4:00 a.m., five hours of sleep was all her body received, and the only rest her mind was allowed to have. Thea prayed Owen was having a restful, healing sleep and she knew she needed to be at the hospital with him, but at the same time she wanted to be far away. She wanted him well enough to experience the consequences of his actions. She rested in her bed for two hours scolding herself for defending him. She cried and used the corner of her sheet to capture her tears. *Ah should've never, under any circumstances, defended his behavior. Oh Lord, help me through this day. Give me strength tuh do the right thing. My vows say 'for better or worse'. Does that mean Ah can't leave him or does that mean Ah can leave him, but Ah can't divorce him?*

By 7:30 a.m. Thea and Malcolm were on their way back to the hospital. The car moved like it was slicing through air as soft music played in the tape deck. Thea had been mourning the death of her way of life. She had been quiet, her eyes closed and her head cradled against the headrest. "Ah been relatively happy most of my life, but now Ah wonder 'bout my remaining years. Ah'm almost sixty. Ah'd say Ah was young by most standards. But Ah'm not young. Ah ain't ol' either. Ah'm just on the far side of middle age. Ah'm gonna hold on tuh as many precious moments as Ah can."

Malcolm was in his own quiet place, but when his mother's soft voice rippled the quiet he glanced at her, momentarily removing his eyes from the road. "Mama, what are yuh talkin' about? 'Yuh ain't young, yuh ain't old, yuh middle age.' What brought all that on?"

Thea opened her eyes and stared out at the road. "Well, its time for me tuh make every moment of every day count. For the last three days Ah been moping around, letting the actions of others cause me pain and steal my precious time, my precious moments."

"Mama, have yuh been wondering what really happened tuh Dad? Yuh know, what the doctor was talking about."

"Ah been givin' that some thought too. Seems kinda funny yuh father has this, so called accident, 'round 'bout the time he's forced tuh confess. Ah believe what the doctor said, and if that's so, then Ah believe yuh daddy deserved a beatin'.'"

"Mama . . . how could yuh say that?"

"Ah think yuh should be stoppin' this car if yuh need tuh be lookin' at me like that. Maybe we need tuh talk, but yuh sure can't eyeball me and drive too."

"Ah'm sorry Mama. Ah'll keep my eyes on the road."

"Ah said what Ah did 'cause Ah'm a mama. Ah know the pain of seein' yuh child hurt. Now hear me good! Ah don't wanna see yuh daddy in the hospital, but Ah can understand how someone could punch him around like that, and even then it don't mount tuh the years of sufferin' that family went through."

"Mama, what about Dad? Ah mean, are yuh gonna leave him? When yuh came home with me were yuh plannin' tuh leave Dad for good?"

"Malcolm, Ah just needed tuh get away. Ah may still leave him for good, but Ah don't know that yet. Ah still need tuh get away so I can think, but Ah'm gonna stay for now, least 'til yuh Dad is better. Nothin's changed. How can Ah stay in this town knowin' what Ah know?"

"Ah know, Ah understand. Can Ah ask yuh something? It's about Johnny," Malcolm said.

"No, Ah don't think Johnny hurt yuh father!"

"Ah wasn't gonna ask yuh that. Ah know Johnny wouldn't do anything like that."

"Okay! What is it?"

"Ah know yuh always liked Johnny. All those years, yuh liked Johnny. Will yuh feelings for him change now?" Malcolm glanced at his mother and quickly returned his eyes back to the road.

"Malcolm, Ah been thinkin' bout him a lot these last few days. Can yuh imagine what he must be feelin'? Ah don't know, Ah think Ah might even like him more. Last night Ah think yuh wanted tuh call him. Listen honey, Owen is Johnny's father too. He has a right tuh know how his father is doin'. After all, he called yuh tuh let yuh know he was in the hospital."

"Yeah, yuh right, Ah called Reverend Turner and asked him tuh call Johnny for me."

"Well, yuh didn't have tuh do that. Yuh call Johnny and stay in touch with him."

"Ah will Mama. Ah just didn't want tuh hurt yuh more."

"Well, Ah want yuh tuh know that ain't what hurt me, and Ah ain't gone let nothin' hurt me again; nothin' is gone steal another precious moment from me."

"Good for yuh Mama."

* * *

Thea knew Reverend Oliver would be better when she arrived at the hospital. She had prayed on it and believed the Lord would be there for them. It also helped that she didn't receive a crisis call in the middle of the night. It was 8:00 a.m. when she and Malcolm arrived in his room. He was awake and his bed had been raised to an elevated position. Tubes and leads for the medical monitoring equipment were still attached to his body, but this time he looked so much better. A liquid breakfast consisting of a high protein substance filled a tall cup. A special straw set on his tray, along with a cup of coffee and a four ounce carton of orange juice. Reverend Oliver's face brightened when he saw Thea and Malcolm enter the room. Thea returned his smile with a smile of her own before she remembered she was supposed to be angry with him.

"Hi Dad, Ah'm glad tuh see yuh better," Malcolm said while leaning over to give him a gentle hug.

"Hi son. Hello Thea." Reverend Oliver's words were slurred. "They wired my jaw so it's hard tuh speak."

"Yuh look better Owen." Thea didn't rush to give him a hug the way Malcolm did. She clutched the handle of her pocketbook and held it close to her chest the way she seemed to do whenever anxiety plagued her, then she double patted his shoulder.

"Ah'm better," Reverend Oliver said. He could see the disappointment in her eyes and looked away.

"How long do yuh think yuh'll have tuh stay in the hospital?" Malcolm asked. He noticed the exchange between his parents and asking about the hospital stay was his way of moving forward to a more positive subject.

"Ah don't know. Ah haven't seen a doctor this morning. Ah don't even know who my doctor is. The last thing Ah remembered was talking to Reverend Lipton, then waking up this morning in the hospital with my jaw wired."

"Well . . . yuh doctor's name is Dr. Parks. We spoke with him last night." Thea spoke to enlighten him. "He said you had two fractures to yuh jaw and yuh pressure is really high. Reverend Turner was with yuh from Sunday night 'til we arrived yesterday evening."

"What day is this?"

"It's Tuesday morning," Malcolm said. "Dad . . . yuh've been unconscious since Sunday night. Last night the doctor told us they kept yuh sedated so they could get yuh pressure under control and wire yuh jaw.

Reverend Oliver rubbed his hand over his jaw and looked up at Malcolm.

"Yeah Dad, we have tuh talk about yuh jaw. Ah don't believe yuh fell. The doctor said yuh got two fractures in yuh jaw. How'd yuh get two fractures by fallin'? Ah told yuh Ah didn't believe yuh fell when Ah saw yuh Sunday, but we'll talk about that later."

"Mal . . . Malcolm . . . Reverend Oliver raised his hand to get Malcolm's attention.

"No Dad, we'll talk about that later, maybe tomorrow. Okay?"

Reverend Oliver gently nodded his head and stretched to turn and look over at Thea.

Thea didn't have anything to say and was comfortable letting Malcolm do the talking. She sat back in the chair and continued to clutch her pocketbook. Reverend Oliver didn't turn to look at her again and Thea didn't position her chair so she would be in his view without his having to strain. She looked relaxed and the wrinkle that creased her brow for two days had relaxed into a smooth blend of her forehead. Malcolm glanced at her several times while he spoke to his father and the calm in her face appeared to remind him of what she had told him earlier. *Precious moments,* her words whispered in his thoughts.

"Tuesday! Ah lost more than a day?" Reverend Oliver said.

"Ah promised tuh call Johnny and give him an update. Yuh look much better, so Ah'm gonna try tuh reach him before he leaves for work."

Thea nodded her head and smiled. Her eyes freed Malcolm to do what he believed was necessary. She continued to clutch her pocketbook and remained sitting in the chair out of Owen's clear view. She didn't try to strike a conversation or give Owen another comforting touch.

Reverend Oliver watched Malcolm leave the room. He didn't speak and he didn't seem to know how or believe he should ask Thea to move her chair so he could see her. He rested his head on his pillow and closed his eyes as soon as Malcolm disappeared from his view.

The beeping sounds from the diagnostic machinery added to the uncomfortable atmosphere in the room. It wasn't Thea's intention to make him feel uncomfortable. She just didn't have anything to say. Speaking to Owen wasn't on her heart and she didn't make an effort to force a conversation. She was there with him because she was his wife. The day before, she was in a frenzy over his condition and was defending his behavior to Malcolm. The day before that, she suffered emotional pain and was fleeing his presence. Now peace consumed her and that made Owen feel uncomfortable.

* * *

Malcolm stood half in the telephone booth and rested against the opened folded door. He listened as the phone rang at Johnny's home and Marion, his 'Edith Bunker' type maid answered.

"May Ah speak with Mr. Turner?"

"Mr. Turner is not available. May I take a message?" Marion responded with a sing-song voice.

"No, Ah'll try to reach him in his office," Malcolm responded.

"May I ask whose calling?" Marion's voice echoed through the receiver.

"Just tell him his brother. He'll know."

"His brother," Marion repeated. She didn't question. She just wrote the message on the pad. "Yes sir, I'll give him the message as soon as I hear from him."

"Thank yuh." It made Malcolm feel good to call Johnny his brother. He didn't wonder what Johnny would think. He wasn't trying to be malicious. A warm feeling filled him when he spoke of Johnny as his brother. He thanked Marion and hung up the phone, all the time knowing he would give Johnny time to get to his office and try to reach him again.

Malcolm slid into the small bench in the telephone booth and pulled the glass folding door halfway closed. He believed it was a good time to call his office, but Randy flashed into his mind. He placed his elbows on the ledge under the payphone and began massaging his eyes, temples, and eyebrows with his fingertips. The thought of Randy's warm greeting was what he always craved from Johnny, but he knew his relationship with him was wrong.

"*Mr. Oliver?*" he remembered Randy saying while positioning his hand for a manly welcome.

"*Yes,*" *he responded, catching Randy's hand for the shake.*

"*How are yuh? Ah'm Randy Lester.*"

In a flash, his mind switched from Randy to a time when he and Johnny were young, to a time when he intentionally attacked Johnny, wanting to hurt him. That was the period in his life when his feelings were jumbled: love, hate, jealousy, wanting attention, needing it, and being confused. He gave no thought as to how or what kind of attention he received. He didn't understand that his feelings toward Johnny were the consequences of a curse inherited from his father.

"Malcolm!" Thea tapped on the glass door and her voice broke through his thoughts. "Dr. Parks is here. Would yuh like tuh speak with him?"

"Yes Mama." He pushed the phone booth doors back and they hurried down the corridor toward his father's room. *Ah still need tuh call my office, but it will have tuh wait,* Malcolm thought. *Ah'll speak with my secretary and tell her when Ah expect tuh return tuh work, then Ah'll have her transfer my call tuh Randy's desk. Ah didn't get tuh see him yesterday. He must be frantic. Ah left right after Ah got the call from Johnny. My God . . . Ah need tuh break this off with him.*

* * *

Thea and Malcolm stood at the entrance of Reverend Oliver's room and watched as Dr. Parks enlightened him as to the nature of his illness. He pointed to the machines around his bed and explained their purpose then spoke briefly of the nurses. "Now, you follow their orders and you'll be on the mend in no time." He smiled and patted Reverend Oliver's shoulder.

"Dr. Parks," Malcolm spoke up and extended his hand.

Dr. Parks stepped back so he could see Reverend Oliver, his wife and son.

"Mr. Oliver . . . Mrs. Oliver." Dr. Parks shook Malcolm's hand and gave Thea a courteous nod. "I'm happy to say Reverend Oliver had a quiet night. His blood pressure is still a little high, but he appears to be stable. He did run a slight fever, but it was normal this morning. We'll be doing some blood work to rule out infection and I've ordered a round of antibiotics, just to be on the safe side."

"How long do yuh think he'll be in the hospital?" Thea asked as she turned to look at Owen.

"Well . . . I'd like to keep him until his temperature and pressure are within normal limits for twenty-four hours. And when he does return home, I want him to rest for at least a week. Of course he'll be on a liquid diet until his jaw is completely healed and the wires removed."

Malcolm glanced at his father and then back at the doctor. "How long will that be?" he asked.

"From six weeks to two months, but he'll need another round of x-rays before we'll know for sure. Did you have a chance to question him about his injury?"

"No sir," Malcolm responded.

"I think he's coming along nicely. If you have any more questions, you can call my office and leave a message and I'll return your call."

"Thank you Dr. Parks," Thea said.

Malcolm smiled and shook Dr. Parks hand again.

"Good day Reverend Oliver." Dr. Parks gently bowed before leaving the room.

"Mama, Ah didn't reach Johnny yet and Ah need tuh call my office. Dad Ah'll be right back." Malcolm glanced at his mother and turned away. *Damn, she doesn't want me tuh leave her alone with Dad, but Ah really need tuh talk tuh Randy.*

* * *

Malcolm reached the telephone booth and finally contacted Johnny at his office. He explained all that the doctor told him, except the doctor's belief that their father had been physically assaulted.

"Johnny . . . Ah want yuh tuh know, Ah'm very sorry for what Dad did tuh yuh mother." He wanted to say 'our father,' but 'Dad' seemed like a better choice of words, not knowing if Johnny had accepted him as his father.

"It's okay man. That wasn't your fault," Johnny said.

"Ah'd like tuh be yuh friend. Ah'm so very sorry for the problems Ah caused yuh when we were kids. Ah'm happy yuh my brother. Can we be brothers?"

"We are brothers Malcolm, but I still have a lot of healing to do. I do want you to understand that this weekend came as a shock. I've always loved your father."

"Our father," Malcolm said. "He's our father, man."

"You're right Malcolm, 'our father'. I'm concerned about his well being. Other than that, I believe it's a little too early to talk about him or what my relationship with you will be." Johnny's voice was cold and as sharp as a shard of ice. It cut into Malcolm, and if his soul could bleed it would require a transfusion.

"Ah understand Johnny. Ah just hoped we could be friends."

"Not now Malcolm. I don't want to talk about it now." Johnny was bothered. "For now, I just want you to continue to update me on our father's condition."

Malcolm squeezed the telephone receiver so tight his chocolate colored fingers turned pale, anger disfigured his face and his right hand balled into a tight fist. He took a deep breath. "No problem man. Ah'll keep you informed." He hung up the phone before Johnny could say another word. Johnny's tone had been hateful and sarcastic. He had been reaching out for more than twenty years and Johnny continuously shunned him. He placed his elbow on the ledge under the pay phone, and buried his face in the palms of his hands. He needed his bearings; he needed control. Randy returned to his mind; Randy, his substitute for Johnny. Johnny was out of reach, but Randy would always be there for him. He picked up the phone again and called his office, and as planned, he had his secretary transfer his call to Randy's desk.

"How's it going man?" Randy said.

Malcolm detected a touch of insecurity in Randy's voice. "Man, this has been a crazy week for my family. Ah know yuh been worried about me and Ah'm sorry, but Ah couldn't get away tuh call yuh. Man, my family is in crisis, my parents, not me and Theresa. Don't worry Randy, Ah'm still here for yuh. It's not about you and me. Ah'll tell yuh all about it as soon as Ah see yuh."

"Yeah man, Ah spoke with Theresa and she told me yuh father was sick," Randy said.

"Yeah, but his doctor just told me he was getting better. Ah may be in Macon for the rest of the week. Yuh can try tuh reach me at my parents' home, but Ah'll try tuh get yuh at yuh home or at the office."

"Okay Malcolm. It was good tuh hear from you. No . . . it was wonderful hearing from you. Just hearing your voice. . . yuh know what ah mean?"

"Yeah man, Ah'll talk tuh yuh later." Malcolm hung up the phone and he began to feel better about Johnny. *God, this isn't right. Why am Ah using Randy like this. Now Ah know the truth about myself.* He sat back in the corner of the closed telephone booth, placed his hand over his mouth and allowed thoughts of Johnny and Randy to twirl in his mind. Minutes slipped away like flashes. It wasn't long before Thea missed him and was tapping on the phone booth door again.

"What's keepin' yuh so long? Aren't yuh gonna spend any time with yuh father?"

"Yes Mama. Ah'm sorry. Ah was just caught up in thought."

"Well yuh father is asking for yuh. Come now."

* * *

"Thea, would yuh mind moving yuh chair so Ah can see yuh better without straining?" It came to a point when Reverend Oliver was forced to break his silence. He had hoped he wouldn't have to ask her where Malcolm was or to move her chair, but he understood, knowing he was the problem. His medication had removed most of his pain, but his tongue and the muscles in his jaw still ached when he spoke. It was hard for him to look at Thea. Shame and dishonor could not be camouflaged under a dose of medication, except when sedated to unconsciousness.

Thea moved the chair and Malcolm took his regular seat. Their eyes searched and waited for Reverend Oliver to say something else. His blood pressure monitor beeped louder when it registered an increase and a mild whistling tone signaled at the nurse's station. He rested his head on his pillow and took deep breaths, trying to relax to quiet the sounds, but the beeping monitor continued.

"Are yuh all right Dad?"

Reverend Oliver didn't speak; he nodded his head and continued taking deep breaths. He looked toward the nurse's station and noticed the lady in white coming in his direction. He knew he had better say what needed to be said before she reached his bedside.

"Listen," he said and he took another deep breath. "Ah have tuh speak tuh yuh, but that nurse is on her way over here. Thea, Ah need tuh leave this town. Ah can't live here any longer."

"Ah agree." Thea nodded her head, but her response was cold and bland. *How dare yuh issue orders at me! He's right, he does need tuh leave town, but not with me. He's acting like nothing happened. If Ah wasn't a religious woman Ah'd be cussin'; No! Ah wouldn't be in this hospital at all.*

"Ah need tuh let the school know Ah'm out sick, and apply for a short term disability leave. Malcolm, would yuh have the school give yuh the forms

Ah need? Ah'll have the doctor fill them out. As soon as my leave is approved Ah'll be free tuh resign." Owen spoke as fast as he could, but his words were slurred, his mouth ached and the beeping sounds seemed louder.

"Sure Dad."

The nurse walked into the bedside area and appeared to inspect the monitor for accuracy. A quaint smile stretched her lips and she walked back toward her station.

"Thea, we have tuh sell the house," Owen whispered.

"Ah knew yuh'd say that. Ah been thinkin' 'bout that too," Thea responded.

"Reverend Oliver," the nurse said. Somehow she returned to the nurse's station and was back at his bedside without being noticed. "Ah have tuh ask yuh family tuh leave. Yuh pressure is up again. It seems somethin' is upsetting yuh. Right now yuh need complete quiet."

"All right Dad, Ah'll take care of everything at the school." Malcolm spoke fast, understanding the urgency in the nurse's voice.

Reverend Oliver looked at the nurse, "Can they come back later?"

"Maybe this afternoon . . . you really have to rest for now." The nurse turned to Malcolm. "I'll give you the extension for the nurse's station. I suggest you call before you come. Maybe if Reverend Oliver tries to stay calm, his pressure will remain under control."

"Okay! Okay!" Reverend Oliver said. He seemed annoyed because he needed to finish giving instructions. "Thea, will yuh check with the real estate office about the house? Maybe yuh both can come back this afternoon?"

"Yeah, sure Dad, we'll try tuh bring back the forms and information yuh need. Don't worry; we'll take care of everything?" He grabbed his hand for a mild shake. "We'll see yuh later."

Thea stood, gave Owen the same bland stare that didn't register her emotions. "I'll do what Ah can." She continued to clutch her pocketbook and simply nodded at her ailing husband. *Dear Lord,* she thought, *heal him and keep him safe. Help me, Lord. Ah need yuh healing hands too.* She walked from the room without looking back at him.

* * *

Malcolm and Thea stood back and casually greeted the two white men wearing suits as they stepped off the elevator. One of the men had his jacket pulled back with the thumb of his right hand hooked in his pants' pocket. A shinning brass police badge was clipped to his belt, which captured Malcolm's attention, holding him in the path of the gliding elevator doors. Thea grabbed his arm pulling him clear and the door slid shut.

"Mama, Ah think Dr. Parks called the police. Those men are here tuh question Dad."

"Well . . . they may be here, but Ah don't think they'll be able tuh talk tuh him. They wouldn't let us stay."

Malcolm pushed the 'open door' button and watched the men as they approached the nurse's station flashing their badges. "Mama, let's walk back tuh the desk and see what happens. Ah don't want them talking tuh Dad without one of us being there."

"No. What happens . . . happens." Thea stood back still clutching her pocketbook with her arms crossed. "Yuh best take yuh finger off that 'open door' button so we can be on our way."

"Just a minute Mama," Malcolm whispered. He watched as the men asked to speak to Reverend Oliver. They told the nurse they were detectives. He heard the nurse tell them his father could not be questioned but she would call Dr. Parks.

"C'mon Malcolm, let's get out of here!" Thea pulled his hand off the 'open door' button and pushed the 'lobby' button. The elevator door slid shut.

Chapter 6

Loretha knew it was Johnny calling as soon as the telephone rang. She could almost hear his voice before placing the receiver to her ear. "Hi Baby. How yuh doing this mornin'? How's Julia? Did yuh call yuh mother last night? Did yuh hear from Malcolm yet?"

"Gram'ma you always ask so many questions. I guess you just like to get it all out," Johnny said.

Loretha threw her head back and smiled broadly at his remark. "Yuh right about that! Ah gotta get it out before Ah forget. My mind ain't as sharp as it use tuh be. Ah guess it's the perils of gettin' old."

"Now what are you talking about? You've been asking multiple questions for as long as I can remember. It doesn't have anything to do with your age, and you're not old."

"Is that so?" Loretha's words were followed by a chuckle and in her mind she saw a smile on Johnny's face.

"Okay, let me see. Hmm . . . I had a good night. Julia had a good night and she is fine. I spoke with Mama and Nat last night, and Malcolm called me this morning. Did I cover it all?"

"No. Yuh didn't tell me how Reverend Oliver was doing."

"Yuh didn't ask." Johnny laughed and waited for the question. It was a game they had played for years.

"Okay, how is Reverend Oliver?"

"He's stable. Malcolm said his jaw was fractured in two places. And you were right about his pressure. Malcolm seemed calm, so I believe he's going to be fine."

"Well, Ah'll thank the Lord for that." Loretha voice had taken on a serious tone, but a smile remained on her face.

She sat at the telephone table and listened while Johnny continued to speak. "Gram'ma, do you think what happened this weekend is what put Reverend Oliver in the hospital? Have you wondered how he hurt his face? I mean, it seems strange that he should hurt his face on the same weekend the truth came out. Do you think someone beat him?"

"Well, anything is possible, but who would do that tuh him?" Loretha said.

"I don't know, but I'd like to see him, and I really hope no one beat him. I didn't speak with him Sunday. I'd hate for anything to happen to him before I have a chance to talk to him. Julia finished her case and we both took a week off. We'll be leaving D.C. Friday evening, so you'll have us around for a whole week.

"Have yuh told yuh Mama yuh comin' home?"

"Yes, last night. She told me Nat had a back spasm and nearly scared you to death. I guess he's okay. I think he went to work today. I called their house before calling you."

"Yes Johnny, it seemed tuh be pretty bad. He acted like he couldn't breath," Loretha replied and she waited to hear Johnny's response.

"He'll be okay. I've seen him have those spasms and it can be frightening. He'll be okay, but in about three days, he'll be pretty sore."

"What yuh mean Johnny?" Loretha said.

"Well Gram'ma, his muscles get real tight, and when the attack is over, he feels better. But his back and neck muscles have been damaged from the spasms. They'll heal, but he'll feel like he's been in an auto accident. I'm surprise he had an attack. He usually knows when one is coming on, and he'll take his medicine."

"Well, this one slipped past him," Loretha said.

"It sure did."

"Johnny, Ah know this has been a difficult time for yuh. Tell me, how yuh really doin'. Now don't yuh be tryin' tuh fool me boy 'cause Ah can't see yuh face. We're here laughin' and jokin' and speakin' 'bout concern for Nat or Reverend Oliver, but Ah can feel yuh pain. So now yuh just tell me how yuh feel. Yuh know, sometimes it helps tuh talk about it and Ah know yuh can't speak on it with yuh mother. But Ah'm here for yuh. Talk tuh me Johnny."

"Ya know Gram'ma, I still haven't adjusted. My whole life has been turned up side down. I feel unsettled. I promised Mama and Nat I wouldn't speak of Reverend Oliver in their presence. Nat has always been there for me, but this time he seems distant. I'm a man, Gram'ma, and I'm supposed to be strong. I feel like I've been turned inside out and tied in a knot. I'm wired, ya know, jittery. Ya know when I feel like that I have to get home and that's why I want to take the week off."

"Yeah Johnny, Ah know yuh have tuh get tuh MaDear's cottage."

"Yeah, my magic cottage. It's like MaDear is still there. Even if she's not, I always feel better after I've spent some time there."

"Johnny, it always makes me feel good havin' yuh home. Ah know Ah ain't MaDear, but when yuh get here let me try tuh help yuh make some sense of your life. Maybe between MaDear's cottage and me, yuh'll find some answers. Ah just want yuh tuh feel better."

"Okay Gram'ma, I'll see you this weekend. Now, I don't want you to be worrying about me. You know me . . . I'm a survivor. I love you Gram'ma."

"I love yuh too. Bye now."

* * *

Johnny leaned back in his chair and used his left hand to massage his eyes. He thought about Sarah and his grandfather.

Johnny picked up the phone and put a call through to Sarah's office. She had given him her direct line, and answered on the second ring.

"Sarah Turner speaking."

"Hello, Aunt Sarah?" Johnny smiled when he heard her voice.

"Hi Johnny, Ah love it when yuh call me aunt. Ah've been thinking about you and Julia."

"You've been on my mind too, so, I decided to give you a call. Julia and I will be at MaDear's cottage this Friday evening and we plan to stay until next Sunday."

"Yuh coming home? Stephen and Ah have a surprise for the family and we were planning tuh be in Rehoboth Saturday. Ah can't wait tuh see you and Julia."

"Stephen? I really have a lot to catch up on. Who's Stephen?" Johnny turned his chair to face the wall of windows that looked out across D.C.

"Stephen is my soul mate. Yuh've never met him, but you are a lot like him. Yuh'll meet him this weekend.

"I'd really like that. Oh! Aunt Sarah . . . Reverend Oliver is in the hospital. That nasty bruise on his face turned out to be a fractured jaw. Malcolm said his jaw was fractured in two places and his blood pressure was seriously high. His condition has been upgraded to guarded."

"Johnny! Yuh mean he is that ill?"

"That's what I've been told. That's another reason I need to get home. I know you don't have feelings for him after last weekend, but I still do. Anyway, I'm looking forward to seeing you and meeting Stephen."

"Stephen and I will be home on Saturday. Ah love yuh, Johnny."

"I love you too. Bye for now."

* * *

It was Tuesday and classes were due to begin on Thursday. Anxiety over thoughts of Reverend Oliver was causing Nat emotional discomfort. Nat knew he was responsible for all the attention Reverend Oliver was receiving and anger, aggravation, and guilt were beginning to weigh him down. He worked quickly, decorating his classroom, designing his bulletin boards with mathematical themes, counting and stacking workbooks, rearranging tables and lining up the chair-desk combos in neat rows. Channeling his anxiety into energy limited his time for thinking about Reverend Oliver. After moving the classroom furniture, he soon found himself at the window. He stopped and rested both hands on the window sill and became angry when he noticed Malcolm getting out of his car in the parking lot of the local school administration building. "Damn!" he whispered. He didn't know if Malcolm was getting disability or resignation papers for his father.

Over the past two days, Nat realized attacking Owen did more harm than good. It would have been okay if he took his beating, resigned his teaching position, and left town, ultimately causing him to lose his pension. Visualizing running him out of town was a satisfying thought. But he knew it wasn't turning out that way and he was to blame. Now, because of his illness, he was eligible for a disability leave and he could resign after that and keep his pension. That fact alone angered him more than the sympathy Owen was receiving. It was his violence that had been the undoing of his own plan.

* * *

Nat concentrated his stare on Malcolm, hoping he would look in his direction, but Malcolm's thoughts were with Randy. He never looked up on the hill where the old Booker T. Washington High School remained standing; where the memories for almost half the years of his life were formed. Instead Malcolm got into his car and drove away.

As Malcolm went about his father's business, busy thoughts clouded his mind. *Ah needed tuh get away from Randy; our relationship should never have happened. Oh God . . . Ah feel sick . . . nauseated. Ah never thought of myself as gay. Randy was just a friend.* He slapped both hands against the steering wheel. His lips clenched and he could feel his hot breath against his upper lip. "Why did Ah go with Randy?" he mumbled to himself. *Ah let him . . . Ah enjoyed it. Ah love makin' love with Theresa; it wasn't the sex Ah loved with Randy, it was being accepted; like being accepted by Johnny. Am*

Ah gay? Ah can stop . . . Ah will stop. Ah'm gonna call Randy and tell him it's over. Damn! He's gonna freak out. Ah can see him comin' here tuh try tuh talk tuh me. It'll be safe for him here . . . no one knows him. Ah think Ah'll wait 'til Ah get home. If he acts out, Ah'll threaten tuh tell his family. Malcolm massaged his face and chin and kept one hand on the steering wheel as he drove. The wisp of newly grown whiskers gave a familiar scratch to his hand. *Ah love Theresa, but Ah won't let Randy blackmail me. Ah'll tell Theresa if Ah have tuh.*

* * *

About the same time Malcolm was getting the disability papers from the school, Thea was supposed to be visiting the real estate office. That was what Owen wanted her to do, but she wasn't sure it was what she wanted. She thought of how, in just two days, her life had changed directions. She tried not to think of how much Owen hurt her. She shivered as she thought about it. *My Lord, my husband hurt that child and then made her face him, her attacker, all these years. He showed no mercy. We could have left Rehoboth by the end of that school year. Owen could have found a teaching position in another state. We could've returned tuh Columbia, South Carolina.*

Thea locked up her home and was on her way to her car, but her mental anguish seemed to drain and weaken her so that she needed to sit and gather enough strength to continue. Her eyes blurred with tears and she sat in the large rocker and closed them. She unlatched her pocketbook and blindly searched for a fresh handkerchief and suddenly she was sobbing. *Oh Lord, tell me what tuh do. Ah've always been yuh faithful servant, give me a sign. Ah need yuh Lord, Ah need yuh now.* She raised her hands and looked up, but the weeping willow tree blocked her view of the sky and spanned the circumference of her circular driveway. The wind blew from right to left and the branches of the tree waved on the current of air. Suddenly the air current changed to the opposite direction taking the draping branches with it. She took in the deep breath of fresh air her body craved, filling her lungs as she inhaled and unconsciously holding it longer than usual before exhaling. It seemed there was a moment when her mind was quiet of rambling thoughts and she felt the aura associated with real peace, and clarity replaced her cloudy thoughts. *Ah'm gonna visit Loretha. Ah'm gonna do what will make me feel better. The real estate office can wait, Owen can wait. Ah hope Reverend Turner is there. Ah know he should share some of the blame for Elizabeth's suffering. Ah remember him telling the congregation at church that Elizabeth was raped.*

He said he didn't know who raped her, but Ah'm sure Elizabeth told him. Just knowing she was raped should've been enough reason tuh protect and love her, but he disowned her for thirty-six years. Ah have my own issues . . . it's not for me tuh pass judgment, that's for his family tuh do. Thank God, Mrs. Collins took her and her baby in. Ah don't know what Loretha and that child would've done. Ah wonder if that's why Elizabeth, Johnny, and Loretha called her, MaDear?

* * *

Thea turned the key, starting her car. When she reached the end of her driveway she turned left for the three mile drive to the Turner's home. She drove down Rehoboth Road passing the Concord Baptist Church on the left. And after another mile she came around the slight bend in the road and she could see the Turner home on the right. Reverend Turner and Loretha where sitting on their front porch. Thea's chest tightened and her racing heartbeat caused her to take notice of the shame Owen had placed on her. She summoned a deep breath to assist in easing her anxiety, but none the less, the shame remained. Holding tight to the steering wheel, she took her time turning into the driveway and parking the car. When all else failed she always had her pocketbook for added security; she held it close to her chest, the way she had been cuddling it since returning to Rehoboth. Using her other hand, she pushed herself from behind the steering wheel and closed the car door behind her.

Loretha had placed two glasses and a pitcher of fresh lemonade on the wrought iron pedestal table. "Hello Thea," Loretha called out. She hurried to pull up another chair, before excusing herself to rush into the house to get another glass for the lemonade. "Ah'll be back in a moment," she called out.

"Hello, Miss Thea," Reverend Turner said, quickly rising from his chair and nodding his head to greet her.

"Hello, Reverend Turner." Thea bowed her head slightly. "Ah hope Ah'm still welcome at yuh home?"

"Of course, of course, yuh'll always be welcomed here. Come, come, have a seat." He placed his hands on the back his chair.

Loretha had returned and was standing at the lemonade table before Reverend Turner could call her.

Thea was sitting when Reverend Turner eased himself back into another chair. Loretha handed her the empty glass and at the same time offered her lemonade.

"Thank yuh," Thea said. She watched Loretha filled her glass.

"Well, well, well," Reverend Turner said. He was at a loss for words and that was all he could think of saying.

Loretha quietly poured more lemonade into her glass then filled Reverend Turner's glass and words escaped all of them in the next awkward moments.

Thea took a sip of her lemonade and remembered asking the Lord for His guiding light. "Over the years, Ah cried for yuh family," she spoke with a trembling voice. "Ah cried for Elizabeth and Johnny. Ah cried for you, Reverend Turner and you, Miss Loretha. Ah even cried for Sarah. Ah kept all of yuh in my nightly prayers." Thea placed her glass on the small table and reached into her pocketbook for her already damp handkerchief. Tears filled her eyes and she quickly blotted them away.

"Please don't cry, Thea," Loretha said. She reached over and took Thea's hands in her own. "Yuh as innocent as 'Lizabeth in these matters."

Thea continued wiping her eyes with her other hand.

Reverend Turner lowered his head so he didn't have to look at Thea. His face was twisted and he turned away.

"Ah had planned tuh be returning tuh Jonesboro with Malcolm. Ah have a sister a short distance from him. We'll be sellin' the house." Sobs blurted from Thea and she covered her mouth with her handkerchief.

Loretha leaned over to Thea holding her head close to her chest. Reverend Turner walked to the porch's support pillar, turned his back protecting himself from what he found to be unbearable.

"C'mon Thea, we never blamed you. Ah'm so sorry yuh had tuh go through that tribunal on Sunday. It was something that had tuh be done so my family could heal. We knew yuh'd be hurt . . . there wasn't no way tuh get around it. We had tuh make sure yuh husband would tell his family. Otherwise, he could've come here and confessed and you would've never known the truth. Ah know he is a part of yuh, but you don't have tuh be wearin' his shame." Loretha's words were meant to be consoling.

"Ah can't help it. Ah keep rememberin' the signs Ah saw in them early years. Even before Malcolm was born, the day after Elizabeth had Johnny, Owen was actin' strange. Then, a few days later, after Malcolm was born, Elizabeth came tuh the maternity ward tuh visit me. Ah still remember the look of guilt on Owen's face. The same look he had the first time Elizabeth bought Johnny tuh church. And when Ah heard Elizabeth was raped Ah should've put it together. When Ah think of the fondness Owen had for

Johnny over the years . . . he treated him better than he did Malcolm . . . Ah shoulda known. That's why Ah'm tuh blame too. Can yuh ever forgive me? The least Ah coulda done was put it tuh Owen. Even if he denied it, Ah'da known. Ah woulda been able tuh read denial on his face."

"Honey it's easy for us tuh look back and put it tuhgether. Ah knew the day after Johnny was born and Ah didn't do anything. It wasn't for us tuh come forward, that was the responsibility of others. Ah'm not gonna blame myself and yuh shouldn't either." Loretha didn't look at John when she spoke. He must have felt his share of blame. He didn't turn to Loretha or Thea. He didn't relieve Thea's anxiety by consoling her. He excused himself from the porch and walked behind the house.

"Miss Loretha, Ah believe yuh, but Ah think Reverend Turner thinks otherwise." Thea's sobs returned as she glanced up at the empty porch where he had been standing.

Loretha turned and noticed John was gone, then pulled her chair even closer to Thea and began to whisper, "Honey, John knows he deserves his share of the blame. Ah know it's been eating at him for years. Ah believe that's why he had to leave. But let's not dwell on that now. How is Reverend Oliver?"

"Well he's still struggling with his pressure. Yesterday they asked us tuh leave 'cause his pressure went up all of a sudden. Ah'm afraid for him . . . Ah mean with that hypertension. They say it could cause a heart attack or stroke. He also has two fractures in his jaw and they're treatin' that. Ah can't imagine the pain he musta been feelin'. Owen told us he fell intuh the banister on the front porch, but the doctor said he thinks someone beat him."

"My Lord . . . beat him! And he has two fractures in his jaw!" Loretha sat forward in her chair. "How did that happen? Who would do something like that?" Loretha asked.

"Ah have no idea. Ah almost don't believe the doctor, but he was so sure it happened that way, he called the police. While we were waitin' for the elevator two men got off. Malcolm said they were detectives?"

"Well, what did Reverend Oliver have tuh say tuh them?"

"The nurse told the detective they couldn't question him, but they could speak with his doctor."

"Is that so?" The news troubled Loretha. She took a deep breath and momentarily glanced off in the distance.

"Yes, Ah know Miss Loretha. It's scary isn't it?"

"My Lord, yes." Loretha's voice was soft, just above a whisper. She turned facing Thea again. "Did Reverend Oliver say someone beat him?"

"No, he said he slipped on the steps and banged his face on the ball at the top of the banister. Ah ain't gonna let no doctor add tuh my troubles. If Owen said he fell, then he fell and that's what happened unless he says otherwise."

Reverend Turner never returned to the front porch while Thea was there. The ladies were taking a pause in their conversation; Thea had no more to say and Loretha was trying to digest what had already been said. They sat back in their chairs and sipped their glasses of lemonade.

After a minute or so, Thea placed her empty glass on the small table and announced she had to leave. "Ya know we'll be leavin' town. Ah was suppose tuh be at Lefferts makin' arrangements tuh sell the house, but Ah couldn't leave without seeing yuh. It's so hard . . ." Thea needed to use her handkerchief again. "Ah mean, when Ah think about it. Just a few days ago Ah was thinking of rearranging the furniture, and now Ah'm thinking about how Ah need tuh rearrange my life."

Loretha reached over to hold Thea's hand again. Tears began to swell in her eyes too. She blinked rapidly and took a deep breath to chase her emotions back into a safe place.

"Ah wish Ah could see Elizabeth and Johnny. Ah just want tuh tell them how sorry Ah am. Ah want tuh hug them . . ." Thea's emotions were still unsettled. Her neck and shoulders were beginning to ache from the tension and stress. She really wanted to be alone so she could drain her body of tears, and just let it all out so she could regain her strength.

"Yuh'll be around a couple of days won't yuh?" Loretha said. Now she used her right hand to rub it over Thea's shoulders, understanding the pain and tightness she was experiencing.

"Yes ma'am. Ah have tuh stay until Owen is out of the hospital, then Ah'll probably drive him to Jonesboro to stay with Malcolm until he's on his feet. Ah know Ah'm gonna stay with my sister in Atlanta until Ah'm ready to make my next move. Right now, Ah don't know when that will be, Ah just know Ah'm not ready tuh be with Owen."

"Ah certainly understand how yuh feel. But, Ah want yuh tuh know yuh always welcome in my house. Johnny and his wife will be home this Friday night and he'll be here until next Sunday. And of course, yuh know Elizabeth will be home after work. Ah hope you'll visit them. If yuh feelin' a little nervous, come by here and we can go tuh 'Lizabeth's home tuhgether."

"Yes ma'am, Ah'd love tuh see them and let them know how Ah feel." Thea eased herself from the chair. "Ah have tuh leave now. It makes me feel better knowing yuh not angry or disappointed with me. Yuh like family and Ah'm gonna miss y'all."

Loretha stood. "We're gonna miss yuh too."

Just then Reverend Turner reappeared from the side of the house. He returned so quickly, most likely he had secluded himself close by until Thea was ready to leave.

"Please keep us informed on how Reverend Oliver is coming along. In spite of everything we'll continue tuh keep all of you in our prayers," Reverend Turner spoke up as he walked closer and stood behind Loretha.

"Ah know yuh will and Ah wanna thank yuh." Thea looked at Reverend Turner. She lowered her head slightly and smiled humbly. "After all that's happened, y'all have still been so kind and thoughtful . . . and Reverend Turner, Ah wanna thank yuh for being with Owen in spite of all that's happened." Thea turned and stepped down from the porch. She turned back and looked up at Reverend Turner. "Thank yuh again and thank yuh Miss Loretha. God Bless Yuh."

"So long honey," Loretha said.

Reverend Turner smiled and took a gentle bow.

Loretha continued to stand in front of Reverend Turner as they watched Thea walked toward her car. As soon as she drove up the road, Loretha and John returned to their seats.

"John, did you hear what Thea said about someone beating on Owen?"

"I don't believe it. Unless he has another dark secret, maybe he hurt someone else's child. I can't think of anyone in Rehoboth who would hurt him.

* * *

Thea returned home and before she drove into her driveway she stopped her car and got out. She walked across Rehoboth Road and stood looking back at what she could see of her house from between the draping branches of the weeping willow tree. She walked to the left side of her circular driveway where the view was clearer. "Oh Lord help me," she cried out. "Ah love it here." The wind picked up and the branches of the tree swayed and danced in her direction. She smiled and hurried back across the road to her car and drove into her yard.

As soon as she parked her car, she walked under the tree and held her hand up. "Oh Dear Father, my Lord, my Savior, only you know my suffering." She lowered herself to her knees and faced the sun as it flickered between the dancing branches. "Guide me Lord. Please Lord, remove this pain from my chest and the clouds from my mind. Ah'm yuh servant and Ah know what's right. Yuh are my strength and from you all my blessings flow." Thea became silent, but her lips were moving like she was holding a conversation with someone. She remain on her knees for almost and hour and still held her hands to the heavens. The ground around the base of the tree, where she knelt, was as soft as a pillow cushion.

"Thank yuh Lord!" Thea emotions were full, but she didn't cry. "Thank yuh Jesus!" she yelled out as she rose to her feet. Her arms were still held high and her head still turned to the heavens. "Praise the Lord," she sang out as she turned in circles. "Ah'm not leaving Rehoboth. Praised the Lord! Ah'm not leaving my home." She dropped back to her knees and held her praying hands to her lips as she spoke aloud. "My job is tuh stand by my husband and help him do the right thing. Ah didn't do anything wrong and Ah won't run away with him. It's time to settle down and take care of our business. My Lord will give me the directions Ah need. This morning he directed me to the Turner home instead of the real estate office. Praise the Lord! Now he just told me tuh stay in Rehoboth and at the right moment he would tell me what to do about my husband." Thea stood, brushed off her clothes and began walking toward her front porch. She knew it was all in the Lord's hands and she was his servant to do His will.

Chapter 7

Reverend Oliver watched as Dr. Parks and the two men spoke while standing at the nurse's station. He had just awakened from a short nap and he didn't realize their conversation was about him. Dr. Parks reached over the desk and picked up a chart. He flipped it open and the men, one standing to his left and the other to the right, looked at the page on the chart. Dr. Parks pointed to sections on the chart, then one of the men pointed to the chart. Reverend Oliver wasn't interested in what they were saying. Looking at them was just more interesting than anything else in his two bed unit. One of the men pointed to the door of Reverend Oliver's room and Dr. Parks said something and at the same time shook his head, which Reverend Oliver interpreted to mean "no." The men, in turn, reached for and shook Dr. Park's hand and walked away. One of the men pulled his jacket back to place his right hand in his pocket and again revealed the brass law enforcement badge attached to his waist.

Reverend Oliver looked up at the clock. It was 1:15 p.m. Thea and Malcolm left about 10:30 that morning. He looked over at the monitor recording his vital signs. His blood pressure was still up, recording readings between 240/166 and 188/142. *Thank yuh Lord. It's still up, but it's better than it was this morning. Malcolm and Thea will be back around three.* He closed his eyes hoping to return to his nap when he felt a hand on his shoulder; Dr. Parks was standing next to him.

"Good afternoon, Reverend Oliver."

Reverend Oliver opened his eyes and looked up at the tall black man. "Hello, Ah just saw yuh talking tuh those two men. Are yuh my doctor?"

"Yes, you should remember meeting me earlier. Don't you?"

"Seems like Ah do, but Ah'm not sure. Weren't yuh here earlier when my wife and son were here?" Reverend Oliver's words were clear in spite of his sore tongue and wired jaw.

"You're right, and if you don't remember, my name is Dr. Parks."

"Thank yuh Dr. Parks. How am Ah doin'?"

"Well your pressure is down a little, let's hope it continues to go down. It was dangerously high. I have a few questions I need to ask you and I don't expect to see any significant change in your pressure." Dr. Parks spoke out defiantly.

"Okay, I'll try to keep my emotions under control."

"Did you see me speaking with those men a few moments ago?"

"Yes sir," Reverend Oliver said. He spoke sharp, using manners left over from an earlier time period.

"Don't call me, sir. I'm too young for that. You're the senior. I should be calling you, sir." Dr. Parks smiled and patted his hand. "Okay remember to remain calm?"

"Yes, ugh … doctor."

"You have two separate fractures to your jaw. You need to tell me how that happened. Your wife and son told me what you told them."

"Then you know what happened."

"Yes, but I need to hear it from you."

"Ah fell on my front porch and hit my head on the banister."

"How many times did you fall?"

Reverend Oliver didn't like the look on Dr. Parks face. His mind flashed to the two men, the detectives, the badge; he remembered Dr. Parks referring to his injury as two separate fractures and he vaguely remembered Malcolm using the same phase. "Ah believe Ah fell twice. Ah remember tripping on the steps and hitting my face. Ah tried tuh grab the rail, but my hand slipped and Ah seem tuh remember slamming the same side of my face on the edge on the top step."

"You didn't tell your family all that."

"Ah know. Ah didn't want tuh tell them anything. Ah'm an ageing man with a history of hypertension. They worry tuh much. Ah tried tuh pretend it was nothing, but Ah guess it got the best of me."

Dr. Parks looked up at the monitor and Reverend Oliver's pressure was 242/168. "Okay, Reverend Oliver, you need to relax. I'm going to increase your medication, but you really need to relax. I don't want you to have any visitors today."

"But what about my wife and son? They'll be back around three o'clock. Ah really want tuh see them."

"If you relax for the next hour, I'll let them see you for 15 minutes."

"Ah'll try."

❋ ❋ ❋

Malcolm returned to his parents' home. Thea was sitting at the kitchen table looking at the telephone number for Gregory Lefferts' Real Estate Office. Malcolm wanted to hold his mother. Her world, as she knew it, had suddenly collapsed. Her face was puffy. A lump had formed at the base of his throat. The ramifications of his father's actions were just sinking in. While he was angry with the Turners for humiliating his father, he hadn't felt his mother's pain. She rarely displayed a disturbing emotion. When she believed her control was weakening, she substituted anger as a camouflage for her more painful emotions, and even then this display was expressed by her saying "damn-it", a stomp of her foot and a frowning face; she would snatch herself around, her words were sharp and her motions jerky, before calming herself, staring out the window or leaving the room. His mother's puffy eyes, a crumpled tissue held in her hands, and the soft spoken words or lack of them caused him concern.

"Hi Mom, how was yuh day?" Malcolm couldn't think of anything else to say. He walked closer to her, placing his hands on her shoulders and gently massaged her tensed muscles.

"Ah went tuh see the Turners and never got tuh the real estate office. If yuh father mentions Mr. Lefferts, Ah'll just have to say Ah didn't get to see him yet."

"Sure Mama. No problem. Well, Ah have Dad's disability papers. We have a little over an hour before time tuh leave for the hospital. What did yuh talk tuh the Turner's about?"

"Ah had tuh see them. Ah had tuh tell them how sorry Ah was over this nasty situation. How sorry Ah was because Ah should've known. Malcolm, there were signs."

"Mom, yuh didn't do anything wrong. Yuh don't have anything tuh be sorry for. Ah'm angry with Dad too. Ah'm angry he put us through this. Ah'm angry he could hurt a child and destroy a family. Ah'm angry he didn't tell me Johnny was my brother." Malcolm removed his hands from his mother's shoulders and walked to the kitchen window.

"Malcolm," Thea called out.

Malcolm was still looking out the window; he appeared to be thinking back and he was caught up in the past.

"Malcolm, do yuh hear me callin' yuh?" Thea walked to the window and rubbed her hand against his arm.

"Yes Mama, Ah'm sorry. Ah was just thinking about Johnny."

They walked back to the table and sat across from each other.

"Ah told the Turners the doctor said someone beat up yuh father."

"Yuh told them that. Ma! Ah wanted tuh speak with Dad before that got out."

"Ah didn't know that. Besides, Ah think someone did beat him."

"What makes yuh say that?"

"Well, last Saturday morning . . . Ah mean early in the morning; sometime about 2:00, 2:30, Ah'm not sure the time, it was just real early. Someone called him. Yuh father said he had tuh go out. He said it was someone in need. Ah thought he had tuh go tuh the clinic or hospital. Ah though he had tuh meet with a family in spiritual need, so Ah told him tuh be careful and went back tuh sleep. The next time Ah saw yuh father was when Ah woke later in the morning. His face was bruised and swollen. That's when he told me he fell and hit his face against the banister."

"If someone beat him Ah hope Ah find him first," Malcolm said.

"Malcolm, please don't bring no more grief tuh this family."

"Yeah!" Malcolm stood and walked away from the table. His attitude tightened his posture and caused his jaw muscles to twitch. "Okay Mom."

"My Lord!" Thea said, this time it was fear she was hiding. "Yuh stay out of it, Malcolm. Let the police handle it."

* * *

When Malcolm and Thea stepped off the elevator they noticed Dr. Parks leaning over the desk speaking with the nurse. When the elevator door was ready to close it sounded off a 'ding' which caused him to turn and look in their direction. He excused himself and walked over to speak with them before allowing their visit with Reverend Oliver.

Malcolm greeted the doctor with a head bow. "Is my father all right?"

"Yes he's coming along, but I must ask you to limit your visit to 15 minutes. It seems any and everything causes a rise in his pressure. He appears to be worrying about something. I have him on the highest dose of the strongest medication allowable, but it continued to linger in the dangerous range and the slightest upset seems to cause it to spike. So please try to keep him calm. Weigh your words carefully to keep him from getting upset."

"We will," Malcolm said. "Ah picked up forms for his disability leave and he will need yuh tuh fill them out. He's a teacher and school begins this week."

"Okay, I'll complete them. He won't be able to work for some time. You can pick up the completed forms at the nurse's station tomorrow." Dr. Parks was looking over the papers as he spoke. "Oh, I want you to know I spoke to him about his injury. I also spoke with two detectives this morning. Your father said he fell on the porch twice. He said he didn't tell you everything because he didn't want you all to worry. I don't believe him. I watched his pressure increase as he spoke. Something is upsetting him, but I can't get inside his head and that's not my job. Right now I want his pressure under control and stabilized. There are other doctors that delve into the psyche."

"Thank yuh Dr. Parks. We'll be careful with what we say and we won't stay a moment longer than fifteen minutes. Could you have the nurse remind us when our time is up?" Thea asked. She was back to holding her pocketbook tight against her chest.

Malcolm nodded and moved to the side so the doctor could pass.

* * *

Reverend Oliver was watching the window when Malcolm and Thea appeared. He smiled when Thea kissed him gently on his forehead and took a seat near his bed.

"We saw yuh doctor," Malcolm began, "and he's only giving us fifteen minutes with you. Yuh doctor said yuh disability papers will be ready by tomorrow, and Mama has Gregory Lefferts coming by the house this Friday. Okay, how do yuh feel?"

Thea glanced at Malcolm, and then frowned at the ease in which he could lie.

"Ah'm comin' along. If Ah do what they tell me Ah'll be out of here soon. Ah been thinkin' . . . can one of you ask Reverend Lipton tuh come tuh the hospital. Ah need tuh talk tuh him and ask him tuh pray with me. Ah don't have Reverend Turner anymore."

Thea shifted in her chair and gave her husband a tiny supporting smile. Owen returned her smile and looked back at Malcolm.

"Dad . . . yuh gonna tell Reverend Lipton about this?"

"Ah already did. The last thing Ah remember on Sunday was the two of us praying together. Ah would like him tuh continue tuh pray with me.

"All right Dad. Ah'll give him a call as soon as we leave here. Oh Dad , Ah hear Johnny is coming home this Friday and will be home for a week. Ah know he's really worried about yuh and Ah been callin' him, tellin' him how yuh doing."

"Is that so?" Reverend Oliver whispered. His eyes glazed over and a tiny peaceful smile brightened his face.

Thea looked up at the monitor. "Owen, your pressure looks much better."

"Yeah Dad, 149/98, that's pretty good. Keep that up and yuh'll be out of here."

"Ah guess yuh fifteen minutes are up, here comes the nurse," Reverend Oliver said.

"Well Owen, we promised the doctor we'd only stay fifteen minutes. We'll see yuh tomorrow. Please rest." Thea reached over and patted his hand.

"See yuh tomorrow Dad. Listen tuh Mama and rest." Malcolm left the room leaving his mother to have a few moments of private time with his father.

"Ah will Malcolm."

Thea turned to Owen when she felt him take hold of her hand. "Ah love yuh Thea. Please stay with me," he whispered. His grip was solid, but gentle enough to make a statement.

Thea tilted her head slightly to the left and gave Owen a gentle smile. "Ah Love yuh too Owen." She allowed him to hold her hand, knowing her release would come soon and pulling away would only upset him. She forced another smile and when he released her hand she rubbed her palm against his injured jaw. She didn't lie when she told him she loved him and she didn't commit herself to remain with him, but like Malcolm, she led him to believe everything was going to be all right; for Thea, that was the same as a lie. She continued to smile while she moved back toward the door. After leaving the room, she stood in front of the large window, glanced at Owen and mouthed, "Ah love you."

Thea's strength waned as soon as she was out of Owen sight. She could see Malcolm waiting for her at the elevator and hurried toward him, believing if he moved, she would lose her direction. She wanted to go home; she wanted to pray; she wanted to cry. Spending just fifteen minutes with Owen forced her to be dishonest and she never intentionally lied in any form in her life. It was a feeling she didn't like and she didn't know how to rid herself of the emptiness she felt.

Malcolm was startled by his mother's appearance. He hurried toward her. "Mama! Are yuh all right?"

Thea felt his hands rubbing her upper arms but she didn't tell him what was bothering her. She knew he would never understand. Malcolm had spent his entire life polishing lies so they resembled the truth to the point that he believed them himself.

"Ah'm all right Malcolm. Ah just want tuh go home."

* * *

Malcolm held his car door open for his mother. She entered slowly, like she was approaching her eighties. Her burdens were heavier than she had ever carried and only her Lord prevented her from bearing the weight alone.

"Malcolm, Ah don't want tuh leave Rehoboth and Ah don't want tuh leave yuh father. But, if anyone has tuh leave it will be him. Lord knows Ah love him and Ah don't know what my life would be like without him, but Ah'm not selling the house." Thea had crossed her arms in a defiant tone.

"Mama, did Ah hear yuh say yuh not leaving Rehoboth?" Malcolm glanced at his mother and placed his eyes back on the road. All he could do was hold tight to the steering wheel and try to get back to Rehoboth safely.

"Yuh heard right. When Ah returned from the Turner's home, I sat under that weeping willow tree and Ah prayed for answers. Ah'm gonna keep on praying, cause the one thing Ah know now is, Ah'm not leavin' Rehoboth. Ah didn't do anything wrong. My life is here. Yuh father is the one who needs tuh leave Rehoboth. Ah want you tuh go home and find a place near you for yuh father." Thea's face was emotionless and her eyes fixed at the windshield. "Just scout out places close by where yuh can visit him regularly. Ah don't believe Theresa will welcome him in yuh home as openly as she did for me. Ah took a vow for better or worse. Ah did nothing wrong. My life is here. Yuh father will have tuh leave me. Ah will not break my marriage vows. He has wronged me and the people of this community and he will have tuh leave, but he will have choices he can make. The Lord will tell me what he has to do and the choice will be his." Thea never looked at Malcolm. Sunlight peeked from behind the dark clouds and alternated in flashes across her face through the windshield. She squinted her eyes and moved her hand to cover her brow like a visor.

Malcolm could only give his mother a few quick glances and continued to drive. "Mama what are yuh talking about? What choice do you have for him tuh make?"

"Ah'm not real clear on that yet, but the Lord will tell me when the time is right."

"Mama . . . what are yuh talking about?"

"That doesn't matter now. Ah just think yuh should go home. Go be with yuh wife. Go back tuh work. Ah can take care of things around here. Ah'll tell yuh father Ah sent yuh home and yuh can come on the weekend if yuh want, but Ah don't want yuh messing up yuh job and yuh life. Ah can take care of things here and when yuh father is well, then he'll really need yuh, especially if he leaves Rehoboth. Ah've given this some thought and Ah can handle things around here. Malcolm . . . listen, everything will be alright, so don't worry."

"Mama, you are not making sense."

"Tuh say the Lord is my Sheppard, is not making sense?" Thea turned toward him placing her right hand on the dashboard and her left on the back of the soft leather seat. "Malcolm, yuh not stupid and yuh have excellent hearing. Ah'm not leaving my life here in Rehoboth. Ah didn't do anything wrong. Yuh father might have tuh leave, but Ah'm not going anywhere. It will be yuh father's decision; if he stays he will pay whatever the price required of him. Ah don't know what that price is yet, but the Lord will speak tuh me. Ah will not break my marriage vows, so Ah want yuh tuh go home and be ready for when yuh father really needs yuh. Please don't make me say it again!"

The air in the car was climate controlled, but Malcolm lowered his window anyway. The scent of the air outside the car warned of a storm, but Malcolm drove with his elbow resting on the door and holding the side of his head against the storm that had already begun in the car. Dark clouds were on the move, blocking the sun like a canopy over the land while the Lord did his work. Flashes of light raced across the distant sky and moments later the thunder roared.

"It seems like we're in for a spell of bad weather. Ah think yuh should pull under that overpass until it passes." Thea pointed at the concrete shelter.

Malcolm did as his mother suggested, and lowered her window halfway before turning off the engine. He shifted his weight and gave her his full attention. "So, when do yuh want me tuh leave?"

"Ah'm not rushing yuh, but it's still early. If yuh leave as soon as yuh drop me off, yuh could be home before dark. Ah'll tell yuh father Ah sent yuh home so yuh could save yuh sick time for when he comes home."

"Sounds like yuh rushing me off." Malcolm reached for the ignition and started the car. The humidity and his mother's compulsive demands were irritating him. He raised the windows and turned on the air conditioner. He wanted to drive off through the furious storm which was far less than the storm that was raging inside of him.

* * *

"Oh Nat," Elizabeth said. "There's Daddy and Mama. Let's stop." Her parents were sitting on their front porch as Nat drove around the last bend on Rehoboth Road.

The passing storm added a crispness to the early evening air and removed the humidity that lingered most of the day. Nat looked at Elizabeth and smiled. She was so excited, like a child. He had been married to her for eighteen years and she never asked to stop at her parents' home when she knew her father was there. He slowed down and took the right turn into their driveway as soon as the words passed her lips.

Elizabeth got out of the car and quickened her pace, hurrying toward the porch. "Hi Mama," she called out, but her arms were reaching out preparing to embrace her father when she was still more than ten feet away.

Reverend Turner stood. He moved slow and steady using his hands against the armrest to push himself up. By the time Elizabeth reached him, his arms were also open wide. They embraced as though they hadn't seen each other in years. Loretha stood, clasps her hands, and smiled. Nat smiled, displaying all of his front teeth and he placed his arm around Loretha's shoulder.

The extra chair that Thea had sat in was still on the porch. "Let me get another chair," Loretha said.

"Ah'll get it," Nat said. "Yuh don't need tuh be luggin' chairs around."

"Grab that old wooden chair in the corner," Loretha called out.

"Ah got it Ma."

"Put it here by me Nat," Loretha said. "Let's let them two get reacquainted. So, how yuh been? The last time Ah saw yuh, yuh nearly scared me tuh death."

"Sorry 'bout that." He held the back of the chair while Loretha eased herself down. "Ah've had a bad back since college and sometimes it causes me tuh have terrible muscle spasms."

"Yeah, Johnny told me about yuh bad back and how yuh gonna be sore from that last attack."

"Yes ma'am, but compared tuh the muscle spasms, the soreness is nothin'."

"Well Ah'll pray all yuh pain leaves yuh."

Nat smiled as he watched the interaction between Elizabeth and her father. A moment of quiet separated his thoughts from Loretha's and she changed the subject.

"Yuh know, Thea visited us tuhday."

"She did? How's the Rev.?" Nat said, sitting back in his chair.

"Ah thought yuh wouldn't care."

Nat sat up and leaned close to Loretha. "Ah don't. Ah'm just a bit nosey." He laughed and sat back in his chair. He interlocked his fingers, placed his elbows on the armrest and allowed his clasped hands to rest against his stomach.

"Thea and Malcolm had tuh leave the hospital early. The doctor said somethin' was botherin' Owen; something was upsettin' him."

"Ah'd say something was upsetting him. He's just lost everything," Nat whispered.

"Yeah, that's probably what it is and the doctor doesn't know about that. It could be that, but his doctor said he didn't fall against no banister. It seems he has two fractures tuh his jaw and that doctor said he was beat up."

Nat sat at attention. "Say what?" He almost yelled, but he was always thinking about Elizabeth. He looked over at her smiling, talking and holding her father's hand. He looked back at Loretha. "Beat up?" he whispered.

"Ma, did yuh say Owen was beat up?"

"Yeah, that's what Thea said the doctor b'lieves."

"Ma . . . yuh have tuh start from the beginnin'. What did she say?" Nat was sitting on the edge of his chair trying to get Loretha's attention. He placed his hand on her hand and she turned toward him.

"Oh . . . yuh ain't just nosey, yuh do care." Loretha chuckled lightly and gave her hands a single clap. "Okay . . . okay . . . well . . . Owen told Thea and Malcolm he fell, but the doctor didn't believe them. He said it couldn't have happened that way because Owen had two fractures to his jaw, so he called the police. Thea said when they were leavin' the hospital they passed two detectives."

"Did Reverend Oliver say someone beat him?"

"No. Ah don't think so. Ah think she said that's what the doctor said."

Nat sat back on his chair and his head rocked like his neck was made of rubber. He could feel his muscles tightening. Loretha was staring at him. He stood and stretched. "Well Ma, Ah think it's time for me tuh leave. It's been a long day. Ah do need tuh rest my back. Beth can stay and spend some time with y'all."

"John . . . Nat is ready tuh leave. 'Lizabeth, yuh can stay awhile, have dinner with us and take Nat a plate. Ah know yuh tired of lookin' at food 'specially when yuh been lookin' at it all day." Loretha patted the back of

Nat's hand. "Is that okay with yuh, Nat?"

Nat smiled.

"Okay, it's settled. Ah'll drive yuh home Nat," Loretha said.

Nat smiled again. "It's okay Beth. Ah'm kinda tired. Ah need tuh take my medicine and take a little nap. Ah gotta help these sore muscles along."

Elizabeth smiled. "Okay, Ah'll see yuh when Ah get home."

Nat could feel his muscles tightening more with each step he took toward Loretha's car. Deep breaths were helpful and he prayed another muscle spasm wouldn't come over him before he could get to his medicine. He opened the door to Loretha's car and sat resting his head on the back of the seat. He took another deep breath and then another.

"Sore muscles getting the best of yuh?" Loretha got in the car and started the engine. "Yuh really look tired."

"Yeah, Ah know. It's all part of the bad back syndrome."

"Well yuh know what yuh need tuh do tuh feel better," Loretha said while driving up Rehoboth Road.

"Yuh so right." As soon as Nat arrived home he eased himself out of the car like a man twice his age, and waved as Loretha drove away.

Ten milligrams of Valium relaxed the muscles in Nat's back and slowed his racing thoughts, reducing his worry over Reverend Oliver's condition. He pulled the lever on his recliner and lowered it so he could stand. His legs felt like rubber. He took a deep breath, and when he felt his strength return, he made his way across the room. Dave Brubeck's 'Take 5' cassette was calling him. He slipped the tape into his stereo system and returned to his recliner. Brubeck's horn sounded 'Blue Rondo a la Turk' and filled Nat's den just as he was resting his head on the back of his chair. He closed his eyes and Reverend Oliver was in his head again. *He will never tell anyone what happened, no matter what. Ah think he believes he deserved to be punished. Johnny will be here in a few days. Ah'll know what's really going on then, but Ah'll have tuh ask him. Johnny would never talk tuh me about Oliver. No matter what Oliver says, Ah'll deny it. It's his word against mine.* Nat's mind rambled on until sleep finally took over and Brubeck played on.

Chapter 8

Theresa expected Malcolm to return home around 8:15 p.m. He had called as soon as he arrived at his mother's home to tell her to expect him that evening. When she heard his car pull into the driveway she rushed out to greet him. He stopped at the beginning of the walk and they smiled at each other. When he reached the top of the porch they hugged and entered the house arm in arm.

"Ah love you, Theresa," Malcolm whispered before he swooped her up in his arms and carried her into their bedroom. He was tired from the drive, but he loved Theresa equally as much as he loved his mother, a different kind of love. Both loves holding residences in different corners of his heart. He felt his mother's anguish from his father's secret. He held a deep and frightening secret of his own.

"Malcolm, what are yuh doing?" The wild look in his eyes excited her.

Gently, he kissed her forehead, her nose and his lips brushed down onto her breast. She slipped out of her blouse and he pulled her bra down and unfastened it. Theresa was weak with wanting him.

In time they lay naked and their love making was taking them into each other's world. If he were tired from his drive or depressed from his father's dilemma or Johnny's aloofness or thoughts of Randy, he pushed those feelings aside and channeled that energy into making love to his wife. He wanted her fulfillment to be more than she knew was possible.

Malcolm laid his head against Theresa soft breast; their hearts pounded to the same beat and he was too tired to speak. *Ah don't need Randy,* he thought. *Ah just made crazy love with my wife and Ah loved it. Ah'll win Johnny over and my life will be complete.*

"Oh my God, Malcolm, that was wonderful. If yuh keep that up we'll be at it again."

"You taste so good," he moaned.

"And yuh loved me like yuh never did. What brought that on?"

He ran his fingers through her hair. "Yuh were pretty wonderful yuhself." He kissed her on the forehead. "Ah love yuh and Ah never want tuh do anything tuh hurt yuh."

"How would yuh hurt me?"

"Ah see how my father hurt my mother. Oh . . . Ah don't want tuh talk about it now. Let's take a bath tuhgether. Yuh lay there just like that and Ah'll fill that big whirlpool tub yuh had installed. We can relax and have a romantic evening. While the tubs filling, Ah just have tuh call Johnny. Now, don't get dressed, Ah'll be right back. Ah should've called him as soon as Ah arrived home, but Ah couldn't resist yuh. Ah don't want tuh miss him."

Theresa pulled the sheet over her naked body and smiled at Malcolm while he reached for his robe and headed for the bathroom to adjust the water. He returned to the bedroom, sat on the side of the bed, and placed a call to Johnny. He closed his eyes. *Please Johnny. Please don't turn me away. We were just kids. Yuh my brother; Ah love yuh. Ah've always loved yuh.*

"Turners' residence," Marian answered.

"Malcolm Oliver callin' tuh speak with John Turner please." Malcolm held the phone to his ear, and looked up at the ceiling.

"One moment, sir," Marian said.

Malcolm sat up straight and waited for Johnny to pick up the telephone.

"Mr. Oliver, Mr. Turner is indisposed. May I take a message?"

"No! Yuh may not take a message!" Malcolm slammed the phone down so hard the internal bells rang. "That pompous son-of-a-bitch, Ah won't call him again!" He rubbed his fingers over his eyes until they met at the bridge of his nose. He was hurt and angry. "What kind of person can hold hatred for years? Ah don't have that kind of energy and Ah thought Ah was the bad guy. The next move will be his."

"It's okay Malcolm. Don't let Johnny ruin our night." Theresa rose up on her knees and wrapped her arms around his neck.

"Never Theresa, c'mon honey our bath should be ready." He looked up and tried to soften his tone, but his disappointment still filtered through.

Theresa eased herself off the bed and positioned her naked body in front of her husband. Malcolm stood and allowed his robe to drop to the floor; he wanted their flesh to meet. He almost allowed his dilemma with Johnny to ruin his evening with Theresa.

"Oh honey! We have a soothing bath waiting for us," he whispered.

They held hands like young lovers and walked into the large bathroom.

The whirlpool tub was just large enough for two people who wanted to be close enough for loving. Theresa turned on the jets and curled up in Malcolm's arms.

"Okay yuh won. Now Ah know what Ah been missing."

"Ah have more for yuh," Theresa teased.

As the water jets massaged Malcolm, Theresa's touch made him want more of her. Lovemaking in a whirlpool tub was a whole new experience; stimulation came at them from all directions.

"Malcolm . . . Ah hate tuh ask yuh tuh have more rough days, this sex is great."

"It's a real tension buster," Malcolm said before thinking. "Oh Ah'm sorry baby. Ah was thinking about yuh all day." His hands were under the water caressing her body.

"That's all right; Ah'll soothe yuh tension anytime." They laughed and held each other tighter.

"Malcolm, tell me what happened since yuh been gone."

"We can talk about that later. Right now let's mess up the guess room."

Theresa tilted her head and gave him a sexy smile.

* * *

Malcolm knew where to find Randy at 7:30 in the morning. He called it 'Randy's quiet place before the storm.' Randy always arrived at work by 7:15 and began surveying Atlanta from the 26th floor conference room's wall of windows at the suite of Landers, Landers & Fine. Malcolm took one step inside the large room and stole a glance at him while he stood holding his coffee mug. He smiled and stepped out of the room, returning moments later with his own cup of coffee. He walked over and joined Randy at the window. Randy shifted his eyes into his peripheral sphere and gave Malcolm a reserved smile before returning to surveying Atlanta. "Hey man," quietly passed his lips before he took a sip of his coffee.

"Morning, now cut the bull. Ah know yuh glad tuh see me," Malcolm said.

"Yeah man. When did yuh return?" He took another sip. "How's yuh father?"

"Last night. He's comin' along. It was best tuh return tuh work." Malcolm flipped back his jacket and slid his right hand in his pants pocket. "He's in good hands and Ah can drive down on weekends. He may need me more when he gets out of the hospital."

The men stood looking out over Atlanta while their minds were busy planning their day or thinking about yesterday or wondering what was to come tomorrow. Five minutes slipped away while they stood holding half empty mugs of cold coffee.

"Well, Ah'll talk tuh yuh later. Ah have tuh see Jack and let him know Ah'm back." Malcolm nodded and hurried to the door.

Randy turned and watched Malcolm leave the room. "Hey . . . how about lunch?"

Malcolm stuck his head back in the room. "Gotcha . . . lunch, Ah do need tuh talk tuh yuh," Malcolm stated.

*　*　*

As soon as Malcolm returned from meeting with his supervisor, Jack Hamilton, he made his rounds of brief meetings with his co-workers to discuss the accounts they were managing for him. There were a few notices on his desk from clients who were willing to wait for his return.

By 11:45 p.m., the secretary called, "Mr. Oliver, Ah have a call for you from Mr. Turner."

Malcolm pushed himself back in his chair, "Tell him Ah'm not at my desk and take a message."

"Yes sir," the secretary said.

Malcolm tapped his pen against his teeth, stood and put on his suit jacket. He glanced across the cubicle and Randy was staring at him. He smiled, nodded toward the elevator and turned to pick up his keys from his desk draw. When he turned back Randy was on his way. He hurried down the corridor and caught up with him just as the elevator doors opened.

"Hey man. How about Emil's? It's on me," Malcolm said.

"What's the occasion?" Randy responded as he looked up at the express elevator indicator light.

"No occasion, Ah just need peace and quiet."

"Hey," Randy said as he shrugged his shoulder, "it's on you, man."

*　*　*

Malcolm tossed his keys to the valet as soon as he stepped out of the car in front of Emil's and he and Randy entered the dimly lit, highly rated restaurant.

"Reservation for two under Oliver. Remember, Ah asked for seclusion."

"Yes sir, Mr. Oliver. Please follow me," they head waiter announced.

Malcolm and Randy were led to a table in the corner of the restaurant. A small antique lamp with a tiffany shade set near the wall on top of the glass top, table. Malcolm asked that the waiter come immediately to take their order. They were familiar with the menu and their time was limited.

Randy ordered the filet of beef with a baked potato and broccoli and Malcolm decided on the rib eye steak with rice pilaf and asparagus. They shared a perfectly chilled bottle of Shiraz wine.

As soon as Malcolm finished his lunch he placed his napkin on the table and set back in his chair. He rubbed his hand over the back of his neck and took another sip of wine.

When Randy was finished with his meal he placed his fork down and lifted his wine glass. He glanced over the table at Malcolm and smiled.

Malcolm smiled back at him then his face turned cold. "Are yuh willin' tuh trade Gail and the boys for me?" he asked Randy and he followed up with a penetrating stare.

Randy's chest heaved in a minor spasm. He coughed and covered his mouth with the cloth napkin. He set his wine glass down. His expression turned bland and he moved back in his chair as if he had been deflated.

"Damn Randy!" Malcolm whispered. "Don't yuh love me?" He placed both hands palm down on the table and leaned over his empty plate.

Randy coughed again and cleared his throat. "Just what are yuh tryin' tuh say." He leaned forward, picked up his wine glass and gulped down the wine like it was water before giving Malcolm his full attention.

"Why don't yuh answer my question?" Malcolm was still leaning over his empty plate.

"Ah love my family more. Ah love our way of life, and yes Ah love you," Randy whispered. He squinted and shifted his eyes, like he wasn't sure what Malcolm was getting at.

"Yuh love me in that order? Yuh don't love me first, then yuh family, then yuh way of life? Now . . . Ah want yuh tuh take a moment and think about it real hard." Malcolm sat back in his chair and crossed his legs and stared at Randy. *God, Ah didn't start this right. Ah sounded like a real bastard,* he thought. *Ah hope this goes over well. The things we did with each other started out as experimental. It was a first for both of us. We have wives, we don't need the sex. God! He's my best friend and Ah want tuh keep it that way, without the sex.*

"Why yuh messin' with my head? We always had an understanding. Ah'm gonna always love my family first," Randy said and he pushed his empty plate toward the center of the table.

"Ah hear yuh man. Ah'm sorry Ah came on so strong, but Ah bought yuh here because Ah need tuh say things." Malcolm backed up in his chair and poured more wine into their glasses. He leaned on his elbows and extended himself over the table into Randy's circle of space. "Randy . . . what Ah'm tryin' tuh say is . . . Ah'm so very happy yuh love yuh wife and family first. Ah love my wife. If yuh could be my friend without being my lover too, it would be ideal, but Ah don't think that's possible."

"Yuh breaking up with me?" Randy placed his trembling hand over Malcolm's hand and his unblinking eyes fixed on Malcolm's face.

Malcolm pushed himself back in the chair and pulled his hand free before signaling for the waiter. "Check please."

"Why'd yuh bring me here tuh tell me this? Why at lunch when yuh knew we'd have tuh return tuh work?" Randy spoke softly, but the expression on his face yelled his words across the table at Malcolm. He looked up to see the waiter standing over them with the black leather folder that held the check.

"Your check, sir." He placed the folder on the table, took a slight bow and walked away.

Malcolm stood and removed his wallet from his back pocket. "Because Ah knew yuh'd be forced tuh pull yuhself tuhgether and think about what Ah've said." He removed enough money to cover the bill and the tip and continued talking. "Believe me Randy, it would tear me up tuh lose yuh friendship."

Both men walked away from the table. Randy was quiet. He knew what he wanted to say, but unlike Malcolm, he knew the timing was poor.

"Let's work on the friendship," Malcolm continues saying as they left the restaurant. He called for the car and one of the valets hurried off to the parking lot leaving the other valet to pretend to not be interested in their conversation.

The young valet drove up with the car. "Ah got it," Randy yelled out as he slipped the tip in his hand. Malcolm was already sitting behind the wheel when Randy closed the door.

"Man, yuh handling this very well. We might just make it," Malcolm said just as he put the car in gear. Randy gave him a coy smile and nodded his head.

* * *

Another message from Johnny had been left on Malcolm's desk while he was at lunch. He sat in his chair and noticed the time of his call to be 12:55

p.m. *Ah'm gonna return his call this time. But first Ah'll find out how Dad is doing.* He loosened his tie and reached for the telephone.

"Hello Mama, It's me. Malcolm," He sat back in his chair, crossed his legs and spoke softly into the phone.

"Of course it's you Malcolm. Ah only have one son. Ah hope yuh callin' from work?"

"Yes ma'am. How's Dad tuhday?"

"A little better than yesterday. Ah got tuh stay a little longer. Ah told him Ah made yuh go home so yuh could get back tuh work and Ah had Reverend Lipton come by and pray with him."

"So Dad didn't think badly of me for leavin'?" He pushed himself back in his chair and propped his feet on his desk.

"Oh no . . . he agreed with me. Ah told yuh he'd understand."

"Thank yuh Mama. Ah'll be there Saturday, but in the afternoon and Ah'll stay through Sunday evening. Theresa might come with me. She thinks yuh makin' the right move and is supportin' yuh one hundred percent."

"Well, yuh just thank her for me. Ah needed tuh hear that."

"Yes Mama. Ah have tuh go now." Malcolm looked up and Randy was looking over the top of his cubicle. "So long Mama. See yuh Saturday." He hung up the phone, stood and searched the nearby cubicles looking for co-workers who might be looking on. "Randy! Why are yuh standing here like this?"

"We need tuh talk." Randy's voice was so weak Malcolm could hardly hear him. He was breathing heavy, perspiration beaded his face like tiny pearls, his body trembled, and the whites of his eyes were pinkish. He looked like he was going to collapse and die at that very moment.

Malcolm rushed to his side, helped him inside the cubicle and to his chair. "Man yuh look terrible. Did yuh do something tuh yuhself?"

Randy shook his head.

"Ah'm callin' Jack. Yuh need tuh go tuh the infirmary." Malcolm picked up the phone and Randy grabbed and squeezed his wrist.

"No. Ah just need tuh rest a minute. Please don't call anyone," Randy whispered before releasing Malcolm's wrist.

"Randy, yuh sick." Malcolm appeared frantic, and his eyes searched Randy's eyes, his face, hands and any and all areas of him that might give him a clue to his ailment.

"Ah'm scared. Ah don't know what's happening tuh me . . . maybe it'll pass."

Tears rolled down his face and he pulled his handkerchief from his pocket.

"Ah think we need tuh get yuh tuh the hospital." Malcolm placed his hand on Randy's chest and his heart was pounding so fast he couldn't count the beats. He backed out of the cubicle and ran toward Jack Hamilton's office.

"No Malcolm," Randy whispered. His weak voice only hastened Malcolm's pace.

Moments later, Malcolm and Jack returned and found Randy sitting at Malcolm's desk, resting his head on his folded arms.

"If yuh can help me tuh the infirmary, Ah promise Ah'll do whatever the nurse says," Randy whispered

"Damn Randy, yuh look like yuh ready tuh drop dead. What happened tuh yuh?" Jack asked. "Malcolm why didn't yuh just call the nurse, then call me? Yuh may have wasted precious time." He took a deep breath, then exhaled before picking up the phone. "Call for an ambulance and meet me at Malcolm Oliver's work station with some oxygen," he bellowed orders at the company nurse."

* * *

It was late afternoon and Malcolm was still at the hospital. He remained with Randy until his wife, Gail arrived. The doctor's assured her they didn't believe her husband was suffering from anything other than severe anxiety, but they wanted to admit him for close observation and to run a few diagnostic tests. Malcolm knew what caused the anxiety. He held Randy's hand, then leaned over and whispered in his ear, "Good-bye."

Randy knew he meant it this time. He turned away and found himself looking at Gail's beautiful and concerned face. He pulled his hand from Malcolm's and rubbed Gail's hands and arms. Malcolm smiled, nodded at Gail and left Randy's bedside.

Malcolm passed the row of telephones as he walked from the emergency room on his way to his car. He was still angry with Johnny, but he wasn't going to allow him to be the better man. It had been a crazy day and he wished he could have stayed in Rehoboth. He reached in his pocket and pulled out a quarter, just enough to reach the operator and charge the call to his home telephone.

"The Legend Bank, Mr. Turner's office," the receptionist sang out.

"Hello, my name is Malcolm Oliver. Ah'm returning a call tuh Mr. Turner."

"Mr. Turner is not available. May I take a message?"

"Yes," Malcolm was quick to answer. He decided not to place himself in a position to be humiliated by Johnny. He asked the receptionist to note that Reverend Oliver's condition was improving and gave her his mother's telephone number so Johnny could call her for updates. He decided if he were to receive a call from Johnny it would be because Johnny wanted to speak with him. He thanked the receptionist and hung up the phone.

* * *

Normally Malcolm wouldn't pick up his office phone until 9:00 a.m., but because of his father's illness, he made an exception. When he heard Randy's voice he started to hang up, but he knew he would only call back.

"Thanks for taking the call. I know it's Friday, yuh busiest day, but Ah haven't spoken tuh yuh since Wednesday. Ah had time tuh think about what yuh said," Randy whispered.

"Why are you whispering?" Malcolm sat with his elbows on his desk and whispered back into the phone. He knew Randy understood he was in the office and had to whisper.

"Gail didn't leave the house yet."

"Then why did yuh call me?"

"She's not in this room and Ah wanted tuh speak with yuh before yuh got busy."

"Listen, yuh may be trying tuh just be friends, but apparently yuh body is rejecting yuh wishes. Yuh need time. Ah'm willin' tuh give yuh time, but yuh got tuh get it tuhgether or Ah'm gone." Malcolm stood and paced the small confines of his cubicle.

"Ah just wanted tuh tell yuh Ah was sorry. Ah felt myself getting sick and Ah could've gone directly tuh the infirmary, but Ah wanted yuh tuh see how Ah was feeling. Ah wanted yuh tuh feel sorry for me and stay with me. Ah'm sorry. Please accept my apology."

"Ah will this time. Ah really want tuh be yuh friend, but yuh have tuh hold it tuhgether man. Yuh   get better and Ah'll see yuh next week." Malcolm looked over the cubicles. He saw Jack heading toward his office.

"Where yuh going?" Randy continued whispering.

"Damn, Randy. Ah know yuh not gonna stalk me," Malcolm scolded.

"Sorry man. Ah'll see yuh next week."

"See yuh man." Malcolm hung up the phone and walked toward the kitchen for a second cup of coffee. He had passed the bulletin board several times since returning to work and had not noticed that Landers, Landers & Fine was opening another office in Northern Atlanta and the firm was seeking managers, supervisors and senior agents. *Damn! This is the last day to file for these positions. Ah'm gonna submit an 'application of interest' for Randy and myself for the manager and supervisor positions.* He removed the thumbtack holding the notice and hurried to the copy room. It seemed to take forever before the copy machine warmed up. Before returning to his desk, he placed the original notice back on the bulletin board.

By the time Malcolm returned to his cubicle the office had come alive with chatter. The workday had begun and that was a great camouflage for his call to Randy. "Hey man, don't talk. Ah just need tuh ask yuh something. Did yuh see the notice for the new office building the firm is opening in Northern Atlanta?" Malcolm didn't have to whisper. He hoped Randy could hear him clearly if he just spoke in his normal tone.

"No. Ah didn't see or hear anything about that."

"Okay, listen man. Ah made copies. If yuh promise tuh behave, Ah'll run the forms over tuh yuh house at lunchtime. All yuh need tuh file is an 'application of interest,' but the deadline is tuhday. Yuh qualify for the manager and supervisor position. The base salary is $10,000-$20,000 more than yuh current base salary and the annual commission ranges from $40,000-$60,000 in a good market year." Malcolm paced the floor of the cubicle as he spoke.

"Man Ah'm okay."

"Okay now, Ah'm just gonna have enough time for yuh tuh fill out yuh paperwork and get back tuh work." He sat back in his chair again and listened to Randy.

"No problem. Damn! They do that shit all the time. The good old boys had that notice for a while and they probably placed it on the board late last night. This is the mid-eighties, and we managed tuh get pass the front door, but they don't plan on letting us get anything else. Look who's still ruling the roost. We have the credentials, intelligence and experience. They fight tuh have us on their team because with us they make their goal and keep their large bonuses, but it's their intention tuh keep us as their Indians, and never allow us tuh be chiefs," Randy preached.

"Okay man Ah'll see yuh at lunchtime. Then Ah'll take care of everything else."

Chapter 9

Thea turned the engine of her car off as soon as she drove under the aging weeping willow tree. She rested her head on the back of the seat and closed her eyes. A sweet summer breeze bathed her face; its coolness was refreshing as it moved across the damp tracks of her tears. Unhappiness came in several forms and at that moment it visited her with many uncertainties of what the near future with her husband and life in Rehoboth would be like.

She had just returned home from visiting Owen. His blood pressure had been under control and stable for longer periods. Reverend Lipton had visited him three times since Wednesday, but his doctor still remained convinced he had been assaulted. It was Saturday and Malcolm and Theresa were due by early afternoon. Thea had plenty of food; several church members had been delivering prepared dishes all week. When she wasn't home they'd leave prepared meals on the porch swing with cards or notes wishing them well. She was thankful for this; at least she didn't have to cook and she knew whom to return the serving bowl to. She decided to make potato salad to serve along with the prepared fresh rolls, collard greens, and sliced ham.

"Thank yuh Lord for yuh many blessings." Thea prayed in her usual soft whisper that was meant only for the Lord to hear. She placed her head back on the car's headrest. "Ah'll be in yuh house tuhmorrow and Ah'll be thankin' yuh folks for their support." She closed her eyes, inhaled slowly, and held the sweet air in her lungs until her body forced it out. One more quick breath of air was taken in before she removed the keys from the ignition and placed them in her pocketbook. The shadow of her weeping willow tree swept across her face and she glanced through her windshield. *If my weeping willow tree can dance then Ah can smile. There ain't nothin' sad about a weeping willow tree. It doesn't weep. Ah think all its moments are precious and it dances; each branch dances in rhythm with the next. Ah been watching my weeping willow tree grow and flourish ever since Ah came tuh Rehoboth, and it's a happy tree. Round about now it seems like it's the only thing happy at the Oliver residence.* She pulled herself away from her thoughts, got out of her car and turned to admire her dancing tree one more time, "Thank you Lord. Ah know yuh let yuh willow tree dance for me tuh remind me not tuh worry. Sometimes Ah do get carried away and let the Devil's misery step in. Ah remember yuh telling me Ah would have yuh guidance. Thank yuh Lord."

* * *

Thea was just placing the prepared potato salad in the refrigerator when she heard tapping on her front door. Her hands were clean and dry, but she wiped them on her apron out of habit and hurried from her kitchen. She saw Loretha standing on the outside of her screen door holding a chocolate layer cake in a plastic cake carrier.

"Hello, Miss Loretha." A smile was already on her face before she unlatched the door.

"Good afternoon, Thea," Loretha said, her greeting was graceful and warm and she smiled as she handed over the cake carrier. "Ah missed yuh. Ah ain't seen yuh since Tuesday and Ah was worried about yuh. Yuh've been in my prayers night and day. How's Owen? Please forgive me for not coming by sooner." She stepped across the threshold and spoke quickly in her usual way.

"Oh thank yuh." Thea held the door while Loretha entered the house. "C'mon in the kitchen," Thea said softly as she led the way. "Owen, well . . . he's doing somewhat better. His doctor seems tuh have his pressure under control, but every once in a while it spikes. His jaw is on the mend. Malcolm and his wife will be here shortly. Ah'm sure they'll like some of this here cake." She lifted the cake carrier and glanced back at Loretha..

Loretha sat at the dinette table and watched as Thea removed the cake and place it on a platter. "How yuh doing, Thea? It was my meanin' tuh ask yuh tuh come with me tuh 'Lizabeth's. Yuh know we talked about it." She watched Thea rinse the cake carrier, wiping it free of moisture and setting it on the table near her. "Johnny and Julia came home last night. They'll be here for a week. Yuh always welcome and Ah know Ah can speak for everyone, but yuh might not feel comfortable around all of them."

Thea continued to listen as Loretha spoke. She smiled and made eye contact with her before returning to the kitchen area to remove the pitcher of ice tea from the refrigerator. Another smile was in order when she placed the two glasses of ice tea on the round dinette table and took a seat across from Loretha. "Well, Ah'm gonna have Malcolm and his wife this weekend. Ah would like tuh visit Elizabeth sometimes next week and Ah would love tuh

see Johnny and meet his wife," Thea said as she looked over at Loretha. "It's
so hard. Owen and Ah don't have much family." She wrapped her fingers
around her glass. "Our parents are dead and we're both the youngest in our
families. Our brothers and sisters are either deceased, tuh old or live tuh far
away tuh travel. Ah forced Malcolm tuh go home and return tuh work. It was
no use him messing up his work keepin' company with me. Right now, Ah'd
be lonely in a crowd." She looked up at Loretha for confirmation that she did
the right thing, and then glanced at her fidgeting fingers that were nervously
moving on the table in front of her. She turned back to Loretha and took a
quick breath. "Anyway, he'll be back tuhday. If yuh askin' how Ah'm doin',
and if it weren't for our Lord, Ah'd be tellin' yuh Ah'm doin' terrible. The
Lord keeps tellin' me not tuh worry, but the future is a little scary."

"Baby, don't be worrin' yuhself until yuh need tuh worry." Loretha took
hold of her hands to comfort her and hold them still. "One day when yuh life
falls back intuh place yuh gonna remember this time and how the Lord
carried yuh over the rough times. Honey, He's carrying yuh now. Just be
faithful and hold on for the ride. When He set yuh down, yuh feet will be on
solid ground again, and yuh'll know what direction tuh take."

Thea looked around the kitchen and dining room like she was seeing it for
the first time. Loretha patted and released her hand and Thea gave her
another timid smile. "We been in this house thirty-seven years and, except for
the time Ah was in the hospital having Malcolm, Ah never spent one night
alone." She returned her attention to Loretha. "Ah never knew what
loneliness was until now. Ah never knew there were two kinds of loneliness,
the physical and the emotional." She beckoned for Loretha to walk with her
into the dining room where they stood at the window and studied her tree.
Suddenly she turned to face Loretha. "Experiencing one type of loneliness is
hard enough, but both . . ." Thea crossed her arms over her chest and shook
her head. "If it weren't for our Lord, the devil would have surely stolen my
soul."

Shivers attacked Loretha and she wrapped her arms around Thea and held
her gently. "Oh Thea, don't ever give up hope. Ah've felt that sense of loss
and hopelessness. And sometimes when yuh think it can't get worse, it does,
but there is a bottom. Yuh'll see the light again and it will shine brighter than
ever. Keep praying and keep the Lord near yuh and the light will return tuh
yuh life."

When Loretha released her hold, tears escaped from Thea's eyes. Thea tried to smile while she removed a napkin from the holder on the table to wipe her face. "Thank yuh Miss Loretha. Ah know of the hardship my husband caused yuh family and yuh still have yuh light."

Thea and Loretha sat in the chairs located at the end of the dining room table, near the large double windows. Loretha had turned her chair so she directly faced Thea and she had also reached for a napkin to hold just in case she needed it.

"Yes honey, yuh husband caused a hardship of unspeakable terms, but once Johnny was born, Ah felt a joy that was indescribable." Loretha sat back in her chair and hugged herself. Her eyes locked with Thea's and she knew she should help to ease her suffering. "Well . . . yuh know, John refused tuh allow 'Lizabeth and Johnny tuh come home. Thanks tuh Mrs. Collins; we called her MaDear . . . well . . . thanks tuh her, my babies had someplace tuh live. Ah tricked John intuh signing emancipation papers, issued by the state of Georgia, and that gave 'Lizabeth the right tuh make her own decisions. Then, when the church questioned John, he wanted tuh have her come home but she refused, and he was furious." Loretha turned away from Thea before continuing to speak. They were painful words and she had never spoken them aloud to anyone. Her eyes searched the dining room area of Thea's home for a safe place to rest before sharing the truthful conclusion she was forced to make about her husband. She turned toward the window and saw Thea's weeping willow tree and the drooping, waving branches charmed her into relaxing and her words flowed freely. "Whenever we were all in public, John pretended he was so proud of Johnny, but in our private lives, he never spoke to him or 'Lizabeth. He forced me tuh live in two worlds. He estranged sister from sister. He kept my light at a dull flicker, so dull, there were times Ah believed it to be extinguished. And the saddest part of all was . . . he always knew who Johnny's father was. 'Lizabeth told him the day after Johnny was born. At first he didn't believe her, but after a couple of years there was no doubt about it, but he preferred Reverend Oliver over his daughter. He refused to question yuh husband or allow me to speak of it tuh him." She turned from the window and looked at Thea. Tears rolled down her face and she used her napkin to wipe her eyes and cheeks. Thea attempted to stand, to go to her and offer her comfort, but Loretha raised her hand, gesturing her to stop. She blotted her tears again. "Yuh see Thea, both of our husbands have injured 'Lizabeth and changed the course of events in Rehoboth. Yuh blessed. Yuh light will never have tuh wait that long tuh shine bright again. So yuh just let the Lord stand by yuh tuh keep yuh company, and yuh won't ever be lonely when yuh in that crowd." Loretha leaned over and kissed Thea's forehead.

Thea wiped her own tears. "Thank you, Miss Loretha. Ah really don't know what tuh say."

"There really is nothing tuh say, and out of all of this we have Johnny. And let me tell yuh . . . he loves yuh husband.

"Did Elizabeth ever tell Johnny, Owen was his father?" Thea stood and began to fiddle with the corner of her apron as she spoke.

"No, only five people in this world knew," Loretha answered. She and Thea walked back to the kitchen. They returned to their seats at the dinette table where their glasses of ice tea were waiting for them. Loretha drank half of hers before continuing to speak. "Only 'Lizabeth, Owen, MaDear, John, and, of course, myself, knew the truth; Johnny was drawn tuh yuh husband like a magnet. We tried tuh keep them apart, but we didn't know what tuh tell Johnny, and this created a problem with Malcolm."

"Oh my Lord, yes, it really got complicated. Now, after all this Ah hope they'll get together." Thea placed her hand over her mouth before moving it to her cheek. She finished drinking her glass of ice tea and looked over at Loretha. "May Ah pour yuh a fresh drink?"

"No, no, this is fine," Loretha replied as she finished her own drink.

Thea stared at her empty glass. "All of this envy and jealousy is a result of a curse my husband brought on our families."

Loretha glances over at her with pleading eyes. "Please don't say that. It makes me feel that my Johnny is the result of a curse. Let's just say we have some influence over our young men. Let's help them get together. It seems like they've both been badly hurt."

"Ah'm sorry, Ah didn't mean it that way." Thea reached across the table and touched Loretha's hand. "Johnny is a wonderful person and Owen loves him so much. For the past three days Johnny has been calling me tuh get an update on his condition. He said Malcolm left my number with his receptionist."

Loretha stood. "It's okay, but now Ah have tuh leave. Ah hope tuh see yuh in church."

"Ah can't thank yuh enough for coming by."

The ladies walked to the front door. Loretha opened the screen door and waved again as she made her way to her car. She drove pass Thea's car and under the gentle branches of the dancing willow tree. Just after she turned left out of the driveway, Malcolm and Theresa arrived.

* * *

Julia and Elizabeth met up with Loretha at the Turner residence, while Nat sat in a straight-back wooden rocker on the front porch at MaDear's Cottage and Johnny sat on the swing. The sun was high over the cottage, casting a shadow over the porch, but shining bright on the driveway.

"Johnny, do yuh remember when we had tuh climb over that fallin' tree and yuh stepped on that snake?" Nat propelled himself in the rocker and smiled. "Ah believe we were right about there," he pointed to the paved road, to where the shade of the trees cut a path across the sun light.

"Yeah!" Johnny said. He threw his head back and laughed. "Whoever said you couldn't take the country out of the man, was wrong."

"Yuh right about that. Yuh didn't have no country left in you." Nat slapped his leg and stopped rocking the chair. "Man Ah didn't know yuh could jump so high as when yuh jumped back on that log. Johnny, why didn't yuh just let me chop that snake with my machete?"

Johnny burst out laughing. "Man, I wasn't trying to save the snake's life. I was afraid you'd miss the snake and hit my foot with that big knife."

"Man, yuh didn't trust yuh own dad." Nat threw himself back in the rocker and laughed out loud.

"I trusted you. It was your aim I didn't trust." Johnny chuckled while pushing the swing with his feet.

It took several moments for their memories of that experience to pass and their laughing to be reduced to just smiles. Nat was the first to break the silence. "Yeah Johnny, we had some good times, even when we didn't know they would turn out tuh be memorable."

Johnny had both arms draped over the back of the swing and controlled its motion to a slight rocking; he never lifted his feet off the porch, and he smiled as he nodded his head.

Nat stopped rocking his chair. "Yuh going tuh see Reverend Oliver tuhday?"

"Yeah man. Ya know, I wanted to go around three o'clock. I hope I get to see him without the rest of his family being there."

"Ah hope yuh get yuh wish. Ah hear Malcolm is due back tuhday, and will be here until tuhmorrow night."

Johnny stood and walked to the edge of the porch. He shoved his hands in his pocket and turned to face Nat. "Your right. Maybe if I go to the hospital right now, I'll have a chance to visit with him before Malcolm gets there."

"That's possible," Nat said as he eased himself out of the rocker and slowly stood erect.

"Man, you're walking like an old man," Johnny commented.

Nat half chuckled as he responded. "This old back makes me feel like an old man. It ain't been right since that last attack."

"Don't you think you should have it checked out?"

"Oh, Ah think if Ah take my medicine and rest, it'll get better . . . we'll see." Nat responded as he limped to Johnny's car.

"Okay Dad. You know your body." Johnny hurried to close the cottage door, but he didn't lock it. He wasn't sure if Julia had her keys. He drove Nat home and turned left onto Rehoboth Road.

Johnny drove pass his grandparents home and only saw his grandfather's car in the driveway. He smiled, believing his mother, grandmother and wife were probably off shopping. Before that thought could leave his mind he passed the Concord Baptist Church on his right, and he thought he would ask his mother if they could attend the grandfather's church for Sunday service. He heard himself say *thank you Jesus* when he noticed Malcolm's car parked behind Miss Thea's in the Oliver's driveway.

✳ ✳ ✳

Johnny stood at the nurse's station outside Reverend Oliver's room within minutes of arriving at the hospital. He saw his father resting peacefully through the large window and he was happy Reverend Oliver had his eyes closed and didn't see him, at least until he had a chance to ask the nurse if he could have a visitor.

The nurse pulled up father's chart, "May Ah have yuh name, sir."

"John Robert Turner. He's my father."

"Yes, Ah have yuh name listed as immediate family. This is an 'Intensive Care Unit' and only immediate family members are allowed tuh visit."

"Is my father's illness considered 'critical'?" Johnny had placed both hands on the desk and his eyes pleaded for the answer he wanted to hear.

"No sir. He is improving and is listed in 'guarded' condition. If he were critical he would be in our 'Critical Intensive Care Unit'." The nurse closed the chart and smiled. "You may visit with him. Ah'm sure he'll be happy tuh see yuh."

Who remembered me enough to list me as his son, he thought. *It was probably Miss Thea.* Johnny thanked the nurse and walked into the hospital room. He stopped when he saw his father hooked up to all the machinery and laying in a motionless sleep. The left side of his face was still discolored and swollen, but it appeared to be a lot better than it was the week before. He walked over to the right side of the bed and placed his right hand over the bedrail and on his father's forearm. Reverend Oliver opened his eyes and looked up at him. Johnny smiled, and Reverend Oliver continued to stare at him.

"It's me, Reverend Oliver. It's me, Johnny."

"Johnny," Reverend Oliver whispered. His cheeks quivered in his attempt to smile.

Johnny recognized the precise moment when his father realized it was him. "Yes it's me, Johnny. Now, may I call you dad?"

Reverend Oliver nodded his head. "Ah'm sorry Johnny."

"We can't change that, and I wouldn't want to. I'm here and you're my dad. I love you now, just as much as I've always loved you. I'm not going to brood about the years I missed out on. All that time is gone. We have each other now and for ..."

"Malcolm . . ." Reverend Oliver whispered in a slow slur. His eyes shifted away from Johnny.

Johnny didn't see Malcolm walk pass the window and now he was standing at the door. As soon as he noticed him he attempted to remove his hand from Reverend Oliver's arm, but his father's grip held him in place. Malcolm walked to the right side of the bed and placed his hand on Johnny's shoulder.

"Johnny, we're brothers. We can both love our father."

Johnny refused to attend to Malcolm. He smiled at his father and relaxed the hand under his father's hold. "I'm okay, Dad."

As soon as Reverend Oliver turned his attention to Malcolm, Johnny cut his eyes at his brother.

Malcolm shifted his eyes away from Johnny and removed his hand. "So Dad, Mama tells me yuh been keepin' yuh pressure under control and Dr. Parks says if yuh keep up the good work over the next week yuh can get out of this ICU. Oh, Ah hope yuh not mad at me, but Mama made me go home." He was walking to the left side of the bed while he was talking.

"Ah know. She told me all about it and Ah understand." He smiled at Malcolm and turned back to Johnny. "So, how long yuh gonna be in town, Johnny?"

"I took the week off. I'll be here until next Sunday, sir."

"Sir? What happened tuh, Dad?" Reverend Oliver gave him a serious stare.

Johnny glanced at Malcolm like he needed his permission to refer to his father as Dad.

"Damn Johnny! He's just as much yuh father as he's mine and Ah love havin' yuh as my brother."

Johnny kept a straight face and thought, *I don't want to be your brother, I only want to be his son. I don't want to upset him. I'll take care of you later.* He gave Malcolm a broad smile. "Sorry yuh have tuh go home, but I'm gonna have Dad all tuh myself all next week." He walked around the bed and patted Malcolm's shoulder, then turned to his father. "Dad, Malcolm only has today and tomorrow. I'll see you tomorrow. I'm gonna let you guys have a little more time together." He leaned over the bedrails and kissed him on the forehead.

"See ya, Dad." Johnny took a couple of steps backward, nodded toward Malcolm, before turning and walking from the room. He waved again as he walked passed the window. By the time he reached the elevator he was so angry he wanted to spit. He balled his hand into a fist and side punched the down button on the control panel. The elevator was waiting and opened immediately.

* * *

Johnny was still angry with Malcolm when he turned onto Rehoboth Road. He wanted to let go of the past, but the past wouldn't let him go. More than twenty years had passed since Malcolm's campaign of hate against him ended. All of the mental anguish he internalized as a child had left deep grooves in his soul and simply could not be smoothed away because Malcolm asked to be forgiven. He thought about all the years he used to hide out in the bushes around Reverend Oliver's home waiting for Malcolm to leave, just so he could steal extra time with his father. Now it angered him that he was continuing to steal time to be with him. He knew Reverend Oliver carried the blame for not confessing sooner, but if he had come forth, he probably would have left Rehoboth and he would have had nothing; it was all so confusing.

Johnny drove all the way down Rehoboth Road, making the first right turn after passing his parents' brick, ranch style home. He drove the remaining stretch down Collins Road to MaDear's cottage. He was experiencing one of his conflicting moments when he needed to be at his country home; his place, where he believed MaDear's memories would be comforting and soothing for him. During his drive through Rehoboth he didn't see any cars at his grandparents or parents' homes. He believed everyone was either off shopping or visiting friends. He was happy to have a few moments alone, and he sat back in MaDear's soft reupholstered chair. He lifted his chin and rested his head on the soft cushion and allowed himself to smile. His arms rested on the wide, soft doily covered armrests and he closed his eyes. *MaDear died on October 17ᵗʰ, 1963. Lord, I guess you gave her to me for as long as you thought I needed her, and I will always be grateful to you for that.* Johnny fell into an afternoon nap and dreamed MaDear was holding him. *"C'mere Johnny-Boy. What be bothering yuh? C'mere, tell MaDear."* Johnny turned to the side, pulling his right leg up under his left. The right side of his face snuggled close to the chair's soft back cushion. *"Johnny-Boy, Ah been tellin' yuh tuh never allow hate tuh enter yuh soul. It'll burrow way down deep inside yuh and hurt yuh, Boy. Yuh don't be needin' that kind of pain. Jesus said, 'Turn the other cheek.' "*

"MaDear, all those years I turned the other cheek, but the bad feelings for Malcolm just piled up"

"Johnny-Boy, didn't Ah tell yuh, yuh needed to forgive too? Boy! Ain't no need tuh be turning the other cheek if'n yuh don't be forgivin'. Yuh ain't never gone forget, but yuh be feelin' a whole lot bettah when yuh forgive."

"Ah can't forgive him and Ah can't forget." He removed himself from MaDear's chair and slid to the floor resting his head against the seat of the chair. *"Ah have tuh keep my guard up."*

"Yuh keep prayin' on it and that day will come. It be takin' more energy tuh hold that misery in yuh heart than tuh forgive."

"MaDear, Ah never prayed tuh forgive or forget. Ah just hate Malcolm."

"Johnny-Boy, hate is the Devil's feeling and it's his word. It'll eat a hole in yuh soul. Yuh don't know how much misery yuh been holdin' until yuh rid yuhself of hate.

"Ah ain't never wasted a prayer on Malcolm."

"Den it gone be eatin' at yuh 'til yuh do. Yuh hear me…"

"Johnny!" Knock … knock … knock … "Johnny!"

Johnny opened his eyes and glanced around the sitting room of the cottage. "Julia!" he called out, but no one responded.

"Johnny!" Knock … knock … knock, he heard coming from the front door in the living room.

"Who is it?" he yelled out as he stood from the floor and smoothed his clothes. His watch told him it was 3:10 p.m. And he immediately wondered where his wife was. He hadn't seen her all day.

"It's me Johnny, Malcolm!"

Johnny opened the door and used his hand to wipe the remainder of sleep away from his face. "What brings you here, man?" He didn't invite Malcolm in the house, but stepped out onto the porch to meet with him. He pulled his shirt tail from his pants and told Malcolm to have a seat while he sat on the porch near the steps.

"When Ah got home Ah met your mother, grandmother, and wife. They were visiting my mother and Theresa, that's my wife. Ah thought Ah'd come tuh see you."

"Why?" Johnny stood and walked behind the house. Malcolm leaped from the porch and followed him.

"Man . . . how many times do Ah have to say Ah'm sorry. We were boys, just kids. Johnny Ah've been trying tuh make up with yuh since Ah was a teenager."

Johnny kept walking toward the overgrown path in the woods. Malcolm stopped midway of the back yard, threw his hands up, and at the same time took a deep breath, before forcefully exhaling. He watched Johnny enter the woods and lowered his hands, slapping them against the side of his legs. He shook his head and broke out into trotting steps to shorten the distance between them. "Johnny, please! Man, we need tuh talk!" He leaped over the tall new growth covering the forest floor. He could see Johnny's white shirt in the distance. He slowed down, becoming concerned over Johnny's intention.

* * *

Johnny sat on a large fallen log and rested his forehead in the palm of his hands. He remembered his dream and MaDear's words returned to him. *Yuh ain't never gone forget, but yuh be feelin' a whole lot bettah when yuh forgive.* Her words repeated in his head and forgiving wasn't something he was ready to do. He knew Malcolm was coming in his direction and he wasn't sure what his own next move would be. Just blaming him for stealing his share of his father added another layer to the suffering he caused. It didn't matter that Malcolm didn't know of this thievery; Johnny believed he stole their opportunity to be friends. If they were just friends, he would have been able to spend time with Reverend Oliver, but from his earliest memory, Malcolm pushed him away and began attacking him.

"Man, can Ah talk tuh you?" Malcolm pleaded.

Johnny raised his head and stared straight ahead. His hands were positioned as if he were praying.

Malcolm stood looking down at Johnny. The log where he sat was almost three feet wide and appeared to be more than fifty feet long. Malcolm wanted to be face to face with Johnny so he backed up against a young Georgia pine and squatted down into a position that put them at the same eye level. "Johnny, Ah've spent the last twenty years of my life trying to tell yuh how sorry Ah've been. When we were very young, Ah was jealous of yuh because Ah thought Dad liked yuh more than me…"

Johnny continued to hold the same posture, except he closed his eyes while Malcolm spoke.

"As Ah got older . . . man . . . Ah had these feeling for yuh. Feelings a boy wasn't suppose tuh have for another boy. Johnny, Ah was so aggressive toward yuh because Ah thought Ah needed tuh keep yuh away from me. Ah was afraid of yuh. Man . . . Ah loved yuh . . ."

Johnny sprang from the log and was on top of Malcolm before he could finish speaking. Both men hit the forest floor. "Johnny!" Malcolm yelled. He grabbed Johnny in a bear hug and rolled over forcefully pulling him to the bottom position, before turning him loose and jumping back to his feet.

Johnny jumped to his feet. "What do you mean you love me?" He yelled and took a swing at Malcolm's head with his right fist. Malcolm ducked and Johnny punched him in the stomach, dropping him to his knees.

Malcolm coughed, bent over and dropped on one knee. He watched Johnny's feet strut around him. As soon as his wind returned, he sprang on Johnny and wrapped his arms tightly around him. He slung Johnny around and turned him loose, causing him to fall backward over the old log. "Johnny stop! Ah only want tuh talk tuh yuh. Ah'm not gonna fight yuh."

"I don't want to talk to you!" Johnny screamed, and he rushed at Malcolm, head butting him in the chest and causing him to skip backward, his arms waving as he fought to maintain his balance. Johnny stood and watched as he landed in a nest of bushes and shrubs before rushing in his direction.

Malcolm hurried to his feet, snatched himself from Johnny's grasp, and circled around a tree until he was behind him. Keeping Johnny in his sight, he stepped back until he reached the clearing. Johnny rushed toward him again, his appearance was frenzied like he was releasing a lifetime of pent up anger in that one moment. Malcolm spread his legs, wiggled his fingers and held his arms wide apart, taking a defensive posture. "No Johnny!" He yelled just as he caught him in a bear hug and held him tight. "Ah don't want to fight yuh,

Johnny!" Johnny was taller than Malcolm, but Malcolm was more muscular and stronger. He locked his fingers around Johnny, pinning his upper arms tight to his side. He could feel Johnny's hot breath passing over his right ear. Malcolm held tighter, pressing his head against Johnny's shoulder. "Please Johnny. Ah don't wanna fight yuh. Yuh my brother, Ah love yuh man!" Malcolm began to cry. "Ah've always loved yuh and now Ah know why."

It seemed like every time Johnny heard the word 'love' he struggled more. "Turn me loose Malcolm!" He struggled, twisting, jerking himself, and swinging his forearms, trying to punch Malcolm, but only tapping him on his sides.

Malcolm continued to feel Johnny's muscles flexing and straining in an attempt to be free. Tears flowed freely from his eyes and he pleaded with Johnny to calm down. They danced around, one holding and the other struggling, one crying and the other seething with anger, one pleading and the other demanding; two forces that were pulling in opposite directions, but Malcolm continued to hold on. Suddenly the fight left Johnny; his muscles relaxed and he let out a wail of a cry. Malcolm released his embrace and backed several feet away from him. Johnny dropped to his knees, bent over resting on his elbows and placed his head on the forest floor. He cried a loud gut wrenching sob. Malcolm stood crying with his hands interlocked behind his head and his elbows directed forward in front of his face. He took two steps toward Johnny, stopped and bent over. "Johnny. It's okay man!" He cried out and took a step backward.

Johnny remained on his knees and raised the upper portion of his body. He lifted his head toward the sky, covered his eyes with his hands and continued to cry. His sobs were loud and frightening, enough to keep Malcolm several feet away. Both men cried, Johnny loud and wailing and Malcolm soft and weeping. Johnny was expelling the hate he had harbored for so long, he believed it was a part of whom he thought himself to be.

Malcolm pleaded for forgiveness and acceptance, and cautiously walked closer to Johnny. He knelt facing him, using his hands to smear tears away from his cheeks. His reddened eyes stared at Johnny for signs of forgiveness, knowing the physical battle was over, but Johnny had a way of inflicting psychological punishment that was far more damaging. Malcolm was willing to accept whatever morsel of recognition Johnny would throw his way.

Suddenly, Johnny reached for Malcolm. His movements were quick and Malcolm raised his arms in a defensive manner, but Johnny managed to

22

capture him in an embrace. "I'm sorry Malcolm," Johnny whispered. "We are brothers."

"Thank yuh Johnny. Ah love yuh man."

The brothers stood and embraced again, giving each other several manly pats on the back. There was nothing else to be said. They released each other; Johnny staring straight ahead and Malcolm looking down, his feet shoving away the debris on the forest floor until he reached the dark earth. Johnny went back to sitting on his log and Malcolm returned to squatting against the Georgia pine. They didn't speak and their faces were still and soft. It was as though their souls had been flushed and they needed to be refilled with new energy before they could move again. After about five minutes they locked eyes and the laughter came; Johnny was first to break the quiet.

"Man, maybe you should clean up before you head home or you better have a lot of answers ready," Johnny said, still laughing and scanning Malcolm's appearance.

"Yeah, Ah hope no one sees you either. Yuh got dry leaves and cockleburs in yuh hair and all over yuh pants, and yuh shirt is ripped and dirty. Man, yuh look like yuh been rollin' on the ground." Malcolm laughed harder and crawled closer to Johnny to retrieve a leaf from his hair.

Johnny started picking leaves and tiny pieces of twigs from Malcolm's hair. They took off their shirts and wiped the perspiration from their faces and bodies, then used them to brush at their pants, knocking away the dried dust and dirt. Finally they inspected each other for minimal present-ability. By the time they made a complete revolution their eyes met again.

They were trying to compose themselves as they walked from the woods. Then the laughter in their eyes grew and they tried to hold it behind their lips, but it burst out in a howl of hilarity and soon they were supporting themselves on each other's shoulders as they staggered along.

"Do you realize we must've looked like monkeys grooming each other?" Johnny said as he continued to rest his arm on Malcolm's shoulder while he caught his breath. "Thanks for hanging in there Malcolm. I hope you feel as good as I do."

Malcolm smiled, "Ah do. It's been a long time Johnny. Yuh know, Ah have tuh take Mama tuh the hospital after church tuhmorrow. Do yuh think we could visit Dad tuhmorrow morning, before church? Ah'll drive, if yuh don't mind."

Johnny nodded and walked Malcolm around the front of MaDear's cottage to his car. Malcolm extended his hand for a shake and Johnny pulled him into his embrace. "I'm happy to have you as my brother, man."

"Me too Johnny." Malcolm patted Johnny on the back. They moved back and smiled at each other as Malcolm got into his car. Johnny stepped from the driveway to the stone walk and gave Malcolm a final wave as he drove away.

* * *

Julia had returned home while the men were in the woods. Now she stood watching them from the living room window, camouflaged behind the sheer curtains. She crossed her arm and smiled. *Oh thank you Lord. Finally my husband can truly be happy.* She walked out onto the front porch and watched Malcolm disappear down Collins Road. "Johnny," she whispered softly so as not to startle him. He turned and walked up the steps of the porch, stopping one step before the top so they would be at the same height. Julia gently kissed him. "I'm happy for you Johnny. Today you've killed your demon."

"It's dead and I feel so alive. Let me get cleaned up and I'll tell you all about it. Malcolm told me he met you at Miss Thea's. It seems like you've had a busy day, too." He took her by the hand and they walked into the house.

Chapter 10

Malcolm pulled up in his parents' driveway, to where his mother's willow tree brushed the right side of his car. "Ah'm home," he called out when he entered the house.

Thea took hold of Theresa's hand after seeing Malcolm's shabby appearance. "What happened tuh yuh?" Theresa said. Both women appeared to be frozen in place.

"Everything is great!" Malcolm hurried down the hall and divided his kisses between them before walking through the dining room. "Life is beautiful."

"What do yuh mean, 'everything is great' and 'life is beautiful'? Yuh look terrible and yuh so dirty." Theresa said moving backward for him to pass.

"Malcolm, yuh smell like a wild man." Thea placed the back of her hand against her nose. "But yuh seem so happy. Why don't yuh go clean up and come back and tell us what's going on."

"Ah'm gonna go, but Ah want yuh tuh know Ah'm so happy because Johnny and Ah made up. Now, Ah'm gonna go. There ain't much more tuh tell after that."

"Yuh made up?" Thea said. She grabbed hold of Malcolm's clammy arm.

"Yeah Ma . . . we went down in the woods and worked out our differences the hard way." He had a closed lip chuckle behind his smile and shifted his attention between his mother and wife. "We fought, but neither of us tried to hurt the other. We knocked each other down, rolled on the ground, Johnny took a couple of swings at me, and Ah swung at him, but we both missed each other. Mostly, we wrestled around until Johnny was ready tuh forgive me and except me as his brother. The next thing we knew we were hugging and pulling dried leaves and twigs from each others hair."

"Forgive you," Thea said, not expecting Malcolm to take on all the blame.

"Yes Mama, Ah've always been the aggressor. Ah was the one picking on Johnny, bullying him when we were children. Ah didn't stop until that night on River Road.

"River Road? What happened on River Road?" Theresa asked

"Honey, that's another story. Ah'll tell yuh about it sometime."

"Anyway, Ah bullied Johnny until we were sixteen years old." Malcolm glanced at his mother. "Mama, Ah made his life hell. He had every right tuh hate me. He's a better man than me tuh except my apology, even now."

"All right Malcolm, if yuh say it was that way. Ah always thought it was both of yuh. As long as it's over, that's the best news Ah've heard in a long time, but it looks like y'all really did it the hard way." Thea gave Theresa an embarrassed glance and waved her hand at Malcolm, "Enough of that for now. Ah'm just happy it's over."

Malcolm kissed Theresa's soft cherry brown, cheek. "Oh Mama, Ah wanna visit Dad this evening. Do yuh want tuh go with me?"

"Yes Malcolm. Yuh think we can leave here by 6:00?" Thea said.

"That sounds good tuh me." Malcolm responded as he hurried toward his bedroom.

Theresa reached in the cabinet for the dishes to set the table, while Thea removed the ham from the oven and turned it off. She placed six rolls on the top shelf of the still hot oven to warm up and remembered the telephone calls.

"Theresa, who's this man … ugh … Randy Lester? He's been callin' here all day. Ah told him Ah'd give Malcolm the message as soon as Ah saw him. Ah forgot tuh tell him when y'all arrived."

"Oh, he's Malcolm's friend from work." She set the plates on the table, positioned the flatware and returned to the cabinet for the glasses. "How many times did he call? Maybe there's a problem. Malcolm told me he got sick at work last Wednesday and they had tuh take him tuh the hospital, but Ah thought he was all right."

Thea sliced the ham and arranged it on a small platter before covering it with wax paper. She placed the potato salad on the table. "Well, he sure sounded desperate. Ah thought the man was gonna start cryin' on the phone. He called here three times; once befor' y'all arrived, then while our company was here, and again just a little while ago. Ah shoulda called yuh tuh the phone."

Theresa scooped the collard greens from the pot on the stove, placed them in a serving bowl with a glass top and set it on the dinette table. "Malcolm can return his call after dinner if he has time."

By the time Malcolm returned to the kitchen the dinner, including the rolls, had been placed on the table. "Ah'm sorry Theresa. Ah asked Mama if she wanted tuh go tuh the hospital, but Ah didn't ask you. Ah didn't mean tuh overlook yuh."

Theresa smiled and nodded, "Now, will yuh bless the food so we can have dinner?"

They held hands and Malcolm spoke softly, "Lord, thank yuh for this food which we are about tuh receive for the nourishment of our bodies. In Jesus' name we pray. Amen."

Thea began passing the serving bowls around the table and it wasn't long before everyone had served themselves.

"Oh Malcolm, Mother said Randy called three times tuhday. Ah didn't speak with him, but he wants yuh tuh call him. Mother said he sounded like it was urgent."

Malcolm checked the time on the wall clock. "Ah don't have time tuh call him before we go tuh the hospital." He diced a section of ham and brought it to his mouth before glancing up at Theresa and Thea.

Theresa reached over and placed her hand on Malcolm's forearm. "Yuh know Malcolm, Randy knows yuh father's sick. Ah really don't think he'd be callin' yuh like this unless it's somethin' important."

Malcolm continued with his dinner, but he could feel his mother and wife's eyes piercing across at him. "All right . . . Ah'll call him as soon as Ah finish eating." He smiled at Theresa and his mother, using his remaining energy to hide his anger. "Ah went by his house Friday tuh take him some papers from work and Ah spoke tuh him yesterday."

Malcolm hurried through his meal leaving the women at the table, while he excused himself to go into his father's office where privacy was available. He heard Randy's telephone ring twice before Gail answered it.

"Hi Malcolm, how's yuh father?" Gail's voice sounded pleasant but concerned.

"He seems tuh be comin' along. How's Randy? He really gave me a scare the other day. Ah thought he was havin' a heart attack. Is he home?"

"He was around here all day, but he promised the boys he'd take them tuh the movies. Ah was happy he left; he's been so depressed and jittery. Ah've really been worried about him."

"Well . . . would yuh tell him Ah called?" Malcolm swiveled around in his father's chair while holding the phone to his ear. "Ah'm going back tuh the hospital now, but Ah'll call 'em when Ah return. He should be back by then."

"Okay Malcolm. Ah'll give him yuh message. Bye now."

"So long Gail." Malcolm hung up the telephone and sat in his father's chair holding his head in his hands. *Breaking up with Randy isn't gonna be as easy as Ah thought. It seems when Ah get one problem worked out another swells up.*

"Malcolm, are yuh ready?" The heels of his mother's shoes tapped against the hard wood floor as she walked toward the study. "Is yuh friend all right?"

Malcolm stepped into the hall. "He wasn't home. Ah spoke with his wife and she said he took the boys to the movies." He placed his arm around his mother. "Why do yuh have a pillow?"

"Because Theresa is drivin', Ah think yuh could use the time tuh rest." Thea hugged the pillow and they walked toward the front door.

"Are yuh ready, Theresa?" He turned toward the kitchen and raised his voice hoping she would hear him. "We'll wait for yuh in the car."

"Ah'll be out shortly," Theresa called out.

* * *

Julia relaxed in Johnny's arms and rested her head on his chest while he combed his fingers through her long, thick, black hair. She couldn't see the serenity that blanketed his face, but the peaceful beat of his heart reminded her of the joy of forgiveness. She rubbed her hand over the t-shirt that covered his chest.

The telephone rang and their cherished tranquil moment was interrupted. Julia reached for the telephone on the nightstand. "Yes, ma'am, I'll tell him," she said as she replaced the receiver on its base. She moaned and snuggled closer to Johnny. "I want to stay right here, just like this, a little longer."

"What is it Julia?" He sounded concerned; his fingers remained in her hair, but were motionless.

"Your grandmother wants us to come to her house. She said she has a surprise and wants us to stay for dinner."

"A surprise? Mama wants us to come to her house for dinner. Well . . . ten more minutes won't matter." Johnny lifted up and kissed Julia on top of her head. "Thanks Julia."

"Thanks?" Julia lifted her head and gave Johnny a puzzled look.

"Thanks for being here with me. Sometimes I wonder if you think my past is a bit unsettling. I'm always talking about Reverend Oliver, Malcolm and my decision to hold on to MaDear anyway I can."

"No Johnny, I'm amazed how your life is coming together. Your MaDear died more than twenty years ago, but the entire life lesson she taught you remains as your guiding light. It took a long time, but I don't believe you would've been able to accept Malcolm without her early teaching." Julia reached up, gave Johnny a passionate kiss, rolled over and was standing before Johnny was able to speak. "Okay, now let's get over to your grandmother's."

Johnny rose up on his elbows. "All right, but you're mine tonight."

* * *

Johnny recognized three of the four cars in his grandparents' driveway, two belonged to his grandparents, and one belonged to Nat. He and Julia parked their car and walked to the house. Johnny opened the door and the sounds of laughter and talking led them to the living room.

"Aunt Sarah!" Johnny called out. He hurried to embrace her. "I knew you would come down." He turned and held his arm out beckoning for Julia to come to him. "I want you to meet my wife, Julia."

"Oh Johnny, Ah met Julia when you were first engaged." Sarah smiled and hugged Julia. "Yuh don't know what a pleasure it is tuh meet yuh again."

"I've heard so much about you. Thank you for keeping our Johnny happy," Julia said.

"Johnny, Ah know Mama told yuh she had a surprise." Sarah locked arms with Johnny and Julia and led them to Stephen Parker. "Ah want yuh tuh meet someone." Stephen was speaking with Nat and didn't see them come up behind him. When Nat's eyes shifted in their direction, Stephen turned and smiled. "This is the surprise Gram'ma spoke about?" Sarah said, moving closer to Stephen. He was a handsome, chocolate colored man with dark brown wavy hair, graying temples and a mixed gray mustache.

"Stephen, Ah would like yuh tuh meet my nephew, John Turner and his wife, Julia." Sarah smiled and blushed like a school girl.

"Nice meeting you, man." Johnny smiled and shook his hand.

"Johnny . . . Julia, Stephen is the surprise. We were married yesterday," Sarah announced.

"Your husband? Hey man, welcome to the family." Johnny shook his hand again, a hardier hand shake, and this time he pulled him into a one arm hug.

Julia's smile broadened. "I'm new to the family too."

"Thank you," Stephen said as he placed his arm around Sarah's waist.

Loretha and Reverend Turner walked close to Nat and Elizabeth. Sarah flashed the rings on her left hand toward her father. "Okay Daddy, Ah'm married now. My new name is Sarah Turner-Parker."

Julia and Johnny walked over near Loretha, Elizabeth, and Nat. "Ah need tuh go tuh the kitchen, but first Ah want tuh see how Sarah and Stephen are gonna handle Daddy with her new name," Elizabeth whispered to the group. Loretha and Nat laughed quietly, while Johnny and Julia gave each other inquisitive glances.

"What's this new thing, the wife keeping her maiden name and just adding her husband's name?" Reverend Turner spoke out.

"That's what it is Daddy, it's a new thing. Aren't yuh happy for us?" Sarah left Stephen and hurried to her father's side. She kissed his cheek. "Are yuh happy for me?"

"Yes Ah am. Yuh married. Ah guess the name isn't important, but Ah'd like tuh have seen yuh married in a religious ceremony," Reverend Turner said. He kissed her on the cheek.

"Daddy yuh can have it both ways. Honey, show Daddy the papers." She patted Stephen's breast pocket and smiled at her father.

Stephen retrieved an envelope and handed it to Reverend Turner.

Reverend Turner unfolded the paper. "Sarah . . . Stephen, you said you were married. This form is an incomplete marriage license application." He appeared puzzled and the space between his eyebrows held a single crease. He looked at Stephen and Sarah and waited for an explanation.

Sarah showed her father a copy of the completed marriage license from the Justice of the Peace and explained that they had until Monday noon to return with a completed marriage license from a religious ceremony.

"Sir, I'd be honored if you'd marry us at the Concord Baptist Church tomorrow after regular service." Stephen watched Sarah hug her father's arm while he spoke. He placed one hand in his pocket and moved the other as if it were doing the talking. "Sir, there was no excuse for the urgency of this situation except that I've been trying to get Sarah to marry me for years. I was stunned when she finally accepted my proposal. I believed I needed to marry her as soon as possible. I was so afraid she would change her mind, so I insisted we have a civil ceremony. Sarah insisted on a religious one, so we compromised and here we are."

Reverend Turner and Stephen shook hands. "Thank you, sir," Stephen said.

"Oh that's wonderful Sarah, but what will yuh wear?" Elizabeth hurried to Sarah and hugged her.

"Ah have everything even my shoes and fresh flowers in the car. Ah just need tuh put them in the refrigerator tuh keep them fresh, and then Ah need tuh ask Mama if she can help with the food. We can get everything else out later."

"Well . . . Ah'm standing right here, ask me," Loretha said.

"Ah'm asking yuh, Mama," Sarah said.

"Of course Ah will, we'll do what we can to get a caterer," Loretha responded.

"Great idea, Mama, but do you think yuh can get someone on such a short notice?"

"Well, Ah'm gonna call the bakery and see if Ah can order a wedding cake. Maybe a small, three tier, vanilla cake with a lemon filling. It's still early and it might cost a little extra because of the late date, but it's worth a try. And Johnny's housekeeper, Gerta and her sister's have a catering business and if they're not working this Sunday, maybe they can cater for us." Loretha picked up the telephone and held it to her chest, closed her eyes and appeared to be praying. "Let me call Gerta first, and then Ah'll call the bakery for the cake." Loretha dialed the numbers while Sarah and Elizabeth stood back holding each others hands. "Hello Gerta? How are you tuhday? Fine . . . fine . . . yes, this is Loretha Turner. Yes, Johnny Turner's grandmother. Miss Gerta, Ah hope you can help me. It's such a short notice. Would you be able to cater a dinner for about seven-five people tuhmorrow after church?" Loretha held the phone with both hands and smiled. "Oh . . . my daughter, Sarah decided at the last minute that she wanted her father to preside over her wedding. We want tuh have a small reception here at the house." Loretha nodded her head as she listened to Gerta speak. She smiled and waved her hands at her daughters and lifted her head and mouthed words thanking God. "Yes, Miss Gerta. How about ham and turkey, string beans and collard greens, macaroni and cheese or potato salad or both, some rolls, oh and some candied yams. If you have a better idea, you may select the menu. Ah'm just so happy yuh can help me. Ah can bring some money by yuh house so yuh can buy the food. After you determine the amount of work that's involved on such a short notice, just give me a bill. Believe me yuh a life saver." Loretha hung up the phone and threw her hands in the air. "Oh . . . thank yuh Jesus, thank yuh Jesus!"

Sarah, Elizabeth, and Loretha screamed with joy at having Gerta's services. "Okay . . . we're not done. We still have tuh call the bakery," Loretha said as she made the next call. Just as she suspected, she could pick up the cake before the bakery closed that evening.

* * *

Sarah approached Elizabeth and placed her arm around her shoulder. Elizabeth flinched and Sarah's arm jumped. It was a subtle move, but enough that the sisters noticed and enough to experience discomfort. Their eyes locked and instantly they knew the toll years of estrangement had taken on both of them. Sarah's eyes were expressing guilt for her impulsive behavior and remorse for years of emotional distance. She knew it was wrong to tell Johnny that Reverend Oliver was his father before first speaking with Elizabeth. She never considered whom she might be hurting; she knew her motives were purely self-serving. Although the outcomes of her actions were positive, it could have turned out differently. Now she realized she had caused an additional rift in her sister's life.

" 'Lizabeth can we take a walk?" Sarah held her head down slightly and allowed her eyes to plead that her request be granted.

Elizabeth's smile was ever so faint and her expression appeared guarded. She nodded and turned to leave the den, but stopped at the sound of Sarah's voice.

"Oh 'Lizabeth, do you think it would be all right if Ah ask Nat tuh take a walk with Stephen? Ah don't think it's a good idea leaving him alone with Daddy," Sarah had leaned into Elizabeth space and whispered in her ear.

Both women turned to see where their father was, then they nodded and smiled when they located him with their mother. Their parents appeared to be deeply engaged in the arrangement for the wedding; the timing was right to leave the house.

"Oh Sarah, now yuh worried about Daddy?" Elizabeth smiled and squeezed Sarah's hand before she could take offense. "Ah'll ask Nat," she whispered.

Sarah watched as Elizabeth approached Nat and Stephen, and she smiled until Elizabeth returned to her.

"Okay Sarah, let's go. Nat's gonna take care of everything," Elizabeth whispered.

* * *

The burgundy blooms of the crepe myrtle bush had developed so majestically and its roots went deep into the soil of the left corner in the front yard. Reverend Turner had reconditioned and painted the rusty bench a white enamel and the beauty of that section of the yard called to Elizabeth and Sarah. It wasn't long before they were sitting on the white wrought iron bench when they noticed Nat and Stephen leaving the house. Sarah smiled and turned to Elizabeth, holding her hands out, palms up, offering herself to her and pleading.

"How can Ah ask for yuh forgiveness?" She pulled the palms of her hands together as if praying. "Ah'm so sorry 'Lizabeth. Ah've caused yuh almost as much pain as Daddy. Ah've been selfish and self-centered."

"Stop Sarah," Elizabeth said as she took hold of Sarah's hands. "Yuh don't have tuh do this."

"Please, 'Lizabeth. Let me finish." Sarah pulled her hands from Elizabeth's grasp.

"All of these years Ah never allowed myself tuh be close tuh you or Johnny because Ah felt like Ah would be betraying Daddy. As a child, that was acceptable, but as an adult that was just plan selfish." Sarah held her head back, closed her eyes and inhaled as much air as she could before exhaling. "Can yuh ever forgive me?"

"Sarah, there is no doubt you and Daddy removed some of the light from my life, but Ah had Johnny, Mama and MaDear and yuh'll never know that kind of love and security. Oh Mama loves yuh as much as she loves me, but Daddy's love offers no security. He can turn on yuh as quickly as he can flip a quarter, but Ah'll always love him. Ah don't know why or how, Ah just do." Elizabeth stood, pulled the burgundy cluster of blossoms from the crepe myrtle bush and held them in her hands. She lifted the flowers to her nose and took a deep breath before turning her attention back to Sarah. "Yuh need tuh understand something." She smiled and sniffed at the flowers again searching for its subtle aroma. "Those first days in the hospital were the worse days of my life. When Daddy disowned me Ah wanted tuh die. Ah tried to end my life. Ah believed the Lord had forsaken me; Ah hadn't bonded with my baby, and Ah was causing Mama so much pain it was unbearable. Ah'm sorry Sarah, Ah never thought about yuh; Ah never thought about yuh feelings. If Ah could live my life over, Ah would have given anything tuh have you and Daddy sharing it with me, but Ah wouldn't change anything else not even the circumstances of Johnny's existence."

Sarah reached over and hugged Elizabeth. "Ah love yuh and yuh have tuh allow me tuh be sorry. No matter what yuh say, Ah know Ah didn't do the things Ah should've."

"Ah love yuh too. Ah don't think we ever said that tuh each other. Sarah, nothing can be gained by dwelling on the past. Yuh've made it possible for this family tuh come tuhgether and move forward and Ah love yuh even more for that. Now come on, let's go find our men."

* * *

Malcolm blocked out the sound of the engine and the conversation between his mother and wife. He propped the pillow against the interior corner of the back seat, crossed his arms in front of him, and closed his eyes. He relaxed his body, but thoughts of Randy prevented him from relaxing his mind. *Damn! Ah've known Randy for ten years and been his lover for eight. That was before his oldest boy was born; before Theresa and Ah were married. Ah'm a selfish son-of-a-bitch. We were best friends, he didn't seduce me; we were there for each other and it just happened. Ah could've let him down easier. We have never been with any other men. Why didn't Ah wait until my father was well and until Johnny and Ah worked out our differences? Randy is my friend and Ah want tuh remain his friend. Right now, Ah just need tuh settle him down.*

Malcolm unwrapped his arms from his chest and raised his left arm over his head to block the sun from his eyes. Otherwise he remained still as if in a deep sleep, but stillness and shut eyes are often deceiving.

"Malcolm . . . Malcolm," Thea called testing his alertness. She glanced back at him checking for a response. "He must really be tired."

"Mother, have yuh wondered who hurt Dad?"

Malcolm peeked at his mother and watched her snap her head around in Theresa's direction. He believed he could feel the vibration of her movements through the motion of the car. *Oh Lord, why did she ask Mama that?*

"Oh, Malcolm told me what the doctor was saying. Ah didn't mean any harm." Theresa had a way of looking pitifully humble. "Ah'm sorry if Ah said something wrong."

"No, no . . . yuh family and yuh husband should be keepin' yuh informed, but Owen said no one hurt him. He said he fell on the porch." Once again Thea grabbed the security of her pocketbook and held it close. "Let's just leave it at that." She glanced down and fiddled with the clasp. She pulled her shoulders up to adjust her posture and stared out the car window.

Malcolm continues to watch his mother. She had reached that place where she could shut out the world. Theresa was alone in the car with two other people and he couldn't allow that.

"Oh, Ah needed that! Ah feel much better," he called out while sitting up. He rubbed his eyes and threw his head back against the seat. "Where are we honey?"

"The hospital is two blocks away." She glanced up at him through the rear view mirror and smiled.

"Why are you so quiet, Mama?"

"Yuh know Malcolm, something happens tuh me every time Ah get near the hospital. Ah want yuh father well and this dilemma over." Thea's posture became more rigid.

"Thank yuh Jesus! Ah thought it was me; Ah thought Ah said something that upset yuh," Theresa said as she checked her side view mirror. She glanced over her left shoulder, and turned into the left lane, before making a left turn at the next corner.

"Mama, Ah know what yuh issues are, but this has been a stressful day for me. Ah'm gonna try and stay as loose as Ah can. This morning Johnny and Ah were here at the same time. The air was so thick in Dad's room, if Ah fainted Ah couldn't fall down." Malcolm sat forward in the middle of the back seat. "Ah wanted tuh tell Dad Ah have a surprise for him, and Ah need tuh see how he's doing after this morning's unpleasant visit."

"Why yuh comin' so early tuhmorrow?" Thea broke her silence and glanced back at Malcolm.

"Because Johnny and I want to visit Dad and then attend the 11:00 a.m. service at Concord," Malcolm responded before pointing at the curb near the hospital entrance. "Honey, why don't yuh pull up over there and you and Mama get out of the car. Y'all can go on up tuh Dad's room and Ah'll meet yuh there. Ah'll park the car," he offered.

As soon as the ladies stepped out of the car, Malcolm drove.

* * *

By the time Malcolm reached his father's hospital room, the nurse informed him his father's condition had been upgraded to satisfactory and he had been moved to the medical unit on the other side of the hospital in the Gerald Milton Building.

"Your mother and wife were here not long ago and Ah gave them directions tuh his new room." The nurse walked from behind the desk and stood close enough to Malcolm to smell his cologne. "Yuh take the elevator back tuh the lobby and walk directly across the hall and take the elevators to the Milton building. Yuh father will be in room M319."

"Thank yuh, ugh . . ." Malcolm leaned in to read her name tag. "Ugh . . . Miss Tomey." He took a slight bow before turning and walking away. Halfway to the elevator, he turned quickly and notice Miss Tomey was still standing at the desk and making no attempt to hide that she was still watching him.

Malcolm smiled and thought, *Ah need a Miss Tomey like Ah need a Randy Lester.* He was successful in taking the elevator in the Milton Building and realized the ladies were already visiting with his father. The visiting hours and rules were posted on the wall near the nurse's station and were very different from the 'all day' visiting hours in the intensive care unit. The new hours were 10:00 a.m. – 12:00 p.m., 2:00 – 4:00 p.m. and 6:00 – 8:00 p.m. and only two visitors were allowed per patient at a time.

Johnny and Ah would only have thirty minutes tuh visit before leaving tuh get tuh church on time. Ah'll call him as soon as Ah get home. Ah'll drive Mama back in the afternoon and Theresa and Ah will start back tuh Jonesboro after visiting hours tuhmorrow evening.

* * *

"Mother, Ah believe Malcolm may be in the waiting room." Theresa stood and walked toward the door. "They only allow the patients tuh have two visitors at a time."

Thea nodded, acknowledging her as she left the room.

"Thea," Reverend Oliver said. "Dr. Parks said if Ah continue tuh do well he'd let me go home by the end of the week or early next week," he spoke slowly. His wired jaw caused his words to slur. His eyes were teary and he waited for Thea to tell him everything would be all right.

Thea turned toward him. She had been quiet, and when she spoke she weighed her words in a serious attempt not to upset him. She gently patted his arm. "Yes Owen."

* * *

Malcolm was just about to step into the room, but instead he placed his head against the wall. He knew how his mother felt and when he heard the long silent pause, he walked in the room with the purpose of changing the subject to spare both parents' feelings.

"Hi Dad, Ah see they took yuh for a little ride since this morning. Ah'm real sorry Johnny left when Ah came in. Ah know yuh wanted him tuh stay a little while."

Owen turned away from Thea and nodded his head.

"Well Owen, Ah see yuh don't have a roommate yet," Thea said without commenting on his earlier statement. Instead, she walked to the window and pretended to be interested in the parking lots and the people walking to and from their cars.

Malcolm shifted his eyes toward his mothers and thought, *I'm gonna have tuh talk tuh Mama about Dad. We have tuh make plans for him.* He turned giving his attention to his father. "So Dad, how do yuh like it over here?"

"Oh, the best thing is Ah can get out of bed and go to the bathroom." He pushed the bed position buttons and adjusted his back and legs. "Ah still have tuh call for assistance before getting out of the bed, but Ah can get up and walk around."

"That's great Dad. Yuh know . . . Ah'm gonna see yuh first thing in the morning, so Ah'm gonna go out tuh the waiting area with Theresa and let you have a little time with Mama, but Ah need just a moment with her."

"Hey, why can't yuh talk tuh her in front of me?" Reverend Oliver said.

"Ah could, but Ah don't want tuh spoil the surprise Ah'm planning for yuh." Malcolm tilted his head and smiled. "C'mon Dad, work with me."

"Okay go, but hurry back. This surprise better be worth it."

Thea waited at the door for Malcolm. They walked from the room and across the corridor, far enough away so Owen couldn't hear their conversation. Malcolm placed his arm on his mother's shoulder. "Mama, Ah know Dad has been puttin' yuh on the spot. He's been actin' like everything is all right. Do yuh think yuh could just play along with him? Ah don't want yuh tuh go through this alone. Ah'll be back whenever yuh call me."

"Thanks Malcolm. Thanks for understanding what Ah'm going through. Ah still don't know what he has tuh do. Ah been praying, but Ah don't know what tuh tell him. Ah'm goin' back now. Ah don't want him tuh get antsy."

"Remind Dad that Ah'll have his surprise for him in the morning."

* * *

It was almost dark outside by the time the Olivers returned home from the hospital. They walked toward the house, but stopped when Thea began speaking.

"Can y'all tell me what kind of tree that is?" She stood admiring the tall tree with the long draping, swaying branches again. "Does that look like a sad tree tuh y'all?"

Theresa stood close to Malcolm and looked up at the mature tree.

"Well . . . it depends on how yuh look at it. Ah been lookin' at it all my life. It's a beautiful tree; it's called a 'weeping willow tree'," Malcolm responded.

Thea smiled and turned to Theresa. "What do yuh think?"

Malcolm rubbed Theresa's back and she felt more at ease. "It's a beautiful tree, and it's certainly not weeping. When the wind blows, the branches sway."

"Would yuh say they kinda dance?" Thea smiled and hugged herself as she spoke.

"Ah'd say they dance as graceful as a ballerina," Theresa chuckled lightly as she spoke.

"Thanks Theresa, because this morning Ah named it my 'dancing willow tree'. Ah never realized how pleasant it was tuh look at. Ah do most of my praying under that tree. Sometime Ah pray on my knees, but Ah did move those chairs out there for when Ah want tuh sit while Ah pray and meditate."

"Mama, Ah've lived here most of my life, and Ah've never seen yuh fall in love with a tree."

"Yuh know Malcolm, when yuh heart is troubled, yuh look for beauty all around yuh. That old tree has always been there and Ah only just noticed its real beauty." Thea crossed her arms and looked up at her tree. "It's like the Lord made me take notice of it. He made it dance for me and it was so soothing. The Lord took my misery up in them branches and flung them away. Ah have a decision tuh make and only through prayer and meditation will Ah find the answer. That old tree is gonna help me find my way."

Theresa gently squeezed Thea's hand and smiled at her. "Ah don't believe Malcolm has enough sensitivity tuh understand the beauty tuh be found in a weeping willow tree," Theresa said.

"Ah prefer to call it a 'dancing willow tree'. The only time it weeps is when it rains and even then it dances on a breeze." Thea glanced over and smiled at Theresa again.

"Whatever works for yuh, Mama." Malcolm smiled and hurried to unlock the door when he heard the telephone ring. "Ah'll get it."

"Malcolm," Randy's voice reached his ear in a whining whisper. Malcolm glanced over his shoulder and noticed his wife and mother standing quietly at the entrance to the study, both appearing inquisitive. He covered the mouthpiece of the receiver with his hand, told his mother it was his friend Randy and watched the ladies walk away.

"Wait Malcolm, Ah need tuh talk tuh yuh now!" Randy continued whining.

Malcolm walked to the door and checked the short hall to be sure the women were not standing nearby before returning to his seat at his father's desk to continue their conversation.

"Listen man, Ah'll call yuh back. Ah just walked in the house. Believe me Ah'll call yuh. Just give me ten minutes. Ah have tuh get my family settled."

"Okay, ten minutes. Please Malcolm, Ah need tuh talk tuh yuh," Randy whined.

"Stay cool man. Ah'll call yuh back in ten." Malcolm hung up the phone and walked into the kitchen. Theresa was sitting at the table and Thea stood near the stove preparing a pot of coffee. Malcolm pulled the wooden chair away from the table and it made a scraping sound against the ceramic tile floor. His body language was as angry as the sound the chair made when he positioned himself to sit down.

"What's the matter Malcolm?" Theresa asked. Concern blanketed her face. She placed her hand on his shoulder and allowed it to tenderly glide down his upper arm.

"It's Randy. He and Gail got into it. Ah spoke tuh Gail earlier and she sounded fine. Ah don't know what's got Randy all crazy." He clasped his hands on the table and lowered his head. "If it was that bad, Gail would have acted differently, even if she didn't say anything. Ah know he's my best friend, but Ah got so much on my mind. He could've at least waited until Ah got home. Ah told him Ah just got back from the hospital and needed to settle in and Ah'd return his call in ten minutes."

"Well yuh ten minutes are just about up. Why don't yuh go call him; try tuh calm him down and come back and have some coffee and cake with us."

"Okay honey." Malcolm took a deep breath and smiled at the ladies before leaving the kitchen. He wanted to speak with Randy, to quiet him before he did something he would regret. He dialed his phone number and heard Randy's voice after the first ring.

"Malcolm . . . Ah've been tryin' tuh reach yuh all day. Ah've been tryin' man, but Ah don't know how tuh go on without yuh.

"Randy . . . man, yuh were okay before Ah came intuh yuh life," Malcolm spoke softly with both elbows on his father's desk. A long period of quiet passed while he held the phone to his ear and placed his eyes on his father's brown leather Bible.

"Are yuh still there man?" Randy spoke in a panicked voice. "When are yuh coming home? Ah really need yuh. Ah'm all nerves."

"Ah won't be home until late tomorrow night. Listen man . . . we've been tuhgether for ten years. Ah'm not going anywhere, but Ah been straight with yuh, Ah will not be yuh lover. How many times do Ah have tuh tell yuh. Ah can't do that anymore. Why can't we just be friends?"

"Ah want everything tuh be like it used tuh be," Randy continued whining.

"Man . . . yuh have Gail and two handsome boys."

"And yuh have Theresa and yuh parents, yuh know what Ah mean?"

"Ah know yuh not threatening me!" Malcolm said. He stood and placed his hand on his hip and continued to look down at his father's Bible. *Damn him, Ah would've put my fist in his mouth if he were here,* he thought. "Yuh really need tuh calm down and listen. Yuh have just as much tuh lose as Ah do, so let's hold off on the threats." He sat in his father's chair again, resting his head against its high back. "Listen man, if Ah get back early enough tuhmorrow, Ah'll call yuh. If not we'll meet Monday morning, an hour before work."

"Ah'll hold on until then," Randy said.

"Are yuh going to be okay?" Malcolm pushed his head back against the chair and closed his eyes.

"Ah'm better."

"Remember Randy, yuh the best friend Ah've ever had. Ah don't want tuh lose yuh. Whose car do yuh want tuh meet at?"

"If Ah don't see yuh tuhmorrow night, come tuh section F-210 on Monday. There's a vacant space across from my parking space." Randy's voice sounded manlier.

"See yuh, man. Ah'll call yuh." Malcolm hung up the phone and hurried off to have his coffee with his mother and wife.

* * *

Johnny and Julia arrived back at the cottage around 7:30 p.m.. While Julia showered Johnny was busy preparing a special love nest. He had to work fast and quietly.

Julia slipped on Johnny's night shirt and pulled back the covers of their bed waiting for him. Johnny had not taken his shower and Julia was concerned. He entered the bedroom, removed his shirt, and stood over Julia. She could never resist his smooth muscular chest and he couldn't resist seeing her perfect body on the bed. But this time he turned away from her or he would have never made it out of the bedroom.

"Stay there Julia. Rest, look at television, listen to music, anything, but stay away from me or you'll ruin my surprise. You know I can't stand to see you looking so good." Johnny grabbed his night shorts and hurried to take his shower.

"Are you ready, Johnny?"

"No, not yet, I'll call you in a minute." He ran from one of the two guest bedrooms carrying pillows out through the back door. He was out doors for a few minutes before he returned to the house. Then he stood in the door looking out. "Okay," he whispered. He smiled and returned to the bedroom.

"Julia, you might think I'm crazy, but I'd like you to come with me. He took her by the hand and led her to the back door and out onto the back porch. "I always wanted to make love under the stars, but this is the next best thing. It's a full length screen."

"Johnny this is so beautiful. You have candles and pillows all around. Where did you get the mattress?"

"It's from the sofa bed. It's new. It still has the plastic on it so I put a blanket under the sheets. Do you like it?"

"Yes, I love it, but I have only one question, can anyone see us out here?"

"We have complete privacy, except for nature's creatures. They'll all be watching us. Will you let me love you under the moonlight?"

Julia reached up and kissed Johnny. He rubbed his hand under her nightshirt and pulled it over her head before, lowering her to the mattress. He removed his shorts and their nakedness touched. Being out in the open and having the night air bathe their skin heightened their sexual excitement.

"Johnny it feels so good to be free like this. I could make love with you out there in the back yard."

"I could too, but I'm afraid of snakes, so I'll settle for the back porch." He laughed and began kissing her body and massaging her private places. And she was quiet and melting under his touch.

Chapter 11

The nurse had just walked from Reverend Oliver's room when Dr. Parks walked in.

"How are you feeling this morning?" He stared up at the monitor before looking down at Reverend Oliver.

"Well, it's the needles. Ah don't want any more needles. Ah know Ah have my mouth wired, but Ah can still take pills, look here." Reverend Oliver used his fingers to pull back his lips exposing the hole created by missing upper and lower molar teeth.

Dr. Parks pulled his small flashlight from his pocket and flashed it around his mouth. "What am I looking at?"

"C'mon Doc, gimme the pills instead of the needles. Ah can slip them in there, in them holes where the teeth are missing." He pointed to the side of his mouth. "And wash them down with the water. Ah'll take one at a time."

Dr. Parks couldn't help laughing. He placed his hands on Reverend Oliver's shoulder. "I don't get many patients that make sense. I'll change your orders to pills as soon as I leave the room, but for now I would like you to talk to Officers Benson and Lewis. They're waiting at the front desk."

Dr. Parks glanced over at the monitor. Reverend Oliver shook his head and reminded himself to relax. "Dr. Parks, why do yuh insist that someone beat me? Ah thought we were through with that."

"We are," Dr. Parks said. "It was my responsibility to report my suspicions. Now, it's you responsibility to convince them they don't have a case."

"Then why don't yuh unplug that machine? It makes me crazy. Yuh can plug it back in after they leave."

Dr. Parks called the nurse's station on the telephone and warned them he would be unplugging the monitor in Reverend Oliver's room.

"My Lord, don't they go tuh church. It's Sunday. Okay, Ah'll talk tuh them, but when they leave, please don't forget my medication."

"Not a problem," Dr. Parks said as he left the room.

* * *

"Officers," Dr. Parks quietly beckoned for the detectives to come to the room. "I'm sorry you had to wait. I just had Reverend Oliver moved to this room yesterday afternoon. I had to examine him to be sure he was up to your questioning. If you'll follow me, I'll introduce you to him."

"Reverend Oliver, these are the detectives I spoke to you about," Dr. Parks said while turning and nodding his head at them. "These are Officers Benson and Lewis."

"It's nice meeting yuh gentlemen, but Ah don't know what yuh want. Ah told Dr. Parks everything. Now, Ah'm sure he told yuh what Ah told him. So Ah'm gonna let yuh ask me the questions, but first Ah need tuh ask yuh something. Now, Officer Benson . . ." Reverend Oliver pointed all of his fingers in his directions. He smiled. "May Ah ask yuh something?"

Dr. Parks smiled while Officer Benson and Lewis smiled at each other.

"Ask," Officer Benson said.

"Don't yuh young men take yuh families tuh church on Sunday mornings?"

"Yes sir, Ah can't meet my wife and kids for Sunday school tuhday, but Ah'll be there for the main service. It was nice of yuh tuh ask," Officer Lewis said. He smiled and turned to Officer Benson. It was like he was telling him it was his turn.

"Ah have five children and three of them are singing in the choir tuhday. Last January Ah was ordained as a deacon. Both Officer Lewis and Ah hate it when we have tuh work on Sunday."

"Well let's get on with yuh questioning. It's after nine o'clock and Ah don't want yuh tuh be late for service," Reverend Oliver said.

"Reverend Oliver, could yuh help us out here. Just tell us what happened," Officer Benson said. He pulled a small black pad and a pen from his breast pocket and was ready to take notes.

Dr. Parks crossed his arms, stood behind the detectives and leaned against the wall. He smiled. It didn't matter what Reverend Oliver told the detectives, he knew he was lying. He had sealed his suspicion when he asked to have the blood pressure monitor turned off because he knew it was like a lie detector. Dr. Parks knew it was his obligation to report his findings and it was up to the authorities to complete an investigation. He smiled because, Reverend Oliver had convinced the detectives they didn't have a case.

Officer Lewis glanced up at the wall clock. "Who were yuh visiting so late at night?"

"All Ah can tell yuh is that it was a parishioner in need of spiritual counsel."

"C'mon Lew. If the Rev. says he wasn't assaulted, then he wasn't. There's no case here. What's the name of yuh church?" Officer Benson said.

"The Concord Baptist Church in Rehoboth, Georgia. Ah'm the assistant pastor, and Reverend John Turner is the pastor."

Officer Lewis opened the door and Officer Benson closed his pad and returned it along with the pen to his breast pocket. They both held their hands up in a still wave as they walked from the room.

"Reverend Oliver, would you like me to leave this door open? Dr. Parks remarked.

"Yes. Oh now, don't yuh forget tuh order them pills for me."

*　*　*

Johnny reached across the mattress for Julia only to find an empty space. He reached for his pajama shorts and after pulling them on he opened the back door and was met with the aroma of fresh coffee and fried bacon. He came up behind Julia and wrapped his arms around her. "Did you enjoy yourself last night?" He swept her hair back behind her ear and kissed her in the nape of her neck.

"You were wonderful and so was your special room."

"I didn't know you knew how to cook." He continued to nibble on her neck.

"This side is feeling a little lonely." She turned her head to the left and used her fingers to comb her long hair over her ear. "It's waiting."

Johnny shifted his weight and began to give equal attention to the left side of her neck.

"I never said I didn't know how to cook. How could I not know that. Baby! I'm a Rocky Mount, North Carolina, girl. You can't leave for college if you can't cook." She turned quickly and her silky black hair fell to her mid back. She threw her arms around Johnny's neck and before she could give him a morning kiss, reality set in.

"Stop!" Johnny yelled out holding his hand over his mouth and backing away. Stay there just like that. I'll be right back. I got critter mouth." He ran into the bathroom.

Julia laughed and continued preparing the small breakfast. "The grits are ready and the rolls are in the oven. All I have to do is prepare the eggs. You need something in your stomach before your leave," Julia spoke loud so Johnny would be sure to hear her even though the bathroom was next door to the kitchen.

Johnny returned from the bathroom looking for his morning kiss, and Julia was scrambling eggs in a cast iron frying pan. "Ya know, I can cook too. Let me help you so I can get my kiss."

"It's all done. I even removed the rolls from the oven" Julia wrapped her arms around his neck and gave him the morning kiss he had been waiting for. "Now, tell me when Gerta will be here."

"So-o-o you can't cook." Johnny pointed at Julia while taking his seat at the table.

Julia laughed. She was trying to place her napkin across her lap, but instead used it to cover her mouth. "Johnny . . . just because I asked about Gerta . . ." Julia continued laughing and held her napkin tight against her mouth. "It doesn't mean I can't cook." She continued to laugh. I knew Gerta would be working on the wedding and wouldn't be working here this morning."

"I'm happy for that. I think it would've been a little awkward for her to find us sleeping nude on the back porch. This has been a crazy weekend." Johnny locked eyes with Julia and smiled.

"I'm so happy for you." Julia reached over and took hold of her husband's hand. "Johnny, I want you to finish up and get ready to leave. What time is Malcolm coming?"

"I'll call him. It's after eight o'clock. I believe we said nine, but I'm not sure. Don't forget to save me a seat near you at church." Johnny hurried to finish eating, wiped his mouth and kissed Julia on the forehead before leaving the kitchen. "Oh Julia," he said returning to the kitchen. "I'm gonna place the mattress back into the sofa bed. I can always take it out again tonight." He smiled, rushed to Julia's side and wrapped his arms around her. "God, I love you!" They enjoyed a passionate kiss.

* * *

Johnny called Malcolm and was informed their father had new visiting hours and had been moved out of the intensive care unit. They agreed to leave at 9:20 a.m. Johnny was sitting on his porch and called to Julia when he heard Malcolm's car coming down Collins Road. By the time he arrived at the end of the driveway Julia was standing by his side. She waved at Malcolm and stood on her tip-toes to kiss Johnny's cheek. "Don't forget to save a seat for me at church."

"Okay Johnny. See you later." She remained on the porch until the car was headed back up Collins Road.

Malcolm reached the end of Collins Road and turned right onto Rehoboth Road. The gospel music played on the radio and the noise of the car in motion were the only sounds to be heard. Both men greeted each other, but they had little else to say. Johnny rested his head on the headrest, closed his eyes and a diminutive smile curved his lips. Malcolm gave him a quick glance and his eyes were back attending to the upcoming curves. He tilted his head and his grandiose smile parted his lips.

"Oh! Ah have tuh pull into my parents' yard for a moment," Malcolm said and he made a hard right turn and came to a skidding halt. "Ah'm not sure what Mama wants tuh do about the wedding. Ah'll be right back." He opened the door and hurried toward the house.

Johnny sat up straight in his seat while his eyes followed Malcolm. "What's up man?" He yelled.

"Ah forgot if Mama said she was going tuh the wedding, 'cause if she is, Ah won't be taking her tuh the hospital until this evening," Malcolm spoke as he hurried toward the house and looked back at Johnny.

Johnny got out of the car and walked between the low branches of the weeping willow tree. He smiled as the branches tickled his face and hands and took him back to the days the tree was much smaller, but still a useful hiding place from Malcolm.

"Hey Johnny!" Malcolm called out.

Johnny backed away from the tree, before turning and hurrying to the car.

"The weeping willow tree . . . Malcolm that tree is as much a part of my life as MaDear's cottage." Johnny's face brightened up.

Malcolm backed the car away from his mother's car and turned on a path that put them directly under the swaying branches of the tree. "See how those branches sweep yuh car. Doesn't it remind yuh of how those sponge strips dance across yuh windshield at the carwash? Mama calls it her 'dancing willow tree'. Yuh know, the more Ah watched that tree, the more Ah agree with her," Malcolm said.

"Well, I could sit on your parents' front porch with a cool glass of lemonade and watch your mother's dancing willow tree for hours."

"Ah never gave that tree a second thought. Ah guess Ah need tuh slow down and take life a little easier. Oh . . . about the wedding, Mama wants tuh see Sarah get married. She wants me tuh tell Dad she'll see him tuhmorrow."

Malcolm pulled up to the stop sign on the main road and turned right.

❋ ❋ ❋

As soon as they arrived at the hospital, Malcolm directed Johnny to the Milton building. All visitors were required to stop by the information desk where elderly women, wearing pink volunteer vests, fingered through large files to locate visitor's passes. Johnny and Malcolm had to wait ten minutes before the security guard would allow them to take the elevator up to the third floor.

"Man, they're really strict about visiting hours today," Malcolm said as he and Johnny took a seat in the lobby area across from the information desk.

"Malcolm, how sick was Dad?" Johnny leaned forward staring at Malcolm.

"When Ah arrived last Monday evening Ah thought he was gonna die and on Tuesday, the doctor would only let us visit him for fifteen minutes. Ah thought it was the last time Ah'd see him alive. Yuh grandfather had been with him more than twenty hours and they never asked him tuh leave, probably because he was in a coma."

Johnny looked up at the large wall clock. "Did Dad ever tell you what happened to his face?"

Malcolm set back on the chair and raised his head until his eyes met with Johnny's. "Dad said he slipped on the front porch steps and slammed his face into the ball on the banister." He sat forward again and rested his elbows on his knees. "Well . . . "

"Is there something else?"

"Well . . . Dad's doctor believes someone assaulted him."

"Assaulted him? Who?"

"That's it, his doctor said Dad had two fractures to his jaw and there was no way he could have got that from a fall. Ah wanted tuh talk tuh Dad about that but his doctor said not tuh upset him. Man . . . Ah think Dad got really upset when he found out his secret was out, and that pushed up his pressure. Ah think it made him dizzy and he fell; maybe he fell more than once." Malcolm stood and looked down at Johnny. He placed his hands on his hips. "Dad's doctor was so sure Dad was beaten, he called the police. Ah don't know what happened with that, but Ah'll let yuh know as soon as Ah find out. Oh, one more thing. Mama said Dad got a phone call and he went out early Saturday morning. When she saw him again his face was bruised."

Johnny listened without commenting.

"Visiting hours," the security guard called out. It was 9:55 a.m..

Johnny and Malcolm carried the blue passes and were directed toward the three elevators to the left, under the large engraved brass sign that read

GERALD MILTON BUILDING.

* * *

Johnny stepped into his father's hospital room first and stood for a moment. Reverend Oliver was reading his bible and didn't pay attention to anyone entering his room. Johnny walked to the foot of his bed and Malcolm entered the room and stood next to him. Finally, Malcolm cleared his throat and Johnny coughed.

"Boys . . . why didn't y'all say somethin'? Ah thought y'all were them hospital workers. Look at y'all here tuhgether; Ah never thought Ah'd see yuh two standing tuhgether in my life time."

Johnny and Malcolm gave their father a warm handshake.

"We wanted you to see us together before Malcolm left for Jonesboro. We have to leave by 10:30 to get to church on time. Aunt Sarah is getting married. She's having a small ceremony this afternoon after the regular service."

"Theresa and Ah will be back tuh see yuh this evening before we leave for home, but Mama won't be here until tuhmorrow." Malcolm began to inspect the room. "Hey Dad, where's all the techno-gizmo yuh were hooked up tuh?

"The last of that stuff was disconnected this morning, but Ah think they will be returning the blood pressure monitor. Ah can even get out of the bed, but Ah have tuh call for help first. Ah'm really on the mend. Yuh know, they must believe Ah'm better, Dr. Parks was back talkin' 'bout that assault stuff. He came with two detectives, but Ah told them Ah fell, which is how Ah remember it."

"Dad, Malcolm told me what happened; is that how you injured your jaw?"

"If he told yuh what Ah told him, then, yes. No one beat me up. It was a terrible time for me. My blood pressure must have shot up, because I felt dizzy. Ah fell a couple of times on the front porch and that's what Ah told them detectives. It's over now; they closed the case."

"Well Dad, that does explain it," Johnny said. He took a deep breath and blew out a rush of air.

"Dad yuh have a mouth full of wire. Does it hurt?" Malcolm said trying to change the subject.

"My tongue was sore but it's better now. The worse is the liquid food. Hospital food is bad enough, but when it's liquefied it's horrible. Imagine sipping a low sodium, bland flavored, liquefied drumstick through a straw." Reverend Oliver laughed harder than he should have. He held his hand to his face, but the pain only subsided a little. He tried to laugh without moving his lips.

Johnny and Malcolm laughed but quickly quieted as soon as they noticed their father was feeling some discomfort.

"How long do yuh have tuh keep yuh jaw wired?" Malcolm asked.

"Yuh know, Ah believe Ah heard them say six tuh eight weeks, but Ah'm not sure. The good part is, Ah'll be out of the hospital by then and even though the food will still be liquefied, it will have more flavor." He smiled and nodded his head.

"Hey Dad maybe yuh'll meet Johnny's wife sometime during the week?"

"Ah'd like that Johnny. Will yuh bring her up tuh meet me? Yuh grandmother told me when yuh got married and Ah hear she's very pretty."

"I sure will."

Instantly Reverend Oliver's eyes welled up. He held his head up and tried to hold in his emotions, but a cough shook tears loose to roll down his face. He was quiet when he pulled the covers back. Johnny and Malcolm helped him sit up, allowing his legs to dangling over the side. Tears continued to crawl down his face, but he tried to smile even as he experienced the heaves of a crying man.

Johnny handed him several tissues. "I've loved you all my life. You can't be any happier than me."

"Look at my two boys." He held out his arms. Johnny and Malcolm hugged him.

"Dad, Ah'm as happy as yuh tuh have Johnny in my life. Finally, Ah feel complete." Malcolm locked eyes with Johnny.

"Please tell me, how did y'all get tuhgether?"

Malcolm held his head down, not wanting to be the one to describe the fight in the woods. He could give his father a blow by blow description if they were alone, but he realized he didn't know Johnny well enough to express his perceived version of the details.

"Okay guys, don't all speak at the same time."

"Dad . . . Malcolm and I kinda duked it out the old way. Well . . . I did the throwing of blows; he ducked and tried not to hurt me. We went around and around until the fight was gone and we were crying and then laughing. Malcolm didn't have the anger; I kept that flame burning all these years. Malcolm just helped me stamp out the fire."

"Dad, why don't you get back in bed? It's almost 10:30," Malcolm suggested.

Reverend Oliver slid his feet under the covers and asked his sons to join him in prayer. Johnny stood on one side of the bed and Malcolm on the other and they held hands.

"Dear Lord, Our Heavenly Father," Reverend Oliver began, "from You all blessings flow. Thank Yuh for allowing my two sons tuh stand here with me as brothers. Thank Yuh for Malcolm and Johnny's forgiveness. Ah continue tuh ask Yuh for Yuh forgiveness. Dear Lord, Ah haven't forgotten my Thea. Please Lord. Please, place forgiveness in Thea's heart and let her forgive me. Dear Lord, Ah ask this in the name of Yuh son, Jesus. Amen."

"Amen," Malcolm and Johnny spoke out at the same time

"Thank yuh guys for comin'. Ah want yuh tuh take yuh time drivin' home and remember how much Ah love yuh."

"Okay Dad, I'll see you tomorrow," Johnny said.

"See yuh this afternoon before Ah return home," Malcolm added.

* * *

Johnny and Malcolm were quiet until they left the hospital. Malcolm believed he should say something, but he didn't know what to say. A pleasant thought softened his face and some of his stress seemed to melt away. He smiled as he fixed his eyes on the clear sky and finally he whispered his thanks to Johnny without looking at him.

"No need to thank me man. I love him, too." Johnny looked straight ahead and continued to walk toward the parking lot.

Malcolm made a right turn down the aisle leading to where he parked the car and Johnny followed. A chirping sound was heard when he released the door alarm and started the engine. Malcolm wanted the air conditioner to engage and do its job. Johnny smiled and Malcolm knew the performance of his car was nothing new for him and his top of the line automobiles.

"It feels good in here."

"Yeah man. It helps to get a head start on the heat." Malcolm backed out of the parking space and they were on there way back to Rehoboth.

"Are you going to the wedding?"

"No . . . Theresa and I really don't know yuh Aunt Sarah, but Mama is going tuh be there. She said she wants tuh play the piano." Malcolm checked the traffic flow before merging onto the narrow highway. "We'll be leaving after the regular service and coming back tuh the hospital, before heading home."

"Good thinking man."

"Johnny, may Ah speak frankly?"

"Speak."

"First Ah'd like tuh say thanks for the job."

"What job?"

"C'mon Johnny, Ah've known for years it was yuh recommendation that got me my job with the firm. Man, if yuh hated me so much, why'd yuh help me?"

"I love our father and he was so worried about you. Man you had completed college and was working as a janitor at the high school." Johnny turned toward Malcolm. "Besides, it's always a brother's responsibility to return to his roots and help another brother."

"Thanks man yuh really changed my life. Yuh know . . . Ah wish Ah could stay in Rehoboth this week and spend some time with yuh . . . that is if yuh would have me. For the first time in my life Ah feel whole. Tuhday, we made Dad happy and Ah've never been so happy."

Johnny turned to look at the highway. "Years ago MaDear told me to forgive. I couldn't do it then. But if we had settled our differences when we were teenagers, we could've had twenty years of friendship, even though we didn't know we were brothers."

Malcolm shook his head. "Yuh know what Ah think? Ah think our lives were supposed to be the way they were. We both were our father's penance."

"Say what you want, Malcolm. I should have let it go before we left high school. All the craziness had ended by then. You had your group of friends and I had mine. We were mature and the childish prank had been over for at least two years," Johnny reasoned.

Chapter 12

Johnny and Malcolm arrived at the Concord Baptist Church just in time for morning service. All of their lives the Turners sat on the right side of the church and the Olivers sat on the left. Johnny did a quick visual scan and noticed Sarah, Elizabeth and Nat weren't in the church. He reasoned that Elizabeth was with Sarah preparing for the wedding. Julia, Stephen Parker and his grandmother sat together and had saved a seat for him on the pew.

Julia leaned over to receive Johnny's whisper when he asked where Nat was. He really didn't expect her to know and accepted her shrugged shoulders and empty glance. He gently squeezed her hand telling her it was okay. They both turned their attention to Reverend Turner as he thanked the congregation for their prayers and support for the Oliver family.

* * *

After the service Theresa and Malcolm stood on the steps of the church and approached Reverend Turner. Malcolm held out his hand and Reverend Turner accepted it. "Thank yuh for everything yuh did for my family, sir. Yuh were there for us even when yuh didn't have tuh be. Yuh truly a man of God." Malcolm took a small bow as he spoke. Theresa smiled and held tightly to her husband's arm.

"Thank yuh Malcolm. Will yuh be stayin' for the weddin'?"

"No sir. We want tuh stop by the hospital before we return to Jonesboro. Oh, please forgive me sir. This is my wife Theresa."

Theresa extended her hand to greet Reverend Turner.

"It a pleasure meeting you, Mrs. Oliver."

"The pleasure is mine," Theresa said. She smiled as Reverend Turner accepted her hand for a slight hand shake.

"Thank you again, Reverend Turner." Malcolm continued to hold to Theresa's arm and he took another bow before walking down the church's steps. "Ah would like yuh tuh meet Johnny and his wife before we leave," Malcolm said in a soft voice as he leaned in closer to Theresa.

✳ ✳ ✳

"Gram'ma where's Nat?" Johnny asked. "Isn't he going to stand with Stephen?" His face wore more concern for Nat than for Stephen.

Loretha stiffened her posture. "Yuh know Ah worry 'bout that man. His back spasms have him in bed again. Ah think he should go to the clinic, but he refuses. Ah was hoping he could stand with Stephen during the wedding. Do yuh think yuh could do it Johnny?"

"Sure Gram'ma." Johnny turned toward Stephen. "Hey man, I feel like I've known you most of my life." The men shook hands.

Johnny noticed Malcolm and Theresa standing on the grass in front of the church. He turned to his grandmother and Stephen and held up his hand. "Would you excuse me, I would like to see them before they leave. Julia would you like to come with me?"

"Sure Johnny," Julia replied. She held tightly to Johnny's hand and hurried off with him.

Stephen placed one hand in his pocket and pleasantly nodded at Loretha.

"Hey Malcolm!" Johnny called out.

Malcolm and Theresa turned when they heard Johnny calling. They searched the crowd and saw Johnny and Julia approaching them. "Before you leave I would like you to meet my wife," Johnny said. "Julia this is Malcolm and his wife Theresa."

"It's a pleasure meeting yuh," Malcolm smiled as he greeted her.

Theresa and Julia smiled and nodded at each other. "It's nice to meet you." They spoke almost simultaneously.

Julia stood back and watched as the brothers spoke before Malcolm walked around the car to the driver's side. Johnny opened the car door for Theresa and waited for her to be seated. "You and Theresa have a safe trip home," he said as he closed the car door. "I'll keep watch over Dad and call you if there's any change," he whispered.

Julia held Johnny's hand and waved goodbye.

"Thanks Johnny. Bye Julia. It was very nice meeting yuh," Malcolm said.

Johnny and Julia stood back and watched Malcolm and Theresa leave the church grounds.

"Johnny! We're ready to start," Loretha called out before disappearing into the church.

"Honey you go ahead," Julia said. "I'll go in the front door. I don't think I can keep up with you, but I'm sure I'll be there before the service begins."

Johnny stretched out his stride and entered the church through the right side door. Stephen was sitting on the front pew waiting nervously. He smiled when he saw Johnny and together they waited for the service to begin. Reverend Turner stood in the pulpit still wearing his maroon robe with the white trim. Julia entered the church and walked to the seat near Loretha. Thea played a medley of piano selections while she watched for her cue to play the wedding march, and the congregation spoke in a hushed tone while they waited for the wedding to begin.

Sarah allowed her father to have his way for most of the service with the exception of two issues. She didn't want him to ask the question, "who gives this woman away." She reasoned with her father that she was her own person and as such, could not be given away. The other issue was 'for the wife to obey her husband'. Sarah was adamant that this be stricken from the wedding vows. Her argument with her father continued until they entered the church for the morning service. Finally Sarah said, "Daddy, if Ah don't have it my way, Ah'll walk out of the church and our civil ceremony will go on the record."

Thea played the first eight cords of the wedding march and Sarah and Elizabeth entered the sanctuary from the choir room on the left side of the church, instead of taking the long walk down the center aisle. Stephen and Johnny stood and took their positions. Sarah walked in slowly and stood next to Stephen and Elizabeth stood next to her.

Sarah was dressed in an off white two piece silk suit and a wide brim hat with a matching band. She wore her white sling back shoes and carried the same bridal bouquet she used in her civil ceremony.

Elizabeth stood with her and wore a light blue dress with white trim on the collar, sleeve, and waist band. She also wore white shoes and gloves and carried a single white rose. She smiled at her father, then looked over and smiled at Johnny and Stephen.

Reverend Turner conducted the service, giving praise to the Lord and Savior Jesus Christ, and asking him to bless His children. The 'I do's', 'do you', 'for better or worst' and 'til death do you part' were said. The rings were blessed and exchanged and the groom was instructed to kiss his bride. Mr. and Mrs. Stephen Parker were presented to the congregation and everyone was invited to the Turner's home for a small reception.

* * *

Malcolm left the hospital, driving with both hands gripping the steering wheel and his face cold with anger. He stared straight ahead, but occasionally took a quick glanced at Theresa. He wasn't angry, he was disappointed; he knew she had every reason to be upset with his father. She just caught him by surprise. She could have explained her feeling earlier and he would have had more time to prepare himself and make an excuse for her. But, to wait until he arrived at the hospital and suddenly refuse to get out of the car came as a complete shock.

"Malcolm . . . just last week yuh father called yuh home and had yuh stand with him tuh witness his confession tuh a heinous crime. A week later he's being treated like a wounded lamb. Maybe yuh have tuh cater tuh him, but Ah don't." Theresa sat in the car with her arms crossed and unwavering in her attitude. "Yuh mother is hurt and confused. Now yuh want me tuh become a part of his scandalous behavior. All Ah want tuh do is go home. Ah'm tired and if it weren't for yuh mother, Ah would've spend this weekend in Jonesboro."

Malcolm drove the car and allowed Theresa to complain. She was quiet for various periods at a time, but her agitation was still with her, picking at her nerves, waiting for her display of emotion. He was angry, but held it in until he was closer to Jonesboro. He needed a reason to argue with her so he could storm from their home and go to Randy.

The road sign read "JONESBORO 5 MILES." Malcolm waited another three minutes and another three miles.

"Yuh know Theresa, yuh could have stayed home. Ah never asked yuh tuh come, and even after yuh came, if yuh were unhappy, yuh could have gone home. Ah even noticed the way my mother treated yuh. Her subtle rudeness and unnecessary sharp attitude was uncalled for. Ah do have tuh thank yuh for understanding what she's going through. Ah would've understood if yuh went home for that reason alone. Ah could have rented a car. Yuh're an independent woman. Yuh made a decision tuh come tuh Rehoboth and tuh stay with me, so stop complaining. Ah've heard enough." His voice was coarse and stern as he shifted his eyes from the highway to give her a momentary glare before attending to the road again.

Theresa turned with a jerk and stared at Malcolm. She seemed to be surprised that he had taken so long to respond to all the things she had said about his father. She was more surprise he had recognized his mother's behavior and all she could do was stare at him.

"Ah didn't know what tuh tell Dad when he asked for yuh. Ah had told him yuh would be visiting him. Then Ah told him yuh wanted to stay for the wedding. Yuh made me lie tuh him."

"Hump . . . does it matter? Yuh father lied tuh yuh for years, like father, like son," Theresa said in a sarcastic tone.

My family is in crisis and Ah don't need yuh attitude."

"Just who the hell do yuh think yuh talkin' tuh?" Theresa screamed at Malcolm. The veins in her neck protruded and her eyes fixed on him.

"Who the hell is sitting in this car?" Malcolm gave her a snarling glance. "Either yuh support me when my family is in crisis, or yuh keep yuh damn mouth shut and yuh opinion tuh yuhself. Ah have enough tuh worry about. Ah don't need bitching from yuh. Ah had tuh listen tuh yuh since we left the hospital. Whatever my opinion is with my father is my opinion! Ah don't ask yuh tuh share it or understand it. If yuh don't have anything positive to say, then keep it tuh yuhself." Malcolm drove the car up in his driveway. "Ah'll wait until yuh safely in the house and Ah'm going out."

Theresa slammed the car door and walked in front of it. Malcolm backed the car to the end of the driveway and waited until she entered the house before driving off to the payphone at the corner convenience store. He called Randy's house and prayed he would answer instead of Gail. The phone rang three times before Randy picked up. "Hey, it's me. Ah told yuh Ah'd call yuh as soon as Ah returned tuh Jonesboro. Where do yuh want tuh meet me?"

"Try The National Park Inn," Randy said.

"C'mon Randy, Ah want tuh be yuh friend, not yuh lover. Pick a restaurant where we can talk."

"Man, The National Park has a restaurant. Nothing has tuh happen and we can talk. Ah can't make yuh do anything yuh don't want tuh do," Randy whispered so Gail couldn't hear him.

"What are yuh gonna tell Gail?"

"Ah plan tuh be home by twelve o'clock."

"What about Theresa?

"Ah don't think she cares when Ah come home. Remember Randy, nothing is gonna happen but talk."

"Okay, Ah guess The National Park is a good spot. It's half way between Tucker and Jonesboro. Lets say Ah meet you in forty minutes."

* * *

Randy had already registered at the motel when Malcolm arrived. He had been successful at making Malcolm feel a heightened level of urgency to return to the Atlanta area to soothe his emotional needs. He had caused a rift in Malcolm's emotional tranquility on the very weekend he was trying to discover himself and form a relationship with a brother he never knew was his.

Randy stood and slowly eased the chair away from him when Malcolm entered the restaurant. Malcolm froze at the entrance; he knew he left Johnny in Rehoboth, but in his old life Randy was Johnny. Now, Randy's appearance held him in place and reminded him how their relationship was sparked.

"Over here Malcolm," Randy called out in a low voice and waved his hand.

Malcolm signaled as soon as he noticed him. Smiling, he walked in his direction and pulled a chair up at the table. "Hey man, Ah'm here. Are yuh all right now?"

"Ah feel better. May Ah order yuh something tuh eat or drink?"

"Ah'm not helpless Randy. Ah can place my own order," Malcolm snapped. He raised his arm to call the waitress.

"Are yuh okay? Yuh sound a little touchy. What's the matter?" Randy leaned in so close he could have kissed him

Malcolm moved back when he noticed the waitress approaching. Randy turned, appearing startled and adjusted his position in the chair.

"May Ah take yuh order, sir?"

"Yes . . . may Ah have a deluxe burger and cola?" Malcolm responded while pointing to the item on the menu.

"Yuh don't want a vodka sour or a martini?" Randy pointed to the bar menu.

"Not on an empty stomach. Ah haven't had anything to eat since breakfast." Malcolm closed his menu, smiled and handed it to the waitress.

"Oh, Miss . . . would yuh bring a whisky, straight up and a vodka sour." Randy handed his menu to the waitress, pushed his chair back and crossed his legs. He placed his elbow on the table and used his fingers to massage his lips.

Malcolm sat back in his chair. His fingers drummed the table and he glared at Randy. "Damn you! Ah'm tired, hungry and confused. My father almost died this week, and my best friend thought his needs should come first. Yuh know, Ah just picked a fight with my wife so Ah could have an excuse tuh be with yuh. This week, Ah found out a man Ah grew up with was my brother. Ah had a relationship with yuh which makes me gay, but my heart and body tells me Ah'm not and neither are you. We experimented; there have been no other men in our lives. We both have wonderful wives and we are best friends. Ah don't want to lose yuh friendship, but the gay shit has tuh stop."

Randy folded his arms across his chest and closed his eyes. It was as though, if he couldn't see Malcolm, he couldn't hear him either. After a few moments, he rested his arms on the table, tilted his head, looked humbly up at him and spoke. "Ah'm sorry. Ah felt so panicky. Ah just couldn't envision my life without yuh." He took a deep breath and exhaled quickly. Perspiration began to bead his forehead. He removed his jacket and hung it over the back of his chair.

Malcolm reached across the table to the empty place setting and retrieved the cloth napkin and handed it to him. "Man, drink some water. Don't you freak out on me! Yuh know Ah love yuh and will always be with yuh," He reached over and whispered in his ear. "But there will be no intimacy of any kind and Ah mean that, so don't try yuh panic act." Malcolm patted him on the shoulder and sat back in his chair.

Randy took a large gulp of water, wiped his face and neck and announced he was going to be all right. He continued to take several deep breaths, and he gave Malcolm a nod and a smile. "Man, where's that waitress with the drinks?"

"Ah say yuh could use one about now," Malcolm whispered.

* * *

Malcolm finished off his deluxe meal and the edge on his spirit had softened. He was still a little sharp with Randy but he believed he owned some of the blame. He knew he had failed him; he didn't take the time to consider that someone else had feelings and now there were consequences to be dealt with.

Randy had crossed his legs and was quietly working on his whisky. He picked up the glass containing the vodka sour and offered it to Malcolm. "Ah'm okay Malcolm. C'mon, relax. Have a drink on me for old time sake."

"Okay man, thanks." Malcolm used the plastic straw to stir the drink before sitting back and taking a sip.

Randy sat back in the chair and uncrossed his legs. "Ah have the room. If all yuh want tuh do is talk, then that's what we'll do. If yuh want more, then the truth will be told."

Randy summoned the waitress to order another round of drinks and the check.

Malcolm sipped his drink, feeling confident there was nothing Randy could do to further erode his manhood. "All right Randy, Ah'll go with yuh tuh the room. We'll just talk. I need tuh explain a few things tuh yuh. Ah'll always love yuh man. Yuh my best friend. Yuh were there for me when Ah didn't have anywhere else tuh turn. That's why Ah don't want tuh lose yuh."

The waitress returned with the extra drinks and the check. Randy overpaid the check allowing for the tip. Each man left the restaurant carrying two glasses and walked toward the elevator. They arrived at room 656.

Malcolm walked to the large window and pulled back the drapes. He could feel Randy standing close behind him, but not so close that he was touching him. "Man, back it up a little! Remember, Ah want tuh talk. Yuh crowding me. Let's sit at the table." Malcolm brushed passed Randy and sat in the cushioned chair near the wall and waved his hand for Randy to sit in the remaining seat.

"Ah need tuh ask yuh something." Malcolm sat back in his chair.

Randy nodded his head.

"Have you ever had sex with another man?" Malcolm was now sitting forward and staring into Randy's eyes for that tell-tale lie.

"No Malcolm, Yuh the only man Ah've ever been with," Randy said and he had no trouble allowing Malcolm to read his eyes.

"Randy . . . we are bisexual. We are gay. We are HOMOSEXUAL. Damn-it man! Why can't yuh see that? Ah tried to soften my words earlier, but yuh just didn't get it, so now Ah'm tellin' yuh like it is." Malcolm rose from his seat, leaned over the table and yelled in Randy's face. "Do yuh understand that is what you are. When yuh do what we've done, then that makes us gay! Is that what yuh want tuh be?"

"Ah'm not gay, Ah'm not a homosexual. Ah just love yuh." Randy stood and returned to the window. He removed his jacket, turned and threw it on the bed. He headed to the bathroom and splashed cool water on his face. He returned to the room and took a gulp of the remaining whisky from the first glass. He sat on the bed and adjusted the towel he had placed around his neck. "Ah love yuh Malcolm, but Ah'm not a homosexual

"Man . . . are yuh blind? Ah'm a man! Man tuh man sex equals homosexuality!" Malcolm yelled out. "Ah'm not going tuh blame it all on yuh. It was both of us, and it was wrong." Malcolm pulled up a chair so he was sitting across from Randy, and reached for his hands. "Randy listen tuh me. Ah don't believe being gay is wrong, if that is who yuh are. If God put me on this earth tuh be a homosexual, then it wouldn't be wrong tuh be true tuh myself. But, Ah love women, not men. Having sex with yuh was wrong and against my nature." Malcolm stood and walked to the table to get his drink. He turned the glass up, placed his hands on his hips and stood staring out the window. "The first time Ah met yuh, Ah was intrigued. There was a boy named, Johnny that Ah grew up with back home. My father adored him and Ah loved him even more. But, Ah was a young boy, and later a young man. Ah wasn't supposed tuh have any feelings for another boy, so Ah took every opportunity tuh fight against my true feelings." He turned around, sat on the window ledge, took a deep breath, exhaled and continued speaking. "We were the only two boys on Rehoboth Road and Ah wanted tuh be his best friend, but Ah was afraid of my feelings. Ah thought Ah was gay. Ah was physically stronger than him, but he was smarter than me. All my life . . . Ah tried tuh fight him, but he always beat me with his wit. One day . . . when we were teenagers." Malcolm licked his lips and looked up at the ceiling. "Ah almost killed him, because of a stupid prank. The older we got the more Ah loved him." Malcolm reached for his second drink and sat on the bed next to Randy. "Ah've loved him since Ah was in the second grade. He's a millionaire now . . . been one for several years, but he never forgot his home. He built a health clinic and supports two churches in the community." Malcolm took a swallow of his vodka sour "He's the person that helped me get my job at the firm. The first time Ah walked into the office and saw you; Ah thought Ah was looking at Johnny. Yuh the same height, the same complexion, the same smile; hell man, the two of yuh even sound alike. For me, you were Johnny. Having yuh as my friend, was like having Johnny in my life." Malcolm returned to the chair and looked across at Randy again. "Ah just gave in tuh yuh when we started having sex. All those years of wanting Johnny's acceptance, Ah thought Ah was gay. Ah didn't know he was my brother. Ah didn't know my love for him was the curse my father had placed on me. Johnny and Ah were born a week apart. Ah'm so sorry Ah let yuh down so hard. Can we please just be friends?"

"Ah'm not gay!" Randy continued to cry out. He held almost a full glass of whisky in his hand. "It's only been you Malcolm."

"C'mere man, did yuh hear anything Ah said? Listen, yuh call it what yuh want." Malcolm removed the glass and placed it on the table before pulling Randy to his feet and hugging him. "Now we understand what our bodies were telling us. We had a long time gay relationship. Ah did things a gay man would do, so Ah believe that makes me gay, but Ah'm not gonna live a double life. Ah prefer tuh be heterosexual and Ah'm gonna pray for the Lord's help. It's okay tuh hug and comfort each other when we feel pain. We have wives tuh satisfy our sexual feelings. Ah love sex with my wife more than sex with you."

Randy pulled from Malcolm's embrace and sat back on the bed. "Thanks Malcolm. Ah understand where yuh coming from. Ah thought Ah could get yuh in this room and yuh'd give in." He reached for his drink again.

Malcolm glanced at Randy and smiled. "Man, Ah'm gonna pray for yuh. Ah know yuh can turn around."

* * *

After the wedding service, Elizabeth was the first to leave the church grounds so she would be at the house to greet the guests. Cars lined up for the procession to the Turner's home. Usually the congregation knew when dinner would be served at church, so this was a real treat, and especially so because they didn't know Sarah or her husband.

Reverend Turner and Loretha were among the last to leave the church grounds and they passed Thea standing near her car. She held her lacy handkerchief and occasionally blotted her eyes. She didn't appear to be making any attempt to get into her car; instead her head followed every car as it drove pasted her.

"John, stop the car." Loretha pointed toward Thea. "Why is she standing there like that? Please let me out. Ah need tuh go tuh her."

Reverend Turner pulled his car up next to Thea, and Loretha got out.

"What's the matter, Thea?"

"Ah don't belong here anymore. Ah don't know where tuh go." Tears flooded her eyes and poured down her face.

"John Ah'll come along with Thea. Could yuh go on and help greet the guests?" Loretha stood with her arm around Thea.

"Sure Loretha, but hurry."

Loretha turned to Thea and removed her hanky from her hand. It was so wet there was no way it could absorb another drop of moisture. She removed a fresh handkerchief from her pocketbook and handed it to her.

"Honey, for years Ah watched 'Lizabeth try tuh make sense of this mixed up world. She was a child during half of those years, and made the best decision she could. Yuh made a decision about what yuh'll do. Ah think that's a fair choice tuh give yuh husband. Rehoboth is yuh home. The Lord will protect yuh and keep yuh happy. Yuh know prayer changes things." Loretha spoke softly and continued to watch Thea wipe the tears from her face and when it was dry all her makeup had been cleaned away. "Okay, get in the car and scoot over. Ah'll drive yuh home so yuh can freshen up," Loretha ordered.

Thea looked over at Loretha and continued to wipe her eyes. She had never shared with her the new direction the Lord had given her to stay in Rehoboth.

* * *

The thick branches of the willow tree brushed against the side of the car when Loretha pulled up close to the front porch of Thea's home.

"My Lord, that tree has really grown. Ah didn't know it was this close tuh yuh house."

"It's not. It's just that the wind is picking up and blowing the branches toward the house. Kinda seems like they're greeting me." Thea reached up to touch the branches as she made her way to the porch. She smiles at Loretha. "Yuh must think Ah'm losing it, talking tuh a tree."

Loretha smiled, raised her eyebrow and glanced at her from a slightly tilted head. "It's a beautiful tree, but yuh joking . . . right?"

"Ah know the tree's not greetin' me. Ah was just jokin', but . . . maybe Ah am losin' it." Thea walked around the car and stood near Loretha to get a better look at the tree. "Since all this craziness began, Ah've been sitting on the porch watching the branches of this tree sway and dance on the wind. It's so relaxing and it helps me think clearly. Sometimes, Ah sit under the tree and block out the world around me while Ah pray and meditate. Ah call it my 'dancing willow tree'."

"There's nothing wrong with yuh, Thea. Ah see the beauty in yuh tree. May Ah come and sit with yuh sometimes?"

"Yuh know yuh always welcome." Thea reached over and gave her a warm hug. "Now, Ah've taken up too much of yuh time and yuh have a reception tuh attend. Let me drive yuh home and Ah'll come along as soon as Ah freshen up. Ah don't know what Ah would've done if yuh didn't come tuh me. Ah was frozen in my own self pity."

"Are yuh all right now?" Loretha asked.

"Thanks tuh you, Ah'm fine. C'mon, let me drive yuh home."

* * *

Only thirty minutes had passed when Loretha arrived at the reception and she quickly stepped into the position as mother of the bride. Johnny's housekeeper, Gerta and her sister, Lucile took care of everything that had to do with the food, even down to the china, glasses, centerpieces, tablecloths and flatware. Gerta and Lucile's husbands delivered seventy-five folding chairs and ten banquet tables. They arranged them under a large revival tent that they set up in the back yard. The beautiful wedding cake ordered by Loretha set on a decorated round table and was placed in front of the bride and groom's table. Soft music played on the stereo tape deck and large speakers had been moved under the tent. The guest mingled, socialized, and congratulated Sarah and Stephen.

Chapter 13

Elizabeth arrived home after the reception and immediately went to check on Nat. It was nice that Sarah and Stephen wanted to visit him before they returned to Atlanta.

"Ah'm sorry man. Ah didn't mean tuh let yuh down." Nat was reclined in his chair. A walker had been placed nearby to help him get around when he had to.

"Honey, Sarah really knows how tuh handle Daddy, and Greta and her family know how to lay out a spread. They even set up a tent and had lacy table cloths. It's amazing what they did in just one day. Ah have a plate of food for yuh and some of Mr. and Mrs. Parker's wedding cake." Elizabeth smiled at everyone and kissed Nat on the forehead. She set the plates on the end table while she continued visiting.

Stephen reached and shook Nat's hand and Sarah gave Nat a hug. "It's late and we really need to get on our way. Don't be strangers. That highway goes both ways," Stephen said. "Nat, see about that back."

Nat smiled and nodded. "Yeah man. Ah plan tuh go tuh the clinic tuhmorrow."

Elizabeth escorted them tuh the front door, they exchanged hugs again and she watched as they walked to their car. When they drove from the driveway, Elizabeth returned to Nat's side.

"Oh Nat, Ah'm so sorry yuh missed it. Johnny filled in for yuh."

Nat closed his eyes and raised his head against the cushion of the chair. His hands clutched the arms of the chair as if he were in pain.

Elizabeth's face was etched with concern. "Honey, are yuh in that much pain?" She leaned closer to him

"Beth, Ah need tuh tell yuh something Ah did. Ah can only tell you, and yuh have tuh promise not tuh tell anyone. It's serious and Ah could go tuh jail, but Ah believe Ah'll begin tuh feel better as soon as Ah tell yuh."

Elizabeth's face was still with fear, but her eyes held all the questions she wanted to ask her husband; they shifted from side to side and stared without a blink to replenish the moisture. Her hands gripped Nat's arm a little firmer, enough to register her concern.

"Honey," Nat began. "Last week when yuh told me Owen Oliver is Johnny's father. Ah was so tore up by the pain he caused yuh Ah felt compelled tuh do something." He took hold of Elizabeth hand. "Remember, Ah gave yuh some medication tuh relax yuh and help yuh sleep. Ah told yuh Ah was gonna take a pill too? Well . . . Ah pretended tuh take my pill. Ah waited until yuh were sleep and called Reverend Oliver. Ah picked him up at his house and drove him tuh old man Jenkins's pasture. Ah told him Ah knew he raped yuh, and Ah punched him in his jaw. He fell tuh the ground and looked up at me. Ah wanted him tuh defend himself, but he wouldn't. Ah picked him up from the gravel road and Ah asked him why he stayed in Rehoboth after what he did tuh yuh?" Nat continued to rub Elizabeth's hand, but the memory of that night caused him to squint his eyes as he tried to hold back his anger. "He didn't answer, but Ah knew it was because he believed he could get away with it. Ah threw him against the car and reminded him this wasn't his home town. Ah asked him why he didn't take his family and leave. He said he stayed because of Johnny." Nat looked at Elizabeth and her eyes were pink and glazed. "Ah'm so sorry Beth, but Ah had tuh tell yuh this."

Elizabeth squeezed out a smile. "Ah need yuh tuh tell me this. Yuh can't carry this burden alone."

"Well, Ah told Owen he didn't know about Johnny until the day he was born and he should've been gone by then. Ah couldn't help it. Ah smashed him in his left jaw again, and threw him back tuh the gravel road. Ah had tuh call on the Lord tuh stop me before Ah killed him. Ah leaned over Owen and told him he better not tell a living soul what happened tuh him. Ah told him . . . Ah wanted him out of town in one week. Ah told him Ah wanted him resigned from the church and the school, or his worst nightmare would come true."

Elizabeth removed herself from the chair and stood behind the recliner so she could kiss his face. "Oh Nat, Yuh did that for me? Ah needed yuh thirty-six years ago. Ah had no one tuh fight for me. It's a little late, but it makes me feel good just knowing you were there for me. Ah know it wasn't right, but Ah love you for avenging my honor." She leaned over and kissed him all over his face.

"Okay Beth . . . okay Beth, yuh eating me alive." He chuckle softly. It was too painful to give her the hearty laugh he held inside.

Elizabeth could almost feel his pain when his body twitched as he simply chuckled. "Oh, but what a heavy burden tuh carry now. No wonder yuh spine is all twisted in a knot. Yuh had all that worry and stress. Yuh back went out when Owen was near critical and his doctor was saying he'd been beaten. Ah can't imagine what yuh must've been feelin'. Anyway he must be better. Malcolm went home this afternoon and Mrs. Thea was at the wedding and reception. She kissed him again and knelt near his chair and looked up at him. "The Lord ain't never gonna let nothing happen tuh yuh. So don't yuh worry; if Owen was gonna talk, the police woulda been here by now."

"Well that makes me feel a lot better. Ah should've just let God's will be done. Now Owen has an excuse for not losing his pension, or being run out of Rehoboth. Ah hope yuh father won't go back on his word and keep him at the church. If he does Ah'll have tuh find some way tuh get Owen out of Rehoboth," Nat continued. "Now, Ah might still be charged if Owen does talk. Oh . . . Ah just made it worse for us."

"Ah'm not gonna let yuh worry yuhself sick about what might happen. Look what it's done tuh yuh already. We're gonna pray on it and wait and see," Elizabeth reminded him. "And no matter what, yuh can never let Johnny believe it was you who fractured his jaw. Ah don't know how he would take it. Suppose Owen speaks out against yuh? Oh Lord . . . Ah want that man out of our lives."

"Ah'll just deny it. Ah'll say Ah was home in bed with my wife. It'll be his word against mine. Besides, he's the one with an ax tuh grind against this family." Nat looked at Elizabeth with that 'don't yuh think the law will believe me' smirk on his face. He nodded his head, convincing himself, then bit his lip as he glanced at Elizabeth hoping he sounded convincing to her.

"Yuh right," Elizabeth said and she smiled just to make him happy. "All right honey, Ah'm gonna warm up yuh dinner and after yuh eat, yuh'll feel even better." Before picking up the dinner plates she sat on the arm of Nat's recliner. "Ah love yuh so much." She kissed his cheek again. "Now yuh have tuh get yuh back functioning again." She picked up his plate and was walking toward the kitchen when the doorbell rang and Johnny and Julia stepped in her house.

"Hey Mama, it's just us," Johnny called out from the foyer.

She hurried to the kitchen and set the plates down on the table and rushed back to the door. "How are y'all doing? Ah was just goin' tuh warm up Dad's food.

Hello Mother," Julia said and she gave Elizabeth a small wave.

"Hey baby. Y'all go on in the den. Ah'll be right back in a minute."

Elizabeth returned to the kitchen while Julia clung to Johnny's arm and followed him into the den.

"Hey Dad," Johnny walked across the room and then extended his hand to greet him.

"Hi Johnny . . . and hello Miss Julia, you are as lovely as ever." Nat met Johnny's hand for a shake, while Julia greeted him and continued to hang onto Johnny's arm.

Elizabeth returned to the den and sat on the sofa. "C'mon Julia, sit here next tuh me." She patted the cushion. Johnny sat in the desk chair nearest to Nat.

"Man, thanks for standing with Stephen on such a short notice."

"Oh let me get yuh dinner." Elizabeth stood and laced her fingers together.

"No, not yet, 'Beth. Ah'm not really hungry. Ah'd rather talk tuh Johnny. He's been here all weekend and Ah haven't had much time with him. Johnny, could yuh help me out of this chair? Ah think Ah would like tuh sit on the front porch. Maybe Ah'll feel better if Ah could stretch my legs."

"Sure Dad."

Nat slowly released the lever on the chair placing it in an up right position. His face churned with pain and he panted like a mother birthing a child. Elizabeth set his walker in front of him.

"Johnny . . . yuh stand . . . behind me . . . and don't let me fall," Nat spoke through his pain. "Ah do . . . feel a little . . . better." He placed both hands on the walker and lifted himself up and out of the chair.

"Honey, yuh don't sound better," Elizabeth said.

Julia positioned herself behind Nat's chair, out of his sight, where she wouldn't be in his way and where he couldn't see how sorry she felt for him. Elizabeth walked in front and held the door open, and Johnny was close behind, ready to catch him if he lost his balance.

It was a warm summer evening and the sounds of the night creatures were in harmony. The front porch was completely screened in so nature and man wouldn't violate each others space. Nat had to take one step down to be on the level of the porch and Johnny placed his arm snuggly under his armpits for extra support. Once on the porch Nat selected a straight high back chair with armrests.

"That wasn't as bad . . . as Ah thought . . . it would be." Nat took a deep breath. "Yuh know Beth . . . Ah feel better already. My muscles are very sore, and Ah still got them spasms, but they're not as bad." Nat turned to Johnny, but his range of motion was still limited. "Thanks Johnny, Ah really needed . . . a little movement. When yuh ready tuh leave . . . Ah'll be ready tuh go back in the house. Ah don't want tuh hold yuh up."

Johnny and Julia sat on the porch swing and Elizabeth sat in a metal rocking chair near Nat. Elizabeth held her head back, smiled and rocked herself in her rocker while Nat asked Julia how she liked the tiny community of Rehoboth. Johnny smiled while Julia was explaining that Rocky Mount, North Carolina was only a little larger. "Well, it a lot larger, but my people live in a small community like Rehoboth, five miles outside of town," she explained.

Elizabeth glanced at Nat and smiled. "Johnny, last week you asked for permission tuh have a relationship with Reverend Oliver. We said it was all right as long as yuh kept yuh relationship with him separate from us." She had stopped rocking and was sitting at the edge of her chair. Her eyes were locked on Johnny and her head was tilted to the side. "Now yuh have tuh tell me something, 'cause Ah'm a nosy woman."

Julia held Johnny's hand, glanced over at him and smiled. "He's been a busy man," she said.

"So Ah hear. Ah heard you and Malcolm just had tuh have a fight in the woods behind MaDear's cottage. Thank the Lord this thirty year feud is finally over." Elizabeth laughed and threw her hands up in the air. "It's over, isn't it?"

"I hope so Mama and it feels good to be over," Johnny smiled as he spoke. He lowered his head like a little boy.

"Yes Lord . . . thank yuh, Jesus! The executive vice president of one of the largest banks in the nation was rumbling in the woods like a school boy. Now, that's something," Nat added.

"Yeah Dad, it was really something. You would've died laughing," he spoke through a broad smile and a few chuckles.

"Ah was kinda scared this morning when Julia told me you and Malcolm went tuh the hospital. That's something, y'all fightin' like that . . . at first Ah didn't know if y'all needed medical attention. Then she told me y'all made up. Ah knew Nat was sick and Stephen needed yuh tuh stand with him. Ah didn't know if yuh would be back in time," Elizabeth sat back in her chair and began rocking again. "Yuh know . . . Ah've been hearing all kinds of frightening things about Reverend Oliver." She glanced over at Nat, but she was very careful not to ask what happen to him. Nat remained quiet with a bland expression when he wasn't twitching with momentary spikes of pain.

"Oh . . . yeah . . . Mama, last Sunday, when grandfather was with Reverend Oliver, his pressure was so high, the doctors thought they were going to lose him. It took three days to get it under control. Then, there were the two fractures to his jaw. The doctor had concluded the only way he could have received those types of fractures would be from an assault. Anyway, it wasn't until this morning that the detectives could question Reverend Oliver. He told them he felt dizzy and fell on the porch, one time hitting his face on the banister and then he said he fell a second time hitting his face on the top step. The detectives marked the case as 'closed'.

Nat gently pushed his head against the high back chair and took a slow, quiet and relaxing deep breath.

"Ah feel so bad about Miss Thea," Elizabeth said as she rubbed her hand up and down Nat's arm. "Mama said she's in so much emotional pain. She was more than willing tuh play the piano for the wedding tuhday, but Mama told me she was standing in the church parking lot after the service crying and in a panic. Mama had tuh go tuh her and convince her she was welcome in her home."

"That's too bad," Nat said. "When did Reverend Oliver say the doctors would discharge him from the hospital?"

"Sometime next week," was all Johnny had to say. He didn't dwell on Reverend Oliver, nor did he realize that his parents wanted to hear everything else he could tell them about his condition.

Johnny and Julia sat with his parents for another fifteen minutes or longer and changed the subject to Sarah's wedding. Elizabeth laughed and shared Sarah's position about her demands with her vows and how that clashed with her their father's position. Nat and Julia laughed mildly, but it was particularly funny to Johnny. They all shared praises with Nat about the quality of Greta's family's catering services, and then Julia spoke with amazement at how it was possible to have such a charming wedding in just one day.

"Well Mama . . . Dad, I believe it's time we get on down the road," Johnny announced. He stood up and looked at Julia. "Are you ready to leave?"

Julia nodded and smiled at Nat and Elizabeth.

"Dad, why don't I drive Julia to the cottage? You just have Mama call me when you're ready to go in the house and I'll return to help you."

"Thank yuh Johnny. It's a beautiful evening. Ah would like tuh stay out here a little while."

"All right, I'll see you later." Julia gave Nat and Elizabeth a gentle kiss on their cheeks before she and Johnny left.

* * *

Elizabeth and Nat were quiet as they watched Johnny and Julia leave the driveway. In the next moment their eyes locked and were noisy with conversation. They didn't have to speak; they were relieved and settled down into their comfort zone.

The spasms in Nat's neck and back began to relax and he was beginning to experience more range in his movement. Nat rolled his head back and around and he could hear and feel his vertebrate snap back into alignment. His muscles were still sore, but he smiled at Elizabeth even as he let out a painful moan. When he arched his back, intense stabbing spikes of pain traveled down his spinal column while its stacked bones found their correct position. He moaned louder and his facial muscles became distorted; he knew his back muscles had just relaxed enough to allow his vertebrate to un-pinch the nerves that were causing him so much pain.

Elizabeth had closed her eyes and was in the mist of thanking the Lord for Johnny's news. Nat moaned louder. She screamed his name and leaped to her feet to rush to his side. "What is it? Do you want me to call Johnny?"

Nat had just caught his breath and his voice was weak. He smiled and shook his head. "No . . . Ah'm better. My . . . back . . . just sn . . . snapped back . . . in place." He took a deep breath and smiled, not just with his lips, but also with his eyes. He lifted his head and stretched out his spine again.

Elizabeth stood over him staring, waiting for him to scream out in pain, but he only frowned. "It's better; my back is better Beth. Ah feel a little weak and Ah don't know how strong my legs are. So far, the shooting pains are gone. Ah think we should give Johnny a call. The sooner Ah get tuh bed, the better. Ah'm gonna be very sore tomorrow, but with some pain pills, Ah believe Ah'll be able tuh walk."

Nat watched Elizabeth enter the house. He closed his eyes and stretched out his neck again before resting his head on the back of the chair. *Oh thank yuh Lord.* The sounds of the creatures that inhabited the late August night serenaded him and the atmosphere held a hint of the sweet warm humidity. He turned, looking at the door for Elizabeth and wished her back to his side, but wishing was not enough; Elizabeth would only return within the normal course of time.

"Okay honey, Johnny will be here in a few minutes. Isn't that something about Owen?" Elizabeth said as she pulled her chair closer to Nat.

Elizabeth held Nat's trembling hand He wanted to talk about Owen, but the words wouldn't come together in his mind in a meaningful way. They were all there, but confused and garbled. His only coherent thought to be transformed into a phased was his love for his Beth.

"Ah love yuh too, Nat"

They were quiet and Elizabeth rested her head on his upper arm and watched the fireflies flicker in the front yard.

* * *

Johnny's headlights slapped across the porch before he parked the car. Elizabeth stood and placed her hands on Nat's shoulders and watched as he got out of his car and walk toward the porch. He pulled at the screen door and stood only a few feet away from Nat.

"So you're ready to go into the house. Maybe you'd like me to help you to your bedroom so Mama won't have to do it later," Johnny suggested.

Elizabeth reached for Nat's walker and placed it close to him. "It's late. Having Johnny help yuh intuh the bedroom is a good idea. What would yuh like tuh do?"

"The bedroom," Nat said as he began to pull himself forward to the edge of the chair.

Elizabeth stood on his right side with Johnny on his left, and Nat pulled himself up. He managed to take several steps and grunted and groaned with each one. Johnny pulled at the storm door and adjusted the brace to hold it open.

"Johnny, stand behind me. Ah think it's gonna be harder for me . . . tuh step up intuh the house than it was for me . . . tuh step down. Yuh may have tuh give me a boost."

Nat held tight to his walker, lifting it up into the house. Elizabeth held the walker steady; she placed her foot on it to brace it against Nat's weight, and Johnny was ready to catch him if he fell. Nat lifted his right leg up on the step and tried to push up to bring his left leg up, but he didn't seem to have enough strength in his right leg muscle.

"Don't worry. Ah'll get it. Let me try my left leg." He bit at his bottom lip as a sign of his determination. He placed his left leg on the step and just as he was rocking his body in an attempt to lift his right leg up, Johnny boosted his bottom up and he had both legs on the step.

Nat did a quick turn-around and looked at Johnny. Johnny held his hands up, his palms facing Nat. "I'm sorry man. I had to do it, but if it makes you feel better, I want you to know I never touched a man's butt before. Anyway you said you'd need a boost."

Everyone laughed. Elizabeth hurried for a chair for Nat. She was laughing so hard, tears came to her eyes and her legs felt weak so she propped herself against the wall for support.

"Yuh know Johnny, yuh always made me feel good. From the first day Ah saw you at yuh middle school graduation. Looking at yuh mama made me feel good too." Nat reached over and took Elizabeth's hand. "But you Johnny; yuh were always special. Yuh've been a joy tuh my life. Ah sat here all day and felt sorry for myself because Ah couldn't be with everyone else and in only moments yuh've made my day. Now will yuh help me get tuh my room, and keep yuh hands off my butt?"

"I love you Dad. It really has been a pleasant evening. I know you're not going to work tomorrow. You need to go to the clinic."

Elizabeth walked to Nat's side, and Johnny continued to walk behind him. The noose and rod that gripped his body and tightened like a tourniquet with the earlier news of Reverend Oliver had unraveled.

Before Nat reached his bedroom he smiled at Johnny and nodded his head, but evaded his questions about work and going to the clinic. He knew Johnny had already treated what ailed him and he had the medication to remedy the after effects. "Thanks for everything, Johnny. Ah'll see yuh tuhmorrow."

Elizabeth walked Johnny to the front door and hugs were exchanged. "Johnny Ah haven't seen Nat laugh in several days. Ah believe a good laugh is a cure-all. Ah want yuh tuh have a good night and Ah'll see yuh tuhmorrow."

Elizabeth watched Johnny pull away from the driveway before turning off the porch light. She remembered Nat's food was still in the oven and returned to the bedroom to ask him if he wanted it. With a final refusal, his dinner plate was placed in the refrigerator. Instead, Nat asked for a slice of wedding cake and ice cream and Elizabeth decided to join him and have the same.

* * *

Elizabeth laid on Nat's chest and he held his arm around her back. She could hear his heart beating steady and rhythmically while he could smell the sweet fragrant from her hair. They were still, but each knew the other was awake and thinking. Each waited for the other to speak first, to hear their position on the subject. Nat believed he had said enough and waited to hear what Elizabeth had to say. Elizabeth believed that after Johnny's information, Nat might have a different position to take. Either way, time passed and they held each other in a quiet comfortable position until Elizabeth broke her silence. "Nat . . . Ah can't thank yuh enough for what yuh did for me."

"Ah acted with my gut instead of my brain. Ah thank the Lord for stopping me, and Ah thank him for saving Owen's life."

"Still . . . it was sweet, and the Lord has saved all of us. Now, we need tuh let Owen's family punish him and we need tuh live our lives. Whenever that man comes near me, he brings pain. Ah'm gonna pray and ask God tuh protect us from him. Ah believe he's evil. The only person that seems tuh have a shield of protection from him is Johnny."

"Ah wouldn't say he's evil. What happened tuh him was my doing. Ah was the evil one. He didn't try tuh defend himself. It was like he wanted me tuh hurt him bad enough so he wouldn't have tuh face the families last Sunday afternoon. Ah almost gave him a way out. The Lord held my hands and threw me in the truck."

Elizabeth rubbed his chest, "Well he's gonna be all right, so we won't speak of him. Yuh need tuh get better."

Chapter 14

Loretha and Thea sat under the willow tree near the trunk, where the branches were thinnest. They had moved a small lawn table and two additional metal rockers out there, and spent many early evenings relaxing, sipping lemonade or ice tea, praying and being mesmerized by the long graceful, dancing branches.

Johnny and Julia had returned to Washington, D.C. and Malcolm had only been down one Friday afternoon in almost ten days. Thea visited Reverend Oliver in the morning and by the early evening she needed to relax under her dancing willow tree to sooth her emotional need.

* * *

During Thea's Thursday morning visit to the hospital, Dr. Parks informed her Reverend Oliver would be discharged the next morning. Owen sat in his bedside chair smiling. "Thea, honey, Ah can come home tuhmorrow," he spoke through his wired jaw. His words were much clearer because his mouth was no longer sore from the wires. He was happy, even jovial. "Won't that be nice?"

Thea sat in a chair across from him and hugged her pocketbook. "Yuh know Owen, we still have a problem. We just put it on hold because of yuh illness." Her appearance transformed from mild mannered to unyielding. "Yuh hold the answer tuh what will happen tuh this family."

"Ah understand Thea." His smile disappeared and his eyes turned sad.

"Ah need tuh call Malcolm and let him know you'll be discharged tomorrow. Ah believe he needs tuh be home. We have tuh have a family meeting."

Owen glanced up at Thea as she rushed from the room. He didn't call to her; he just took a deep breath and exhaled slowly. He rested his arms on the chair and shook his head. *Whatever has tuh be, will be. Ah need this tuh be over. If Thea and Malcolm want tuh have a meeting with me, then we'll meet. Ah know Ah don't want tuh lose Thea,* he thought. He looked up and Thea was standing at the foot of his bed.

"Malcolm said he'll be here after work tuhmorrow. Ah'm going tuh leave now."

Owen stood from the chair and walked closer to the bed. "It seems like yuh just got here."

"Yes, it seems that way doesn't it." That was all Thea could say as she leaned over and kissed Owen on his cheek.

Owen took hold of her arm and peered into her eyes. "Ah love yuh, Thea. Please believe me.

"Ah know yuh love me; Ah never questioned that. Ah love yuh, too." Her voice was quiet and cold and she appeared to be fighting her own battle to remain composed. "Ah have tuh go." And she hurried from the room.

* * *

After meeting with Dr. Parks and receiving the discharge orders, Thea and Reverend Oliver left the hospital and arrived in Rehoboth just before noon. Thea set out to prepare his low sodium, lunch of baked chicken breast seasoned with substitute salt, garlic and onion and chicken drippings, string beans in its liquid, and rice, all of which was liquefied separately in the blender. She was sure to prepare enough for several meals and freeze the extras for later.

Reverend Oliver sat with her in the kitchen while she prepared his meal. He wanted to speak, but he couldn't find the words and Thea didn't make any attempt at initiating a conversation. He watched her as long as he could, but his emotions became too heavy. He pushed himself from the table and walked from the kitchen and into the den. The telephone rang, but Thea answered it before he could reach it.

He returned to the kitchen and stood in the doorway. "Oh yes, Miss Loretha, Owen came home tuhday. Ah feel so much better knowing he's well enough tuh be home. Malcolm will be home later this evening. He's coming directly from work." Thea walked into the dining room and looked out at her willow tree. She was listening to Loretha telling her how much everyone cared for her and would support any decision she made. She didn't see Owen watching her. "I'm gonna miss yuh sitting under the tree with me." When Thea turned around, Owen was still standing at the kitchen door. "Miss Loretha, may Ah call yuh later? Ah was just preparin' Owen's meals." She listened for a brief moment nodding her head and smiling. "All right," she responded. "Thank yuh for callin'. Bye now." She hung up the phone.

"Owen, Ah didn't know yuh were standing there. Yuh must be hungry. Ah guess Ah'll have tuh place yuh food in coffee cups."

"That'll be fine."

Thea turned and watched her husband hover over his lunch, sipping it through one of the special straws he brought home from the hospital.

"Owen, Ah need tuh be alone. Ah'm going to sit under the tree, please don't come out. Ah'll be praying."

As soon as Thea left the house, Owen walked to the window and watched her hurrying to the tree. She held her arms out in front of her and parted the branches. He never realized how long the branches were and when she walked between them, he felt like he was ducking down to get a better view. He watched as Thea bowed her head, and then moved it back as though she were looking at the heavens. He walked away from the window believing she was praying and continued with his meal.

* * *

Thea lowered herself to her knees and held her arms up; she cried out, "Dear Lord, give me strength. Ah love my husband, but Ah can't stand tuh see him in his own home. Lord, help me find peace with him. Help him tuh do what's right so he can find peace . . . Ah pray tuh yuh . . . hear my prayer Oh Lord . . ." Thea continue to hold her head high and tears crawled down the sides of her face as she prayed and pleaded for direction. After a while she returned to her rocking chair and used her apron to wipe her face. Soon she wasn't crying any more, or rocking her chair, she was just being soothed by the rhythmic movements of the dancing branches of her tree. She dropped to her knees again and lifted her hand high. "Thank yuh, Lord," she whispered as if the Lord himself had spoken to her. "Yes Lord . . . Ah'll tell him yuh words, Lord. Owen has tuh confess tuh the church. He has tuh leave Rehoboth until he is ready tuh confess. Yes Lord . . . if he confesses, Ah'll forgive him and never speak of his transgression again." Thea lowered head but continued to hold her praying hands high. "Thank yuh lord for hearing my prayers. Ah know Owen will hear yuh word too. Thank yuh, Lord, Thank yuh . . ."

* * *

Reverend Oliver stood from his chair and walked to the same window where he stood before. He watched Thea on her knees under the willow tree. She rocked back and forth on as she continued to pray. He wanted to join her, but her orders played in his head, *Ah need tuh be alone, please don't come out,* she had said. Her words brought shivers to him and his head and shoulders quivered. He needed to talk to her, but there was nothing he could do or say to soothe her. He checked his watch. It was time to take his medication and then he would take a nap. His medication always made him sleepy and he hoped Malcolm would be home when he woke up.

* * *

It was 3:00 p.m. when Thea returned to the house; she had been under the tree for three hours. Her hand shook when she reached for the latch on the screen door. It startled her and she pulled it back quickly as if she had touched something hot. She rubbed her hands together and held them over her face as she backed into the side of the house. *Such foolishness,* she thought. *There ain't nothing wrong with my hand . . . it's Owen Ah'm afraid of. It's the way he looks at me with those sad and pleading eyes.* She opened the screen door and entered the house. When she didn't see Owen sitting in the kitchen she began to search the house and soon located him in their bedroom sound asleep. After closing the bedroom door, she hurried to the telephone and sat at the kitchen table facing the hall leading to the bedroom. She dialed the number and the telephone only rang once before Malcolm picked up. "Hello, Mr. Oliver," she spoke in her most professional voice.

"Mama?"

"Yes, it's me Malcolm. Yuh Dad's fine. Yuh know how it is when I call yuh job. Ah don't know who might answer yuh phone. Anyway, Ah just wanted tuh prepare yuh for when yuh came home," Thea spoke softly and kept her eyes on the hall.

"Prepare me for what, Mama?"

"Ah'm gonna tell yuh father he has tuh confess tuh the church this Sunday or he has tuh leave Rehoboth. He just came home and Ah can't stand bein' in the same house with him. Ah can't stand lookin' at him. He depresses me." Thea rubbed her eyes. "Malcolm . . . Ah didn't do anything wrong. Ah'm carrin' this heavy burden and it's not mine tuh carry. He's got tuh carry his own burden . . . he's got tuh pay. Ah believe the Lord spoke tuh me, and He told me yuh father would confess and I would forgive him. He told me it was yuh father's choice, be it this Sunday or later. If later, yuh father would leave Rehoboth until he was ready tuh confesses tuh the church."

"But Mama, what if he refuses?"

"Then he will have tuh leave this house. You will have tuh take him away from here."

"Mama, that's not fair. Ah didn't do anything wrong either. Ah can't make him do something he doesn't want tuh do."

"Oh . . . Ah can make him leave. He'll leave or Ah'll tell him Ah'll go tuh the church," Thea warned. "Just think about it Malcolm. Ah'll see yuh when yuh get here."

"Okay, Mama. Ah'll see yuh later. Try tuh relax and get some rest. Ah love yuh Mama."

"Be careful driving. Ah love yuh too."

* * *

Malcolm kept a bag packed for the weekend in his trunk. He never knew when he would have to return to Rehoboth to deal with a family crisis. He knew if his father didn't confess in thirty-six years, it was unlikely he would do it now. He was overwhelmed with the decisions to be made and found it difficult to work because he was so worried about his family. *What will Ah do with Dad? He needs an assisted living apartment, but they cost a fortune and most have a long waiting list.* He sat back in his chair and placed his feet on his desk. He picked up his writing pad and pencil and placed a call to Johnny's office. After giving the perception of working he was able to speak freely with Johnny.

The secretary announced, "Mr. John Turner's Office."

"Would yuh tell him it's Malcolm Oliver and it's urgent?"

"Hey, Malcolm, what's urgent?"

"Dad is home and my mother wants him tuh confess this Sunday before the church. If he doesn't, she said he has tuh leave home. He's still medically fragile and my wife has lost all respect for him. Ah can't put him in a motel. His jaw is still wired and he sucks his food through a straw." Malcolm tossed the pad and pencil on the desk before he removed his feet. He leaned forward and placed his elbows on his desk and supported his head with his fingers. "He needs an apartment with round the clock nursing until his jaw is healed. He's on a special low sodium diet, his food had tuh be liquefied and his pressure has to be monitored on a regular basis. Ah wish Mama would wait until he is well, but she said he's draining her. She said if he confesses tuh the church, she can start tuh heal."

"Man, your mother has a right to be hurt and she is a better woman than most to forgive him on any level. We have to help her, so she doesn't have to worry about him. He's my father too and I'm happy you called me. Now, are you sure he's not going to confess?"

Malcolm looked up and glanced around the office to see if anyone was taking a particular notice to him. "No Johnny. Ah just know our father. He hasn't confessed yet, so why would he do it now? Ah could make arrangements for him tuh stay with a friend for a day or two and Ah'll have Mama prepare a few days supply of food. If we have tuh, do yuh think we could get him in an apartment by Tuesday?"

"Ya know Malcolm. You mentioned a motel before, but I'm thinking a hotel suite. There's the new Concordian Hotel in downtown Atlanta. I'll have my staff call to confirm that a suite will be available. I can reserve one for two weeks and longer if we need it. I'll hire an agency to meet his dietary needs and supply nursing staff around the clock, so that all his medical orders are followed. I'll have everything ready and waiting for your call. If I'm not home, you have my car phone number, and my housekeeper always knows how to reach me."

"Johnny thanks for stepping up. Ah hope he does what's right and puts an end tuh this lifetime saga. It will be a sharp blow, but then it will be over and we all can live."

"Malcolm, tell him I'll stand with him. Please call me if he decides to confess so I can be there. I can always cancel the hotel reservation and the special arrangements."

"And I'll stand with him too," Malcolm said. "Then there will be nothing to whisper about. Thanks Johnny. Ah'll keep yuh informed. We'll talk later"

"Yeah, man."

Malcolm sat back in his chair, closed his eyes and exhaled. He felt emotions creeping up on him that he feared he might not be able to control so he left his work station and went to the men's room. Just as his reflection bounced back at him from the mirror, tears left his eyes. *A man ain't supposed tuh* cry, he told himself before he splashed cold water on his face and took a deep breath. *Thank yuh Lord for Johnny and please let this matter be settled.* The paper towels were coarse but effective at blotting away the moisture.

"Malcolm, are yuh all right. Ah saw the way yuh came in here and yuh didn't look well," Randy said as he entered the men's room.

"Yeah, Ah'm fine. Just more problems at home, but my brother helped me with some planning. Ah was a little shaken. Only a friend like you would notice. Thanks Randy."

The two men left the men's room together and returned to their work stations. As soon as Malcolm sat at his desk his telephone rang.

"Malcolm . . . it's Jack. Can yuh come tuh my office?"

"Yes sir," Malcolm answered. *Damn! He probably wants tuh get on me about the time Ah've missed from work. Ah guess Ah have tuh kiss ass.*

Malcolm grabbed his suit jacket, glanced over at Randy and walked briskly to Jack Hamilton's office.

"Come in, come in Mr. Oliver. Have a seat," Mr. Hamilton said as he leaned back in his chair and pointed to both of the chairs in front of his desk. He smiled, then sat forward and picked up an application form.

Malcolm nodded and quietly took a seat without speaking.

"Only three people from this office applied for a position tuh the new Northern Atlanta office building. Ah've been appointed manager tuh that office and Ah've selected you as the supervisor. Mr. Lester will be promoted tuh supervisor in this office."

Malcolm's smile spread across his face. "Ah can't thank yuh enough for making this promotion possible for us. Ah don't want tuh just thank yuh for myself, but for my family, and Ah'm sure Mr. Lester will feel the same way. Sir . . . would it be possible if Ah accept the position in this office, and Mr. Lester be promoted tuh the Northern Atlanta office. Yuh see, sir . . . Ah live in Jonesboro and Mr. Lester lives in Tucker."

"Not a problem. Just give me a minute tuh clear it with Mr. Greco first. Yuh can stay right here while Ah call him." Mr. Hamilton pushed the speed dial number on his phone and reached his manger's secretary. After she announced his office, he asked to speak with Mr. Greco. Mr. Hamilton allowed his chair to rock back as he spoke and explained the situation. "Yes sir, it is a good point. Ah'll take care of the paper work and contact Human Resources. Thank yuh for understanding." Mr. Hamilton pushed his chair back and away from his desk, stood, reached over the desk and shook Malcolm's hand. "Ah'll give yuh a week's training in this position before Ah leave and of course, yuh know where Ah'll be, should yuh have any questions."

"Yes sir, thank yuh, sir." Malcolm smiled and continued shaking his hand. "Sir, may Ah ask yuh one more thing?"

Mr. Hamilton nodded.

"Ah hope Ah didn't speak tuh soon and Mr. Lester would have preferred tuh remain in this office. It makes a difference tuh me, but he may have wanted tuh stay here."

"Ah know where yuh going. Ah won't mention how the assignments were made. Now, would yuh ask Mr. Lester tuh come intuh my office?"

"Yes sir, and thank yuh again, sir," Malcolm said. He still had a big smile on his face and he was careful to close the door gently. *Damn,* he though, *maybe they didn't hide the job announcement tuh keep the African Americans from applying. Ah was just lucky finding it. When Ah run this office Ah'll make sure all promotional opportunities are mailed tuh everyone.*

Malcolm walked over to Randy's desk and stood looking down at him. "Hey Randy, lunch is on you tuhday. We gonna celebrate! Hamilton wants tuh see yuh right now," he sang out.

"Now?"

"Hurry man. He's waiting for yuh."

* * *

"Good morning Mr. Lester. Did Mr. Oliver tell yuh what this was about?" Mr. Hamilton glanced up at Randy over his bifocals and barely smiled.

"No sir, he just told me yuh wanted tuh see me." Randy stood between the two chairs.

"Yuh may take a seat." Mr. Hamilton sat back in his chair and smiled. "Yuh applied for the new office in Northern Atlanta. Actually three people from this firm applied for a promotion, you, Mr. Oliver, and myself. Because of yuh seniority you have been selected as supervisor for the Northern Atlantic office. Ah was promoted as the manager, and as soon as we move out, Mr. Oliver will be the supervisor of this office. Human Resource and the manager worked out the locations of the supervisor positions." Mr. Hamilton could see Mr. Lester wasn't as happy as Mr. Oliver. "Don't you want the promotion?"

"Oh, yes sir. Ah was just caught off guard. Will the revenue earned at the new office equal the earning at the headquarters? Ah don't want tuh lose commissions."

"Actually the company model will change with the opening of the new building. There are too many accounts to manage in this one location, so there will be an even distribution." Hamilton stood from his chair and walked to the window. He turned and faced Randy. He pointed to the floor. "This location will be known as Landers, Landers & Fine South and the new location will be Landers, Landers & Fine North. The executive offices will be located in a suite of offices in the Crystal Building."

"Thank yuh sir. It will be a pleasure working with yuh." Randy smiled and stood to shake Mr. Hamilton hand. As soon as he reached the door he turned. "Mr. Hamilton, Ah hope yuh understand how grateful Ah am for this opportunity and Ah want tuh thank yuh again for yuh consideration." He smiled again and bowed his head slightly. Mr. Hamilton nodded his head and smiled. Randy left his office and walked back to his desk; his face appeared as if it had been chiseled out of stone. *That's why Malcolm bought me those papers. It was just another way for him tuh get away from me. Why does he hate me so much? Ah've always been there for him. Now he expects me tuh go out and celebrate because Ah'll have less time with him. He already spends all his time on the weekend with his father. Ah hardly see him anymore. Ah look forward tuh coming tuh work just tuh see him, now he's made sure he's changed that.* His thoughts stabbed at him and robbed him of all reason. He reached his desk and sat stiff and stared at his computer monitor, but he was blind to only his mind's eye. His hands were placed palms down on his desktop and he continued to listen to the same unreasonable thoughts of an obsessed man.

Malcolm was waiting for him to return from Hamilton's office. He was ready to go to his cubicle and they would exchange handshakes, but when he noticed the bland, blood drained expression on Randy's face he wondered if he was fired instead of promoted. He knew he had to do something. So he went to him.

"How about that Randy, we got the jobs. Now let's go celebrate." Malcolm walked up behind Randy and placed his hands on his shoulder and slid down in the extra cubical chair. "Man, think of the money we can make. Do yuh realize we'll get a percentage of what every agent in the office makes?" he whispered.

"It's not the money. You just want tuh get away from me," Randy whispered back at him.

Malcolm stood up and looked around the office and sat back down. "C'mon man! Let's go tuh lunch. Or if yuh want tuh talk about it, let's go sit in the car, but yuh can't do this here . . . man . . . think about yuh family."

Malcolm checked his watch. *11:30 a.m.* He returned to Hamilton's office. The door was usually open so he felt comfortable stepping halfway in. "Ugh, excuse me, Mr. Hamilton, would it okay if Randy and I left early for lunch? We promise not tuh celebrate tuh much."

"Sure. Ah understand. Ah'd come with yuh, but someone has tuh hold down the fort," Hamilton replied.

Malcolm retuned to Randy. "Let's go!" He was demanding and didn't give him an opportunity to have an opinion. He placed his hand under his right armpit, spun his chair around. Randy stood and walked toward the elevator with Malcolm walking beside him, ready to push him along if he had to. They were quiet while in the elevator and didn't speak until they reached Malcolm's car.

Malcolm sat behind the wheel and put the car in gear. He drove down the ramp of the garage, while Randy rested his head on the head rest, with his eyes closed.

"Before yuh get nutty on me again, Ah need yuh tuh just talk tuh me so Ah know where yuh coming from," Malcolm said, as he gave Randy a quick glance.

"Ah can't stop loving yuh, and yuh keep pushing away from me. That's why yuh brought those papers tuh my house for the promotion. It was just another way tuh get away from me."

"Randy yuh need tuh stop this. Ah'm not going anywhere unless yuh push me away. Ah'll stay away from yuh if Ah think Ah'm causing yuh more harm than good." He held the steering wheel with both hands and continued to maneuver the ramps. When he came to the next level he pulled the car into an empty parking space and turned to face him. "Damn Randy, we're best friends and that's why Ah didn't want yuh tuh miss out on any promotions. That's what friends do for each other and Ah'd hope yuh'd do the same for me. Now, if yuh don't want the damn promotion, tell Hamilton, not me. They'll post it again and select someone else from the office and yuh can stay where yuh are. But think about the money and the luxury yuh holding back from yuh family, just so yuh can look in my face all day. Man if yuh do that, Ah'll lose all respect for yuh."

Randy stared at Malcolm for several minutes. He appeared more anxious than angry and his eye shifted from one insignificant thing to another. "Yuh right Malcolm! Why am Ah acting so stupid?" He took a deep breath, and exhaled through his tight lips. "When Ah went tuh the hospital the doctor prescribed anti-anxiety medication. It helped me feel better and Ah was able tuh return tuh work. He suggested Ah continue tuh take it once daily, but Ah didn't think Ah needed it. After last Sunday and tuhday, Ah'm a believer. Ah'll be taking my medication. Ah believe it will help me keep things in perspective."

"Okay let's go celebrate and plan for our good fortune. Where do yuh wanna go?" Malcolm threw his arm over the seat and checked that there were no cars passing behind him before backing out of the space. He put the car in drive and continued on to the next ramp.

"Let's go tuh Michael's for lunch. A little wine will help me mellow out."

"Michael's it is," Malcolm said. "Yuh know what Ah'd like tuh do? How about you and I go in tuhgether and buy one of those travel campers. We could take our wives and yuh kids, on camping trips. Or maybe Ah'll buy the camper and yuh'll buy the boat, and we can share the adventures."

"Hold on Malcolm, we can't spend our money until we make it."

"It's just good tuh think about making it and all the possibilities we'll have. My brother is a millionaire, but when yuh meet him at home you'd think he's just an ordinary guy. Ah had more opportunity than him and Ah threw it away. He gave me a second chance and Ah'm gonna make the best of it."

* * *

Malcolm parked in the lot across from Michael's and they noticed they were among the first of the lunchtime crowd. They decided to take a table in the open air section because they didn't want their conversation to be captured by the walls and carried to the ears of other lunch timers. The first thing Malcolm did was order Randy's favorite cream white sherry wine. He didn't care what they had for lunch or if it was the proper wine for his meal; he just wanted to knock the edge off of Randy's nerves.

"My father was discharged from the hospital tuhday and Ah have tuh leave after work tuh go tuh Rehoboth."

"Yuh have tuh leave tuhday? Ah thought we could all hang out tuhnight, you and Theresa and Gail and me. Ah thought we could really celebrate."

"Man that's impossible. Ah have tuh go directly tuh Rehoboth tuhnight. My parents need me. We can make plans for next weekend and really do it up in a big way."

"For now, let's have our lunchtime celebration."

"Yuh know, yuh right, Malcolm. Ah'm gonna spend this weekend with my wife and boys and that's the way it should be. Thanks for helping me get the promotion." Randy waved his hand to summon the waiter.

Chapter 15

The blender was grinding away at eight hefty slices of roast beef when Malcolm walked up behind his mother and kissed her in the nape of her neck. She made a startling sound and spun around holding a large prong serving fork.

Malcolm jumped back. "It's me Ma!"

"Boy, don't do that tuh me. Yuh best be speakin' up. Ah'm a little touchy these days. Anyway . . . give me a hug. Ah'm so happy yuh made it home safely. How'd yuh get here so fast? It's only six o'clock."

"Ah left straight from work. Where's Dad?"

"He's sleeping in the den. Thank the Lord his medicine makes him sleepy. Ah ain't got much tuh say tuh him. How yuh been doing?"

"Oh, Ah had a wonderful day tuhday. Ah have tuh tell yuh about it." Malcolm blew a kiss at his mother and left for the den.

Reverend Oliver was stretched out on the sofa. Malcolm picked up the folding chair and set it up so he could speak with him without disturbing his position. He and his mother had decided they would discuss the matter of the confession when the three of them were together. Malcolm just wanted to be with his father in that moment and let him know he was there for him.

Reverend Oliver stirred when he felt a hand rubbing on his arm. "Thea," he whispered.

Malcolm lowered his head and wished he could turn himself into his mother, just for his father's sake. He knew his father longed for her. "No Dad, it's me. Malcolm."

Reverend Oliver opened his eyes. "Malcolm. What day is this?"

"It's Friday evening. Ah came straight from work."

"Why?"

"Because Ah knew yuh needed me," Malcolm replied. "Don't get up. Yuh need yuh rest."

"Nonsense, that's all Ah been doing all day is sleeping. Yuh Mama will hardly speak tuh me. Ah feel like a stranger in my own house. Ah'm happy yuh here. Would yuh like tuh go out and sit under that tree? Yuh mama been sittin' under it most of the day."

Thea wiped her hands on her apron and walked to the dining room window. When she saw Owen and Malcolm walking toward her tree she began to scream. She ran pass the front door, pushing the screen door open so hard, it made a loud clap as it slammed shut. She screamed, "Owen, yuh can't sit under my tree! My tree is special and only the pure at heart are allowed tuh sit there. Yuh unclean!" she cried out and ran behind him, pushing him back and away from the trunk of the tree. "This is a special tree. God has given me strength through this tree. Only the clean at heart are allowed tuh sit here and be tranquilized by its dancing branches! When yuh confess and cleanse yuhself yuh may join me under this tree. That's when we'll start our life over. " Thea continued to cry while she tried to explain.

* * *

Reverend Oliver kept his eyes on Thea as he walked backward from the willow tree he had watched grow for all the years he lived in Rehoboth. His eyes glazed over because unintentionally, he had hurt his Thea again. What does she mean, *'confess and cleanse yuhself and yuh may join me under this tree.' Ah already did that. 'That's when we'll start our life anew.'* He watched Malcolm standing under the swaying branches of the tree, holding and soothing his mother until she stopped crying. He removed his handkerchief and wiped it over his face before returning to the solitude of the den.

* * *

Malcolm and Thea sat in the chairs under the tree. The wind blew and passed through the branches and made them sway.

"Mama what's so special about this tree? It's just an old weeping willow tree. But in the last couple of weeks yuh put some special significance tuh it, like it has a special power."

"It's my special place. Ah've noticed the beauty of the swaying branches. Yuh father bought a curse upon our home, but Ah found this tree tuh be clean and untouched. It's like the Lord said, 'Go out tuh the tree and watch my branches dance for yuh and yuh will find peace.' Ah sit here and meditate as the branches sway. My thoughts become ordered and Ah can think about what Ah want for my future. It was here that Ah decided Ah wouldn't leave Rehoboth, that Ah wouldn't be punished for something Ah had no part of."

Malcolm sat back in the chair and watched the branches sway and move in unison, but he failed to experience the tranquilizing affect his mother spoke of. "Mama," he said as he stood and took hold of her hand. "Ah think we need tuh have that talk with Dad. He's hurtin' real bad. Yuh hurtin' . . . Ah'm hurtin' . . . and yuh tree is not soothing me like it's soothing you."

Thea nodded and while still holding Malcolm's hand she walked between the branches to the house. She took a seat at the kitchen table while Malcolm went to the den to get his father.

Malcolm stood at the entrance to the den and looked in at his father. He was sitting in a chair and appeared to be just staring off at empty space. Malcolm swallowed like he had a lump in his throat; his chest felt heavy, forcing him to take a deep breath before he entered the room. "Dad, are yuh all right?"

"Ah can't live like this. Ah need Thea. Ah want us tuh be the way we were. Ah know Ah sound selfish and Ah'm the cause of all this misery." He continued to stare off into the emptiness of the room.

"There is a way tuh make this better. You and Mama can start anew. Mama wants tuh talk tuh yuh and me in the kitchen. C'mon, Ah'll help yuh up."

Reverend Oliver searched Malcolm eyes for an explanation of his last statement. He continued his visual hold even after he was standing and allowing Malcolm to escort him into the kitchen.

Malcolm suggested his father sit in a chair across from his mother and he sat at the end of the dinette table.

Thea had her head bowed and didn't raise it when Owen sat down. She turned to Malcolm. "Ah'm a bit emotional, will yuh speak for me?"

"Yes Mama." Malcolm took hold of his mother's hand then reached for his father's hand.

"Dad," Malcolm whispered as he looked directly at his father. His mother glanced up at him. "Mama wants our lives tuh get back tuh normal, but first . . ." he squeezed his mother's hand. "But first, yuh need tuh do something."

"What? What else can Ah do?" Reverend Oliver's eyes shifted between Malcolm and Thea.

"Dad, Ah'm not gonna hold it back. We want yuh tuh stand at Concord Baptist Church and confess that yuh violated Elizabeth Turner and yuh're Johnny Turner's father."

"No!" Reverend Oliver yelled out. He snatched his hand from Malcolm's hand and slammed it palm down on the table to assist in pushing himself up to a standing position. "No! No! No!" he yelled out again. He took long strides, leaving the kitchen and strutting down the hall toward his bedroom, and then returning to the kitchen. "No!" he yelled out again. "Ah already confessed tuh Reverend Lipton and the Turner family."

"That's not the same Dad. Johnny and Ah will stand at yuh side."

"No! No!" he yelled out louder and balled his hand into a fist. He walked over to the table and slammed it down.

"Yuh should ask for the church's forgiveness when yuh step down as assistant pastor. After that we are all free of this burden, even Johnny and Miss Elizabeth. Yuh say yuh love Johnny, but he can't even call yuh his father when he's here in Rehoboth," Malcolm yelled out louder than his father. He stood and met him eye to eye.

"Johnny is not in Rehoboth that much and he'll understand. Ah'm gonna step down. Ah told Reverend Turner Ah would step down. How could yuh ask me tuh suffer any more! Haven't Ah had enough!" Owen backed up again and screamed out from between the wires in his mouth.

"Dad, please calm down, try tuh stay calm. Ah don't want yuh pressure tuh go up."

Thea's chair scraped the floor as she pushed it back to stand. She moved quickly around the table and stood face to face with Owen. "Yuh have brought a terrible burden on our marriage and life tuhgether. Yuh have choices." She spoke softly to keep Owen calm, but also to get her point across. "Yuh will stand at the church on Sunday and we can begin tuh have a new life, with the past behind us. All of us can share Johnny's love and we can move on with our lives."

"Stop it, Thea." Owen dropped to the chair and held his head in his hand. "Ah won't do that."

Thea stood over him. She didn't cry or yell, and her soft firm words rested on his ears. "Yuh next choice is yuh will leave this house by Sunday afternoon and stay away until yuh ready tuh confess at the church. The way Ah see it, yuh can do it sooner, rather than later."

Malcolm was quiet. He had never seen his mother so authoritative and his father so submissive.

"Yuh final choice is, if yuh refuse tuh leave this house, Ah will stand at church and speak of yuh transgressions. Ah will keep my marriage vows and never leave yuh. Yuh will have tuh be the one tuh do that. But Ah wonder what a silent and broken marriage is like? Yuh think about it, Owen." Thea left the kitchen.

* * *

Owen raised his head and watched her leave. He didn't speak. He could see Malcolm watching him and he knew he was waiting for his next move. He watched Malcolm correct his posture when he stood to leave the kitchen, but then he turned and sat down again. He stood, left the kitchen, and walked toward the front porch. He could feel Malcolm following him with his eyes. *He thinks Ah'm gonna return tuh his mother's tree just for spite,* he thought. As soon as the screen closed behind him, Malcolm opened it and peeked out on the porch.

"Come on out. Ah was expecting yuh." Reverend Oliver didn't turn toward him; he just waved his hand, extending him an invitation.

Two high back rockers were placed side by side with a small table separating them. Reverend Oliver sat in one and Malcolm sat in the other. They were quiet for a while and Malcolm waited for his father to break the silence. They rocked at the same pace, the two moving back and forth together; the chairs were assaulting the same porch board and making a creaking sound.

"Ah can't do it Malcolm." Reverend Oliver stared off at the swaying branches of the tree.

"Yuh will do it, sooner rather than later, like Mama says. Why don't yuh think about it? Sleep on it. Let me know tuhmorrow so Ah can call Johnny. The two of us want tuh stand with yuh." Malcolm stopped rocking in his chair. "It'll be gossip and then it'll be over. That's the way it was for Miss Elizabeth all those years ago and Johnny had tuh live through it, too. Now it's yuh turn, but yuh got us tuh stand with yuh."

Excellent point, Reverend Oliver thought. *Ah remember how she suffered and Ah wanted tuh go tuh her, but Ah was sick with fear. She tried tuh commit suicide. She thought even the Lord had forsaken her. Her father disowned her. Ah have my wife and two sons. All the children at school spoke of her like she was scum. Ah remember how Johnny cried when he found out his father was mailing money every month tuh his mother. He didn't know it was me, but he cried in my arms. He said he was 'rich and he was loved,' but he wanted a real father. He came tuh me and he felt like he was stealing me away from Malcolm. And Ah caused all that pain and suffering and he still loves me. Ah need tuh stand and make it right.* He turned toward Malcolm and continued rocking in his chair. "Ah need tuh pray for strength and direction. Yuh said some things that helped me. Now it's my turn', and yuh right. Yuh mother won't let me sit under her tree, but Ah seen how the long branches dance and sway. It's relaxing, it seems tuh clear my mind so Ah can think. Ah'd like tuh be alone for awhile. Ah'll give yuh my answer in the morning."

Malcolm stood and gave his father a gentle bow. "Ah love yuh, Dad."

✳ ✳ ✳

When Malcolm entered the house, Thea was busy gathering a few of her personal items and moving into the guest room. She had just completed turning down the bed when she heard Malcolm call.

"Mama, Ah'm proud of yuh. Ah haven't seen yuh take charge like that since the incident on River Road when yuh practically saved Johnny's life."

There was a sadness to Thea's smile. She walked past Malcolm and into the kitchen to finish preparing the liquefied meals and placed them in the freezer. "Ah still have tuh be sure yuh father has the proper meals. His doctor gave me a strict diet for him, but we can talk while Ah work."

Malcolm gently placed his hand over his mother's hands and she stopped preparing the meals. "Mama let me hug yuh." He wrapped his arms around her shoulders, placed his cheek next to hers and gave her a gentle squeeze. "You are a most remarkable woman," he said before kissing her on the cheek.

"Oh Malcolm, yuh go 'way from here." Thea gave him a chuckle.

Malcolm took hold of her hands again. "Mama, after all Dad put yuh through, yuh love him so much Ah can read yuh mind. Yuh thinking if yuh have tuh send him away with me, how will he eat?"

Thea tried to pull her hands away, but Malcolm held them tighter. "That's why yuh fixing all this food. Yuh know Theresa is not gonna let him stay with me, so yuh wondering where will he stay?" Malcolm hugged his mother again and he could feel her trembling. "C'mon Mama, enough with the food. Let's sit at the table."

Thea sat and Malcolm pulled his chair close so he could tell her the plan he and Johnny had developed if they needed to use it. He spoke quietly and brought a smile to his mother's face. He continued to hold her hand and occasionally he rubbed her arm. She rubbed the side of his face and told him she wished Johnny was there so she could personally thank him for reducing her burdens.

"Dad's doing some powerful thinking out on the porch. He's been staring at yuh tree. Yuh wouldn't let him go under it, but he's just looking at it and he's mesmerized."

"The tree is relaxing him. Yuh father is praying and asking the Lord for direction," Thea said.

"Okay, let's let God work on Dad, and we can relax."

"Can Ah just put the food away?"

"And while yuh do that Ah'm gonna call Theresa."

* * *

Theresa picked up the phone on the second ring. She was sitting at the kitchen table grading essays from her honors English class at the high school. She put her marking pen down when she heard Malcolm's voice. "Hi honey," she said. "Baby, Ah'm sorry for the way Ah've been acting. Ah have no right tuh judge yuh father. This is a family matter and we should all stand tuhgether. Will yuh forgive me?"

"Thank yuh Theresa, yuh really don't know how much that means tuh me. We've been going through some really hard times, but pray Dad will stand at church and confess before the congregation. We're asking him tuh do this and he's been praying and meditating. If he does, Johnny and Ah will stand with him. Mama said she'll forgive him and Ah hope you will too."

"If he says he will, Yuh might see me at the church," Theresa said.

"Oh honey, if yuh standing then Ah want yuh tuh sit down."

"Just a minute honey . . . okay now Ah'm flung out on the sofa, pretending yuh in my arms." Theresa was laughing.

"Ah got the promotion tuh supervisor in the office. It means a $10,000 pay raise and from $40,000 to $60,000 in commission, depending on the market year."

"Oh Malcolm, Ah'm so proud of yuh. Do yuh think yuh can come home, just for tuhnight? We can do a little celebrating; Ah want tuh feel yuh body next tuh mine."

"Ah think that can be arranged. Let me call yuh back," Malcolm replied.

* * *

Malcolm hurried into the kitchen and stood near his mother. "Mama, do yuh think yuh'll be all right the rest of this evening. Ah want tuh go home and spend time with Theresa. Ah was promoted from agent tuh supervisor of my office today and we want tuh celebrate. You and Dad seem tuh be okay and Ah'll be back before noon tuhmorrow."

Thea eyes shifted and she gave Malcolm a smile. Malcolm knew she was hiding her disappointment, but she knew she really didn't need him.

"Ah believe Ah'll be able tuh manage just fine. Yuh go on home; be careful driving." Thea took a deep quivering breath. "We'll see yuh tuhmorrow."

"Ah have tuh speak with Dad and make sure he's all right before Ah leave."

Malcolm could feel his mother's eyes on him as he walked down the short hall to the front door and left the house. He held the screen door, easing it shut with one hand as he made his way closer to his father. The loose porch board was still making goose sounds under his father's rocking chair and he joined him sitting in the second chair. Talking to his father was easier than talking to his mother and he explained his reasons for returning home.

"Congratulations Malcolm. Ah'm so proud of yuh. Ah'll see yuh tuhmorrow."

"Thanks Dad." Malcolm stood and caught his father's hand for a hearty shake. "Have a good night. See yuh tuhmorrow."

Malcolm returned to the house and his mother was standing at the end of the hall. He knew she was watching them from the dining room window and he wanted to hug her, to tell her everything would be all right. He blew her a kiss and stopped at the entrance to the den. "Mama, Ah'm gonna call Theresa and let her know Ah'm on my way."

"Okay baby," Thea said as she wiped her clean hands on her apron out of habit and to sooth her haggard nerves.

Moments later Malcolm waved as he drove away.

* * *

It was late evening and Thea left the front door open with the screen unlatched. She worried about Owen sitting on the front porch for so long. It wasn't a screened in porch. She wondered what was protecting him from the insects. *Maybe the Lord placed a net over him, but Ah'm going out and ask him if he'd like an ice cream thin shake. At least Ah can see if he's all right.*

Reverend Oliver looked up at her and smiled, but shook his head when she offered him an ice cream shake. When she asked if he was all right, he nodded. His face was peaceful and he had a small understanding smile. Thea returned to the house and to the dining room where she had a clear view of his back. She pulled out the dining room chair from the table, the one with the arms, and turned it so it faced the window. She was prepared to sit in that chair all night and watch her husband if she had to.

Reverend Oliver's chair had been still for at least ten minutes and his head was still even longer, long enough to cause Thea to be concerned. She quietly walked to the window and glanced down at his fingers and they fiddled against the rocker's arm rest. She exhaled slowly and lifted her head to the Heavens. *Thank yuh Lord. Ah believe yuh speakin' tuh him now.*

The phone rang and Thea hurried to the kitchen to answer it.

"Ah'm home Mama," Malcolm announced.

"Yuh know, it's 9:45 and yuh left here two hours ago?" Thea whispered.

"Sorry Mama, Ah been home for fifteen minutes."

"Okay baby I'll see yuh tuhmorrow," Thea said.

* * *

Thea returned to her chair in the dining room and continued to watch her husband. When she saw him getting up from the rocker she quickly walked to the guest room and slid under the covers. Reverend Oliver went to his bedroom and when he didn't see her, he checked the guest room. She heard the door open and remained still even after she heard it close again. She heard the toilet flush and footsteps leading to their bedroom. She wanted to go to him, but decided it was best that they remain separated. He knew what she wanted and if he couldn't give it to her there would be many separate nights.

Chapter 16

In all the years of living on Rehoboth Road, Thea never slept anywhere other than in her own bed, so she didn't sleep at all that night. When the morning came, she bathed, dressed, and prepared breakfast. She had to wake Owen at eight o'clock so he could take his medication. The door to their bedroom was slightly open, she entered, touched him on the shoulder and he opened his eyes slowly.

"Good morning Thea," he said. His voice was serene and reassuring. "Ah love yuh." He gently took hold of her hand when she handed him his medication and a glass of water. He looked up at her and his eyes begged her for forgiveness.

Thea pulled her hand back and held it against her chest. She glanced down at Owen before turning away. "Ah love yuh, too," she replied. She acted like she was afraid of him and backed up against the wall near the door. "Yuh breakfast will be ready when yuh come tuh the kitchen." She could feel her heart racing and the air was heavy. In the next moment she knew she would be crying; she slouched her shoulders and slipped quietly from the room. The farther she got from him, the cooler the air seemed and she could breathe again. Tears rolled down her face and she lifted her apron to blot them away.

* * *

Owen was startled by Thea's actions. He set the empty water glass on the night stand, threw back the covers, and leaped to his feet. A slight dizzy spell came over him; he reached for the night stand and lowered himself back to the bed. He remained still for several minutes until it passed. Slowly, he stood and checked his balance before reaching for his robe. He placed his hand against the wall and walked down the hall to the kitchen. Thea was standing at the kitchen sink when he approached her. *Ah'm not gonna touch her,* he thought. "Ah love yuh Thea. Ah love yuh tuh much tuh lose yuh. Ah'll do whatever yuh want me tuh do. Ah don't want tuh cause yuh any more pain. Ah love yuh tuh much tuh continue tuh hurt yuh."

"Do yuh mean it Owen?"

"Yes, Ah mean it. May Ah kiss yuh?"

Thea wrapped her arms around his neck and he just held her.

"Ah have tuh call Malcolm," Thea said.

"Let me, it'll be my pleasure." He gently released her and walked over to the wall phone.

Thea sat at the table, laced her fingers and bowed her head. *Thank yuh Lord.*

Owen returned to the table and to Thea. "Is everything all right?"

"Yes Owen. Ah was just thanking the Lord for helping yuh make yuh decision."

"Malcolm and Theresa will be here around noon. They are very happy for us."

* * *

As soon as Malcolm finished speaking with his father he called Johnny. The reservation at the hotel and the private agency had to be cancelled and Johnny needed to make arrangements to get to Rehoboth. The information for the cancellations sat on the desk in Johnny's study. He made the necessary calls and reached for his personal directory. "Julia!" he called out. His voice was loud with excitement as he fished through his telephone listings searching for the travel agent's number.

Julia stood in the door to his study. "You called me, Johnny?"

"Yeah baby, we need to go to Rehoboth. My father is confessing at Concord tomorrow. Can you help me? I can't find the agent's number and we need a flight out today." Johnny's hands were trembling and he thumbed forward through his directory, then backward, and then forward again until Julia pulled it away from him.

"Just let me do this. Why don't you get your bag ready?"

Johnny gave his seat to Julia. "Thanks honey, I'm gonna do just that. I still have to call my mother and Nat, but I need to get myself together first." He left the study and walked down the hall to their bedroom. He stood at their window and looked out over the south side of Washington, D.C. *I guess I should be happy this is going to finally be over. I don't know how Mama stood up to this craziness all these years. It's only been a few weeks for me and I feel like I've been trapped in a steel tomb. I have to call Mama and tell her about the confession. She needs to be warned that she's about to be thrown back in time. She needs to have time to decide if she wants to be present at Concord. It has to be her decision if she wants to expose herself to the stares and glares again. All the gossip that was quieted all those years ago will sound louder than ever and she and Nat have to live and work in the community. She's gonna be terrified.* Johnny turned his back to the window and sat on the window sill.

Julia entered the bedroom. "Okay, the arrangements have been made; we have a limo to and from the airport, our flights and a rental car. Our pick-up time is 3:00 p.m. and we should arrive in Rehoboth before 8:00 this evening." She turned and searched the room. "Where's your bag?"

"I have to call Mama and then I'll grab a few things."

"All right, I'm going to pack my bag." Julia slid the doors to her closet open.

Johnny returned to the study and sat on the sofa holding the telephone in his hand. He closed his eyes and rubbed the back of the phone's cool surface against the side of his face. He remembered how he asked his grandmother to tell his mother that he knew Reverend Oliver was his father. He never really knew what affect that had on her, and he never asked. He only knew he was too afraid of hurting her to tell her himself. He dialed his mother's telephone number and held his breath.

"Hi Mama."

"Johnny, how are you and Julia?" Elizabeth's voice was always bubbly when she heard Johnny's voice.

"Julia and I will be home tonight around 8:00. Mama, I hope you won't be upset, but Reverend Oliver will be confessing to the congregation of Concord during tomorrow's service." Johnny spoke quickly knowing if he paused the words might stick in his throat.

"Oh my Lord!" Elizabeth said.

Johnny thought his mother was upset and he felt weak. He pushed himself back on the sofa and panted for air.

"Johnny that's the best news Ah've heard in yuh entire life. Ah will definitely be at Concord tuhmorrow. Ah can't wait tuh see yuh tuhnight."

Johnny smiled and sat forward. "Mama I was so worried it would be bad news for you. Malcolm and I will stand with him when he confesses. Will that be all right with you?"

"Ah don't care who stands with him, as long as he confesses tuh the congregation."

"I love you, Mama. We'll see you tonight. I know you'll call Gram'ma. Bye now."

"So long Johnny. Thanks for making my day."

Johnny hung up the telephone, hurried back to the bedroom, lifted Julia up and swung her around. "I love you, Julia! We're gonna go to Rehoboth and this is all going to be over soon."

"Okay . . . and I love you too."

* * *

Thea and Owen sat on the front porch and waited for Malcolm and Theresa. Owen moved the small table and pulled the two rockers close together and away from the loose porch boards. He placed the table at the edge of the porch and Thea set a serving tray on it with two glasses and a pitcher of ice tea. They held each other's hand as they rocked their chairs. They could have sat on the swing, but the swing didn't face the tree, so the high back rockers were the better solution.

"When can Ah sit in one of those chairs under the tree?" Owen nodded his head in the direction of his interest.

Thea stopped rocking and stared at Owen. "Ah believe that tuh be my scared place. Yuh can join me there tuhmorrow after the confession, but not before."

"Yuh know Thea, Ah think there's something tuh that tree. Ah prayed and cried and asked the Lord tuh show me the light. The next thing Ah knew the wind was blowing and the long branches of yuh tree began to sway. At first Ah just looked at them the way yuh look at anything, but then my eyes began tuh follow their movement. Ah rested my head on the back of the chair and only my eyes moved. All Ah saw were them branches and then Ah felt like Ah was inside of myself and my life played out before me. Ah felt like Ah was only on the porch for a half an hour after Malcolm left, but when Ah came tuh my true senses, four hours had passed."

"Did yuh hear me when Ah was speaking tuh yuh last night?"

"Yes, but yuh were flashing through my thoughts."

Thea placed her hand on top of Owen's. "Ah was so worried about yuh, Ah sat in the dining room and watched yuh until yuh got up tuh come in the house. Ah ran tuh the bed and Ah was pretending tuh be asleep when yuh looked in on me."

Owen lifted his head and smiled.

* * *

Malcolm blasted his car horn when he drove up in the circular driveway;

he parked behind father's car.

"Hey Mama, Dad," Theresa said as she waved. She hurried to Thea's side and they were first to enter the house.

Malcolm sat on the porch with his father and they were quiet for a while. The rocking chairs creaked, but the scraping sound from the loose porch board was gone; Owen smiled when Malcolm looked down at the floor of the porch for it.

"Thank yuh for coming back." Owen whispered. "Yuh know, when Ah confessed tuh Reverend Lipton Ah told him Ah would confess tuh the congregation of the Concord and Bethlehem Baptist church if yuh mother would come back tuh me. Ah had forgotten Ah said that until Ah was doing all that thinkin' last night. The thought of losing yuh mother is far greater than confessing tuh the church; now, that don't mean Ah ain't scared tuh death."

"Ah know it's hard and this will be yuh longest day. Just remember we'll be standing with yuh, even Johnny. He's flying in this evening."

"Thank yuh Malcolm. Ah don't know how Ah'd get through this without you and Johnny standing beside me. Ah don't want yuh mother tuh stand with me and be humiliated. Ah only need my two boys."

"Ah understand Dad." Malcolm held onto his father's arm and led him into the house.

* * *

Saturday morning was always Nat's favorite day of the week. It was almost noon when he came in the kitchen for breakfast. Elizabeth didn't want to spoil his day with the news that Reverend Oliver would be confessing at the church. He was on his feet again and they had resumed their lives, hardly speaking of Owen or the Olivers. Elizabeth knew this would be the final chapter.

"It's a beautiful morning, Beth. Why don't we take a ride into Macon for dinner and take in a movie this evening?"

"Yuh know, Ah believe yuh're the most thoughtful man in Georgia. Yuh think we can leave a little early and do some shopping too?" Elizabeth batted her eyes, smiled, and placed her hand over his. "Oh Johnny and Julia are coming home tonight. Ah need tuh call him and let him know we may still be out when they arrive."

"Ah'll tell yuh what . . . yuh can shop and Ah'll sit in the store and wait for yuh. Yuh have everything, why do yuh need tuh shop? And why is Johnny coming home, he just left here?"

"Oh yuh know how Ah like tuh look around and pick up some things here and there. Besides, Johnny called a little while ago and told me Reverend Oliver was going tuh confess everything at Concord tuhmorrow."

"Oh Beth . . . Ah hope he doesn't confess everything," Nat said as he took a deep breath

"Oh Nat, it's gonna be all right. Ah don't think he'd do that. Ah think he wants this tuh be over. He knows how much Johnny loves yuh and he doesn't want anything tuh come between the two of them." Elizabeth squeezed Nat's hand. "Now promise me yuh not going tuh let Owen ruin our day.

Nat shook his head. "No . . . no, Beth. We're gonna have a wonderful day, Ah promise."

"Ah want yuh tuh take yuh medicine tuh reduce yuh anxiety. Ah don't want yuh having any spasms. Think about it, what could he say? He told the detectives, his family, the doctor, and just about everyone that he fell. Do yuh think he would suddenly tell the congregation yuh assaulted him? If he did, it would be yuh word against his, and no one would believe him. "

"Yeah, Ah know what yuh mean." Nat took several more deep breaths and he could feel the tension leaving his neck and shoulders. "Thanks Beth. Ah feel better."

"Are yuh all right?"

"Yeah, Ah'm fine, let's eat. Enough about Owen, he's not gonna consume our lives again," Nat replied.

"As soon as we have our breakfast Ah'm gonna call Mama, but yuh right, enough about Owen now." Elizabeth waved her hands as if she were pushing him aside to make room for new business. "Okay, we have salmon and sausage patties, fried apples, home fries, scrambled eggs and hot biscuits. Would yuh like some pancakes?"

"No honey, this is a banquet. Let me bless the food so we can eat."

Chapter 17

Thea turned over in bed and reached for Owen. In the previous weeks and while in her twilight sleep she moved to feel the security of his touch and remembered he was still in the hospital. She rubbed his place in their bed where he should be laying and never opened her eyes. She pulled her hand back and curled it against her chest, while her twilight sleep pulled her in deeper. Suddenly her eyes popped open and she sat up. *Owen is home. Where is he?* She slipped from beneath the bedcovers, pulled on her robe, and hurried from the room. The house was dark, except for the small night lights in the hall and kitchen. She walked to the dining room to look out the window. Owen was sitting on the front porch in the rocking chair staring at the willow tree. The moon was like a fluorescent light shining against his body and casting a shadow against the window curtains.

Thea slumped down in the same dining room chair where she had sat the night before. *Oh Lord, please give him the strength tuh do what's right. Ah know what he has tuh do tuhday is hard, but what he did was terrible, and now he has tuh pay. Please Lord, don't let him change his mind. We're all suffering and it has tuh end. One way or another, it has tuh end.*

It was 5:00 a.m. when Thea decided to return to bed. *Oh Lord, why do Ah feel like Ah did something wrong?* Tears rolled down her face. She removed herself from the chair like every bone in her body was dislocated. The walls supported her as she returned to their bedroom. It would be a little over an hour before she would rise again.

* * *

Johnny purposely left the drapes in the bedroom pulled back and the blinds open to reflect the light upward into the room. He didn't want the daylight to jolt him awake no more than he wanted to hear the sound of his alarm clock. The morning light was a soft way to wake up. He looked over at Julia and she was hugging her pillow like a child hugged a stuffed cuddly animal. He smiled and pulled the cord, closing the drapes hoping she would sleep longer. There was no need to wake her so early. He picked up his grooming kit and headed to the bathroom. He tested the shower water and closed his eyes when it hit his face and ran down his body. *I wonder how Nat is doing. Mama is trying to act as if she's happy to finally hear Reverend Oliver's confession. Ah know she really doesn't want to have her life opened to the church again. I told Reverend Oliver I would stand with him, now I need to be standing with my mother. Mama said it didn't matter as long as he confessed, but I know it does. Once again Ah'm caught in the middle.*

By the time Johnny completed his grooming routine, and made a pot of coffee, it was 7:30 and time to wake Julia. They were expected at his mother's for a 9:00 a.m. breakfast and he wanted to give her ample time to get ready. He returned to the bedroom and allowed the daylight to penetrate the room. Julia was facing away from the window and didn't move. He knelt on the floor and kissed her on the tip of her nose. She smiled.

"Good morning Johnny." She stretched her arms out before hugging him.

Johnny combed his fingers through her silky hair. "I know you slept well. I only hope you had pleasant dreams."

"I hope I did. I don't remember, but it doesn't matter because I'm in your dream house," she cooed.

Johnny smiled and kissed her on the forehead. "You always know how to make me feel good. Okay honey, the bathroom is yours and the coffee is ready. I'll wait for you. Would you like your coffee on the front porch? Mama is not expecting us until 9:00 o'clock."

"It's bathroom duty first and I'll meet you on the porch," Julia whispered.

* * *

Thea got out of bed and pulled up the covers. *Owen, she remembered. Oh my Lord, I hope he's not still on the porch again.* She reached for her robe and hurried down the hall and out the front door. "Owen, have yuh been out here all night?" She spoke to him, but he didn't turn to look at her; he didn't make any conscious movement. Only his chest moved when he inhaled. She felt her heart skip and slowly tipped towards him. He didn't flinch when she rubbed his hand and she was startled by his cold clammy touch. "Owen," she called out again, her voice trembling with fear.

He turned his head just enough so his eyes could meet with hers.

"Are you all right?"

Owen closed his eyes, nodded subtly and returned to his previous position.

Thea rubbed her hand over his back, shoulder, and down his arm until she touched his hand again. "Owen, yuh robe is damp from the night's dew. Yuh been out here most of the night, and could catch yuh death from pneumonia. Please come in and change into something dry and warm up. Ah'll fix yuh a nice hot cup of coffee."

Owen didn't move; he stared straight ahead in the direction of Thea's dancing willow tree. Her eyes followed the direction of his stare and then she stepped in his visual path. He still didn't move; not even to shift to look around her. He maintained this frozen position and closed his eyes as though he had captured enough of the image of the magic tree in his mind's eye for him to continue to meditate without interruption. Thea stood watching him, and waiting for him to open his eyes, but after fifteen seconds, he began to move his lips and tears rolled down his face. She took several steps backward until she felt the porch railing. Fear gripped her. She thought Owen would die before he could leave the porch. She rushed into the house.

"Malcolm, wake up Malcolm!" Thea knocked hard on his door. "Malcolm!" she yelled out. "Yuh father needs yuh!"

"Mama, Ah'm coming!" After a few seconds he opened the door.

It's yuh father. Ah think he's been sitting on the front porch all night."

"All night?"

"Well . . . Ah don't know if it's been all night, but Ah know he wasn't in bed at 4:45 this morning so Ah came into the dining room and saw him on the porch. I went back to bed at 5:00 and he never returned to bed. Ah'm scared, Malcolm."

"Don't worry Mama. Ah'll see about him."

Theresa came through the bedroom door wrapping the belt of her robe around her. "Ah'm gonna put on some coffee," she said in a weak voice.

"Yes, thank yuh, Theresa." Thea walked to the dining room window. She could see Malcolm and Owen, but she couldn't hear anything. Theresa placed the box of tissues on the table and Thea pulled a hand full and wiped her tears. She stood at the window directly behind Owen.

Malcolm spoke to his father, while concern and frustration distorted his face, his hands moved to emphasize his words.

Thea continued to watch Owen sit motionless. She could read Malcolm's lips and she knew he was pleading with his father before he eased himself away and returned to the front door; she hurried to meet him.

"What happened Malcolm? What did he say?" She caught him just as he entered the house.

Malcolm stepped across the threshold and checked that the screen door latched. He placed his arm around his mother's shoulder and led her down the hall and into the kitchen. "He didn't say anything . . . that is, not tuh me. He was crying and his lips were moving . . . and he kept staring at the willow tree. Ah'm gonna call Johnny. Maybe he can get through tuh him."

"Well, Ah'm gonna wrap his mother's quilt around him and Ah'm gonna stay with him until someone comes tuh help us."

Thea went to their bedroom and removed the quilt from the cherished items in her old hope chest. It carried the scent of lilac and mothballs. As soon as she reached the porch she shook it out before draping it over the rocking chair and Owen. He still didn't move, even when she wiped the tears from his face. She sat in the rocking chair next to him, stared out at her tree, and in her soprano voice she began to sing, softly and in perfect pitch:

"What a friend we have is Jesus, All our sins and grief tuh bear!
What a privilege tuh carry, everything tuh God in prayer!
O what peace we often forfeit, O what needless pain we bear,
All because we do not carry, everything tuh God in prayer!

Have we trials and tribulations? Is there trouble anywhere?
We should never be discouraged, take it tuh the Lord in prayer.
Can we find a friend so faithful, who will all our sorrows share?
Jesus knows our every weakness, take it tuh the Lord in prayer."

Just as Thea began to sing the third verse she heard Owen singing along with her. She was surprised that he had come back to her, but she didn't stop singing, rocking her chair or staring at her tree. His voice was weak and slurred, but she understood him.

"Have we trials and tribulations?" He repeated the second verse and Thea sang along with him before continuing on to the final verse:

"Are we weak and heavy laden? Cumbered with a load of care?
Precious Savior, still our refuge, take it tuh the Lord in prayer.
Do thy friends despise and forsake thee? Take it tuh the Lord in prayer;
In His arms He'll take and shield thee. Thou will find a solace there.

"Thank yuh Thea. Ah'm so scared." Owen removed his hand from beneath the blanket and wiped his tears.

"Honey, yuh gonna be all right. Yuh been out here all night taking yuh troubles tuh the Lord in prayer. During all that prayer and meditation, did the Lord tell yuh not tuh confess tuh the church?"

Owen dropped his head like a child being scolded and gave it a slight shake.

"Okay honey, after tuhday that burden yuh been carryin' will be gone. And yes, the church folk will talk, but soon all that will go away. And yuh know what? Ah'll be side-steppin' the gossip, too. "

"Ah hope Ah can do it," he whispered.

"Yuh can."

Thea watched Owen look up at the road and she followed his movement. "Is that Johnny coming? Oh c'mon Owen, yuh need tuh get inside and take a warm shower and change into some fresh clothing. Yuh don't want Johnny tuh see yuh like this."

Owen moved quickly through the front door, while Thea stopped to gather up her precious quilt. By the time she reached the kitchen, he had disappeared into the bedroom. She stopped to compliment Theresa on the sausage patties and bacon frying in the large black skillet.

"The coffee is ready, Mother."

"Thank yuh baby. Ah'm gonna wait for Owen and Malcolm, but you may have yours if yuh like."

"No ma'am, Ah'll wait with you."

* * *

Malcolm ran from the house and met Johnny's car as it pulled up in the driveway. He didn't give him a chance to get out of the car. Johnny rolled down the window and spoke first. "Thanks for calling man. I saw your mother and Dad going into the house. I hope he wasn't trying to hide from me; he seems to be better."

"Yeah man, but he gave us quite a scare. Mama was singing tuh him and he seemed tuh come around, then he noticed yuh car. Ah know he didn't want yuh tuh see him like that. Man it was weird, he was in another zone. Ah'm still worried about him. Ah'd like tuh have him checked out before we leave for church."

Johnny got out of the car and checked his watch as he and Malcolm walked toward the front porch. "Well, it's just a little after 8:00. I promised Julia I'd be back before 9:00. We're due at my mother's for breakfast. I dropped everything when you called and after what you told me, I'm very worried."

Both men stopped at the base of the steps. Johnny pushed his suit jacket back and placed his right hand in his pant's pocket. Malcolm leaned against the banister post.

"Johnny, it was really bad. At one point Ah thought Dad had a stroke. He just came around minutes before yuh arrived. Hopefully, he's taking a warm shower and will look and feel even better. Ah know he needs tuh be checked by a doctor.

"Then why don't we get a doctor out here? Do you think Dad will object if I call the clinic and have a doctor pick up his chart and whatever emergency medication he might need and spend the day with him?"

"You can do that?"

"C'mon man, I'm the Founder and Chief Executive Officer at the clinic. Besides, I won't be using on duty staff. I'll ask an off duty physician to do me a favor. Favors go a long way, you know what I mean?"

"Yeah man, why don't we go in the house? Ah think yuh're on tuh something and Dad might just agree if you tell him. Ah've been with him all his life, so he just pushes me around, but you, Johnny, he wants tuh please yuh. He'll do just about anything yuh ask him tuh do. Yuh saw how he got up off that porch didn't yuh?"

Johnny nodded and followed Malcolm up the steps. When they reached the kitchen Theresa had finished preparing breakfast and Thea was sitting at the dinette table.

"Johnny, you remember my wife?"

Johnny smiled, and Malcolm led him closer to Theresa. "Theresa? Yes I met you at church just before my Aunt Sarah's wedding."

"That's right. How are yuh this morning?" Theresa asked.

"I'm fine and I hope you are too."

Theresa nodded and smiled.

Malcolm caught Johnny's eye and he gave Theresa a tiny bow before glancing over his shoulder when his father entered the room. "Would you excuse me?" Johnny said.

Theresa's eyes shifted over at Reverend Oliver and back at Malcolm and Johnny. Her lips formed a gentle smile and she nodded her head again. Thea stood when she realized her husband was standing near her.

"Miss Thea, may Malcolm and I have a few words with Dad? We'd like to go in the den."

Owen rubbed Thea's hands but, anxiety lines still etched her face. Malcolm walked back to his mother and wrapped his arms around her. "Don't worry.

We just want tuh make sure Dad is okay. Johnny wants his permission tuh have a doctor from the clinic spend the day with him to monitor his health."

Thea nodded her head and smiled.

Malcolm hurried down the hall, entering the den with an apologetic expression on his face. "Ah'm sorry," he whispered as he pulled the desk chair next to his father's lounge chair. Johnny was standing with his arms crossed and leaning against the window sill.

"Not a problem," Johnny said. "Malcolm, would you speak first?"

Malcolm glanced up at Johnny. *My God he's doing it tuh me again. Why is it that he always wants me tuh look like the fool. This was his idea. He knows Dad will listen tuh him. Ah told him that!* He rubbed his hands together and brought them to his lips like he was praying; he was nervous and felt a bit shaky, but he began to speak. "Well Dad . . . Johnny and I were worried about yuh. We know the stress yuh must be feeling . . . ugh . . . about . . . tuhday's church event. Yuh know . . . and after yuh experience last night . . . well . . . ugh . . .we . . . ugh . . ."

"Dad, what Malcolm is trying to say is we want to have a doctor examine you this morning."

"Ah'm okay. Ah don't need tuh see the doctor. Ah had a bad night, that's all." Reverend Oliver's voice carried a slight slur, and he demonstrated an adamant attitude.

Malcolm stood, so psychologically he'd feel at the same level as Johnny. *It's just Johnny's way. He didn't mean any harm. He was giving me the chance tuh show our father how we were going tuh help him.*

"Dad, you know I've loved you all of my life. I can't bear to lose you now. Malcolm and I have had more difficulties than I care to count, but we finally found each other. He told me about your dangerous and anxious night and that's why he called me."

"Yeah Dad, now Johnny wants tuh have a doctor from the clinic come here tuh examine yuh. And that's not all ... he's having the doctor stay with you all day, even while yuh at church tuh make sure yuh okay," Malcolm spoke up with the same kind of confidence Johnny had.

"Johnny, Ah don't need a doctor!" Reverend Oliver took a deep breath and stared at him.

"Yes you do Dad. I have to return to my wife and mother. They're waiting for me to have breakfast with them. I already called for the doctor and he's on his way. His name is Dr. Michael Clayton. He's about our age.

He'll probably give you medication to reduce your anxiety and he'll keep a close watch on your pressure."

Malcolm stepped in front of Johnny and in his father direct view. "Well Dad, maybe yuh don't, but the rest of us do. Yuh been so sick, we need yuh tuh have a doctor with yuh so we'll have peace of mind. Please don't give us a hard time."

Reverend Oliver slumped back in his chair. "My Lord, everyone is always overpowering me. Okay, Okay, Ah'll go along with what yuh ask. Ah don't want anyone worrying about me."

"Thank yuh Dad." Malcolm turned and shook Johnny's hand. "Thank yuh Johnny."

Johnny reached down and hugged Reverend Oliver. "Thanks Dad. I have to leave now."

"Dad Ah'm gonna ask Mama tuh come in and yuh can tell her about Dr. Clayton while Ah walk Johnny tuh his car," Malcolm said.

"I'll see you in church, Dad," Johnny said as he and Malcolm left the room.

Johnny waited at the front door until Thea arrived at the den. "I'll see you later Miss Thea. And Malcolm, tell your wife it was nice seeing her again."

"Thank you for coming, Johnny," Thea said.

Johnny smiled, opened the screen door and walked toward his car. As soon as he was seated in the driver's seat he closed the car door and threw his head against the headrest. Malcolm placed his hand on the open window frame and bent over to see Johnny's face while he spoke.

"You didn't tell me Dr. Clayton was on his way," Malcolm whispered.

"He's not. He lives over near the clinic. I called him before I left home and asked if he could help me out today and he said he would. I told him I'd call him back around 9:00. So look for him around 9:30. I just wanted Dad to believe he was on his way so he'd think he didn't have a choice."

"Damn, Johnny. Yuh know him better than me." Malcolm slapped his hand against the door frame and laughed out loud.

"No man, it's just human nature. Thanks again for calling me. I have to leave. Julia is waiting for me. I'll see you at church."

"Thanks man." Malcolm watched him drive away.

Johnny smiled and waved.

* * *

When Johnny and Julia arrived at Elizabeth and Nat's home, there were four cars in the driveway, two belonged to his parents, one to his grandfather and the other belonged to Stephen and Sarah. Johnny didn't pull into the driveway, but left his car on the side of Collins Road. He opened the car door and took hold of Julia's hand, holding it until he reached his mother's front door.

"Hello my favorite nephew and his wife," Sarah sang out as she held her arms wide open.

"Yes, Aunt Sarah, I'm your only nephew," Johnny replied. He and Julia greeted her and Stephen, and the four of them walked into the dining room together.

Johnny held his hands up high and waved. "Good morning everyone," he called out. "I'm sorry we're late. I hope we didn't hold you all up." He walked over and kissed his mother's cheek and shook Nat's hand. Then he gave his grandfather a gentlemen's bow and his grandmother received a loving hug.

"I love you Gram'ma." He squeezed her a little tighter and rocked her from side to side.

"If yuh don't turn me loose yuh won't have a gram'ma," Loretha said and she smacked at his arms.

Elizabeth began clanging a butter knife against a glass until she got everyone's attention. "Nat has already blessed the food and it's getting cold. Ah don't know about y'all, but Ah'm gonna fix my plate."

* * *

Malcolm stood on his parents' front porch and waited for Dr. Clayton. His mother was sitting in the den with his father, while his wife was dressing for church. The draping branches of the weeping willow tree danced on the morning breeze, while the sun cast flickering shadows across the driveway.

Mama wouldn't let Dad sit under her tree because she said he was a sinful man. But Ah sat under her tree, and Ah'm a sinful man, too. Ah'll never tell Theresa about my relationship with Randy, and Ah really don't have to . . . it's over. Thank God, Ah haven't heard from him since work on Friday. If he takes the medication, it's probably gonna take a couple of weeks before it starts to work on him. By that time he should be in the new office. We'll talk on the phone and catch up with each other on weekends and at special events, but at least we'll act like normal men. Ah'll call him later this afternoon and see how he's doing.

Malcolm looked up and a white medium sized car turned into the driveway. He adjusted his posture and waited for it to come to a stop. "Hello,

Dr. Clayton?"

"Yes . . . is this the home of Reverend Owen Oliver?"

"Yes." Malcolm stood back while the doctor got out of his car and they greeted each other with a handshake. "Ah'm Malcolm Oliver, Reverend Oliver is my father. He's been waiting for yuh."

Dr. Clayton reached in the car for Reverend Oliver's medical folder and his medical bag. "Mr. Turner said Reverend Oliver was his father. Is he your brother?"

Malcolm continued to lead the way into the house and turned once to look at Dr. Clayton. He smiled. "Yes, Reverend Oliver is our father and Ah'll introduce yuh tuh him. Ah know my wife and mother will want tuh meet yuh, but Ah believe they're still dressing for church."

Dr. Clayton was a tall handsomely built man with a pleasant smile. Malcolm admired his confidence and his take charge personality. Johnny knew he was the right person to confront his father's combative attitude. When the men reached the den, Reverend Oliver was reclined in his chair and appeared to be asleep. Malcolm walked over and rubbed the back of his hand to get his attention. "Dad . . . Dad," he whispered.

Reverend Oliver opened his eyes.

"This is the Dr. Clayton Johnny told yuh about."

"How do you do? Ah hope my sons didn't have you come out here for nothing." Reverend Oliver was only in a light sleep. The slightest sound or touch brought him to full attention.

"Well, it's not a problem. I'm happy to help out whenever I can. The first thing I'd like to do is take your blood pressure. I see you were just released from the hospital." Dr. Clayton smiled at Reverend Oliver, as he set the pressure cuff in place and using his stethoscope took the necessary reading.

"Reverend Oliver . . . your blood pressure is reading in a dangerous range. Are you taking your medication?"

"Yes, Ah take it right on time," Reverend Oliver replied.

"It says here you were discharged from the hospital only two days ago. If we can't get your pressure down and stabilized, you will have to be re-admitted."

"No, not now, Ah have tuh do something very important today. After that, if I have to, I'll go back tuh the hospital," Reverend Oliver looked at Malcolm with pleading eyes.

"Reverend Oliver is there something bothering you? Extreme stress is sometimes responsible for an elevated pressure. Sometimes it helps to talk about it."

"Dad . . . tell him. Yuh may as well, yuh gonna talk about it later anyway. It might help yuh tuh talk about it now," Malcolm said.

Malcolm and Reverend Oliver turned toward the sounds of the women coming down the hall. "Excuse me," Malcolm said as he stepped out of the room.

"Mama, Theresa, the doctor is here. May we have a few minutes alone? I'll come for yuh as soon as he's finish examining Dad. Okay?"

"Sure, we'll wait in the kitchen," Thea replied. She looked over her shoulder as she and Theresa walked away and Malcolm was still standing at the door to the den.

Malcolm smiled at the women again and returned to the den.

The door was slowly closed and Malcolm stood against it watching as his father finished telling Dr. Clayton the circumstances of his employer's existence and the years that followed.

"I certainly understand how that could be the cause of your anxiety, and you have an arduous task before you today. I do believe as long as this issue lingers over you, you'll continue to struggle with controlling your pressure."

Malcolm walked over and stood next to his father's chair and Dr Clayton looked up at him. "Ah'm happy our father explained his problem and I agree, Ah'm sure it's the culprit to his failing health."

Dr. Clayton turned his attention back to Reverend Oliver. "Absolutely . . . now, since you're all ready being treated very aggressively to control your blood pressure, I'd like to treat your elevated stress level by starting you on anti-anxiety medication. It will make you a little tired, but you'll be able to function. I'll monitor you blood pressure and if we can't get it within a safe level you will have to return to the hospital."

Dr. Clayton locked eyes with Reverend Oliver and it was evident to Malcolm, the doctor didn't like the visual response he received from his father. "Dad . . . we all love you. We'll do what we have tuh do tuh keep yuh safe. We want yuh tuh go tuh the church today. Maybe yuh can't go for the entire service, but if yuh relax and get yuh pressure under control Dr. Clayton and I will make sure yuh get there. But, Dad, if yuh pressure is too high, we're not gonna have yuh risk yuh life so yuh can say a few words. You will have tuh return tuh the hospital." Malcolm stared at his father causing him to close his eyes, clench his lips and nod his head.

"Okay . . . Reverend Oliver, I want to give you an injection to quickly get medication into your system. I'm only giving you half the dose I'd give you if you were in the hospital because I know you want to go to church, but it's enough to make you feel sleepy. I want you to rest. I'll monitor your pressure and if all goes well, your son and I will get you to the church on time."

"All right Doc, Ah'm yours," Reverend Oliver said as he watched Dr. Clayton prepare the injection.

Malcolm helped him remove his shirt and hung it up in the closet. "Dad . . . how about arriving at church for Alter Call? That should be around 1:00 o'clock. Yuh could go tuh the church at 12:30 and wait in the car. Johnny can come out and let us know when it's time for you tuh come in."

"That's a great idea. It's almost 10:00 o'clock now. That would give you about two and a half hours to rest and to get your pressure under control . . . how about it Reverend Oliver?" Dr. Clayton asked as he was giving him the injection.

"Whatever yuh say as long as Ah get there." He rested his head back on the chair.

Dr. Clayton began wrapping the presser cuff around his arm. "I'd like to keep this on your arm so I can check on you while you're resting."

Reverend Oliver nodded his head.

Malcolm smiled. "Thanks a lot Dr. Clayton. May Ah bring yuh anything? Have yuh had yuh breakfast? Would yuh like a cup of coffee?"

"No, I'm fine. I'll come to the kitchen in a minute," Dr. Clayton said.

"All right, Ah'm going tuh call Johnny now; Ah want tuh catch him at his mother's house."

* * *

When Malcolm entered the kitchen Thea eased herself from her chair at the dinette table. She pressed her praying hands to her lips and waited for him to give her acceptable news.

"Mama, Dad's okay. Dr. Clayton will be in soon tuh explain everything, and yuh can listen while Ah call Johnny. Ah need tuh catch him before he leaves his mother's house."

* * *

"Hello Mr. Baker, this is Malcolm Oliver. May Ah speak with Johnny?"

"Sure, Malcolm, hold on a minute," Nat said and he placed the telephone down on the table.

A few moments later Johnny picked up the phone. "Hello Malcolm is everything all right?" Johnny placed his finger in his other ear to filter out the background noise from his family. "Thank God I called the doctor." He was quiet as he listened to all Malcolm had to say. "Okay man, 12:30, now if the doctor still believes it's too stressful for him, or if he decides he should return to the hospital, will you drive up to the church and let me know?" Johnny nodded his head as he listened to Malcolm. "Okay, man, I'm praying all goes well and I'll see you and Dad during Alter Call, so long for now." Johnny rested against the wall and massaged his eyes with his thumb and forefingers. *I want to go to him. I know Malcolm doesn't need me, but I want to be with him. Maybe if I call him back and let him know I'm coming. I'll only stay a few minutes. Julia can ride up to the church with Mama and Nat.* The telephone at the Oliver residence only rang once before Malcolm picked it up. "Hey man, may I stop by before I go to the church?"

"Sure," Malcolm said.

"Thanks," Johnny said before hanging up the phone.

Johnny returned to the dining room and spoke quietly with Julia before asking for everyone's attention. "Okay family, I have a bit of news. Reverend Oliver is still very ill, but he insisted on being at church today. I have a doctor from the clinic staying with him, and he tells me he is not well enough to attend church, but . . ." He held up his hands to tell them the rest, but they had already determined what he was going to say.

Sarah let out the first set of whining child-like moans; Elizabeth covered her mouth with her hands trying to hide her disappointment, while Nat wrapped his arms around her; Reverend Turner clamped his lips into a frown and looked up at the ceiling. Loretha, Julia and Stephen glanced around at the others and back at Johnny.

"Please, may I continue?" Johnny said in a raised voice. Everyone focused on him. "Thank you. Now, Reverend Oliver continues to insist on confessing today. He refuses to return to the hospital until he does. Dr. Clayton is from the clinic, and he has sedated him. Now, if his pressure is under control by 12:30 this afternoon, he will come to the church for Alter Call, confess, and ask for prayer. The doctor will remain with him at all times."

Julia hurried to his side. "Don't worry Johnny. I want you to go to your father. I can ride to church with your mother. I'll save you a seat."

"Thank you honey, I'll see you at church."

✳ ✳ ✳

Johnny reached Reverend Oliver's front door just as Theresa and Thea were leaving for church.

"How's he doing Miss Thea?"

"He's restin' peacefully. Malcolm and Dr. Clayton are sittin' in the kitchen having coffee. Go on in. Ah believe they're waitin' for yuh. "

"I'll see you in church," Johnny said as he nodded an acknowledgement toward Theresa."

"See yuh," Theresa said.

Thea nodded as she and Theresa stepped down from the porch.

Johnny entered the house and walked to the kitchen. "Hi Malcolm, okay Doc, so how's he doing?"

"C'mon Johnny, sit. You look like you need a sedative," Dr Clayton said.

"No, I can't sit. I just came by to see Dad. How is he?" Johnny placed both hands on the back of the chair.

"Your father is doing better. His pressure is down somewhat, but he's only been sleep an hour. There is no doubt, that this confession and his perception of the community's reaction to it, is the cause of his extreme stress, and that stress is affecting his pressure. He really needs this confession, but worrying about it could cause him to have a stroke, and even take his life."

"C'mon Johnny, he's asleep, but yuh can see him." Malcolm stood and led the way down the hall.

"Is it okay Doc?" Johnny asked.

"Sure, just don't wake him."

Malcolm opened the door and he and Johnny stepped in the den. Johnny pinched his eyes at the bridge of his nose, where his tear ducts were located. Seeing his father in a dead sleep, in his t-shirt and with a pressure cuff around his arm was alarming. Malcolm placed his arm around his shoulder and they left the room.

"Doc, are you sure he's gonna be all right? He really looks bad," Johnny said.

"Johnny, the medication will begin to wear thin in another hour. I believe he'll be fine for church. His blood pressure may stabilize on its own after he has his confession. We have to wait and see, but I'm prepared to act aggressively to protect him and if needed, he'll be back in the hospital before he has a chance to object."

The men returned to the kitchen and sat around the dinette table.

"Oh God," Johnny said. "I wish I could have some of whatever it is you gave my father. I believe Malcolm and I have had a rough three weeks."

"Well, I have an extra cuff in my bag. I can check your pressure. The both of you are your father's sons," Dr. Clayton said and smiled.

"Man, I like the way you put that, but some other time. I don't need another thing to worry about," Johnny said. He began walking toward the door.

Malcolm held up both hands. "No thanks man, maybe next time."

"I have to go. I'll meet you in the parking lot at 12:30 and we'll sit in the back of the church until the time comes. I'll see you later." Johnny raised his right hand, but stopped when Dr. Clayton began speaking.

"Now hear me. If his pressure is not good we will not be at the church. I will have to have him readmitted into the hospital," Dr. Clayton warned.

"I understand," Johnny said.

Malcolm nodded his head.

Chapter 18

Reverend Oliver could hear Malcolm calling him in a voice so far away it sounded like a whispering song. Then he felt a hand rocking his arm and the rocking turned to a shaking; Malcolm's clear baritone voice call out, "Dad, it's time tuh wake up."

"Yes Malcolm, Ah'm awake."

"Do you want tuh get ready tuh go tuh church?" He stood over his father looking down at him.

"Yes . . . yes, Malcolm."

Dr Clayton was removing the pressure cuff from his arm. "You're going to be a little groggy, but your son has prepared a fresh cup of coffee for you. A little caffeine will help you wake up, but the anti-anxiety medication will continue to reduce your stress for at least another four hours. You're going to feel clumsy and sluggish most of the day, so you'll have to take it easy. So far your blood pressure is in the high, normal range. So let's try to remain calm."

"Is he ready tuh stand, Dr Clayton?"

"How about it, are you ready? I'll stand on one side and Malcolm on the other. We'll walk with you to the kitchen and you can have your coffee."

Reverend Oliver took a deep breath and pulled the lever, placing the chair in an upright position. He bent forward and used his arms to help lift himself up. "Okay . . . stand close, but don't hold me. Ah'll lean on yuh if Ah need tuh," Reverend Oliver whispered as he pulled himself to a standing position.

"Now, just stand still a second. Do you feel dizzy?" Dr. Clayton asked.

"No. Ah just feel tired."

"Okay let's start walking to the kitchen," Dr. Clayton said. "I'm going to walk in front. You can put your hands on my shoulders if you need to and Malcolm will walk behind you."

"Ah feel fine. Ah believe Ah'm gonna be all right," Reverend Oliver announced. He stood tall and his stride was slow and steady. When he reached the kitchen, he eased himself into the chair.

"Here's yuh coffee Dad. Ah hate tuh rush yuh, but we only have thirty minutes before we have tuh meet Johnny at Concord."

Reverend Oliver sipped his coffee and watched Malcolm leave the kitchen and return a few moments later, dressed in his suit jacket and adjusting his tie. "Ah just need tuh see which pants yuh're wearing. Ah'll be back in a minute," Malcolm said. He returned with the matching brown suit jacket, tie, and a fresh pale yellow shirt. "Did yuh finish yuh coffee?"

Reverend Oliver glanced at Dr. Clayton and smiled. "He's really keeping me on schedule."

"While yuh were asleep Johnny was here and he wants tuh meet yuh in the parking lot at 12:30," Malcolm said. He stood waiting for his father's response.

"Johnny was here again? We better get started. Ah don't want tuh be late." Reverend Oliver reached for Malcolm to hand him his shirt.

Malcolm smiled, removed the shirt from the hanger and handed it to him. "We should have kept Johnny here with us. Dad really listens tuh him," Malcolm said.

Dr. Clayton returned Malcolm's smile. "I see what you mean."

"Okay men, Ah'm going tuh the bathroom, Ah feel strong, just a little tired. Ah believe Ah can do this alone. Ah'll leave the door open," Reverend Oliver announced.

"Okay, that's the way I want you to sound, but Malcolm, would you stand outside the bathroom door?"

"Sure," Malcolm responded.

"Ah'm ready . . . Ah just need my jacket." The bathroom door pulled open wide and Reverend Oliver stepped out with his shirt tucked in his pants, and his tie neatly arranged. He walked pass Malcolm and glanced back, then returned to the kitchen and lifted his jacket off the hanger. His steps were guarded, but the three men left the house, and were on their way to the church.

* * *

The Sunday morning service at the Concord Baptist church opened with a soft musical prelude by Thea Oliver. The order of service was followed according to the program and none of the family members thought it unusual that Reverend Turner chose to preach his sermon on the topic of forgiveness.

"People, we will read from Matthew 18 verse 21 to 35." He waited until those who wanted to read along with him had found their place.

Then Peter came tuh Jesus and asked, "Lord, how many times shall Ah forgive my brother when he sins against me? Up tuh seven times?"

Jesus answered, "Ah tell yuh, not seven times, but seventy-seven times."

Matthew 18:21-22

Reverend Turner continued to read the verses along with the congregation, only to stop to emphasize the reading. "Our Lord likened an earthly king to the kingdom of heaven." He placed both hands on the podium and leaned forward like he was ready to leap from the pulpit. "The Lord likened him tuh the kingdom of heaven because he was merciful. Now, this king called on his servant when he couldn't pay his debt. The servant begged for more time and fell down to worship the king. But, instead of selling his wife, children, and worldly belongings, the king forgave him." Reverend Turner raised one hand and jumped up. "Ah said, he forgave his debt. He was likened tuh the kingdom of heaven because he was a merciful king. People, he forgave the servant." Reverend Oliver strutted across the pulpit and wiped his face with his handkerchief.

Thea was intrigued by Reverend Turner's sermon. She had heard the Parable before and read the verses in Matthew. She knew the moral he was trying to communicate. She nodded her head and shouted, "Amen," several times to reinforce his preaching.

"Well . . . well . . . well," Reverend Turner continued. "Now, that same servant went out and found a fellow servant. 'Pay me that thou owest,' the first servant said." Reverent Turner wiped the perspiration from his face and leaned on the podium shaking his head. "How 'bout that, folks? The first servant had his fellow-servant at his feet, begging for more time. 'Pay me that thou owest' or go tuh prison; and the first servant had his fellow-servant thrown in prison." Reverend Turner was momentarily quiet, walking across the pulpit shaking his head. "Well . . . well . . . well . . . people, when his king found out what the first servant had done he called him a 'wicked man'." Reverend Turner shook his head, stepped from behind the podium and shouted, "He was a wicked man!" He stomped his foot and pointed his finger at the congregation. "He was reminded how mercy had been bestowed on him and his debt cancelled." Reverend Turner balled up his fist and banged it down on the podium. "In anger!" he yelled out. "The merciful king yelled out in anger and turned the unmerciful servant over tuh the jailer tuh be tortured until his former debt was paid."

Thea led the congregation shouting, "Amen." She turned and watched

Johnny hurrying down the center isle of the church and out the door. Her eyes shifted back to Reverend Turner who seemed to be hung up on his next word as his eyes latched on to Johnny.

"Ugh . . . ugh . . . now people . . . ugh . . . verse Matthew 18 verse 35 tells us . . . This is how my Heavenly Father will treat each of yuh unless yuh forgive yuh brother from yuh heart." He wiped his face with his handkerchief again and turned the pages of his Bible. "Folks, Ah want yuh tuh stand and repeat those words after me. Ah want yuh tuh say them loud. Raise yuh hands and speak from yuh heart."

"This is how my Heavenly Father will treat each of yuh unless . . ." Reverend Turner raised his arms and shouted. The congregation raised their arms and shouted, repeating after him.

"You forgive yuh brother from yuh heart," he raised his hand and shouted even louder and the congregation shouted more passionately.

"Now while Ah have yuh all standing, Ah would like tuh read another scripture. When Ah finish Ah want yuh tuh feel free tuh move about the church and hug each other. Tell each other, 'God loves yuh and will forgive yuh'."

Reverend Turner continued to hold his arms up as he spoke. "Yes people, Ephesians 4:32 tells us . . . 'Be kind and compassionate to one another, forgiving each other, just as in Christ God forgave you.' Oh thank yuh Lord for Yuh sacred words."

Thea took it upon herself to play an upbeat version of 'What a Friend We Have in Jesus' on the piano. The church was busy with people moving about telling each other God loved them and forgave them. They hugged and smiled and laughed then moved on to the next person. Some remained in their pews while others worked their way to the other side of the church. Johnny, Reverend Oliver, Dr, Clayton and Malcolm had taken seats in the last pew at the back of the church.

After a few minutes Reverend Turner nodded for Thea to begin playing the 'invitational hymn' and she struck the chords leading up to "Pass Me Not O' Gentle Savior." The congregation began to settle down and return to their seats. Reverend Turner made a smooth transition from his sermon to Altar Call as he spread his arm wide and extended an invitation to the congregation, for anyone wanting to join the church. The choir sang softly and everyone waited to see who would come forward.

"Anyone in need of special prayer . . ." he spread his arms out again. The draping sleeves of his robe fanned out like the wings of an angle. "Please come forward." He watched as Johnny, Reverend Oliver and Malcolm stood and walked from between the pews. Johnny and Malcolm stood shoulder to shoulder as they followed their father down the aisle. Thea stood from the piano and sat on the pew next to Theresa. The congregation rumbled with inquisitive noise; heads turned and hands covered their mouths as they whispered and shushed each other.

Reverend Oliver spoke quietly to Deacon Jordan before turning to speak to the congregation. "I hope yuh can hear me, Ah can't speak loud because my jaw is wired."

The spontaneous whispering and shushing broke out again. Malcolm tapped his father on the shoulder, while Johnny handed him the microphone.

"Thank you," Reverend Oliver said. The congregation was quiet enough to hear a fly landing on the head of the microphone. "Ah just have a few words tuh say, but first Ah would like tuh thank yuh all for the prayers and support yuh've given my family. Now Ah stand here asking yuh tuh continue tuh pray for us and tuh forgive me for what Ah'm about tuh tell yuh." He glanced around at Malcolm and then at Johnny. "Yuh see these two young men standing with me. Most of yuh know them, but yuh didn't know . . . they're both my sons."

All the deacons stood, Elizabeth stood, and Reverend Turner stepped down from the pulpit and wringed his hands nervously. Thea and Loretha stood. The congregation cried out, some yelled, "No, not you!" Others moaned, some waved their hands

"It's a terrible thing tuh say. Some of yuh were too young or weren't born, but many of yuh remember. Yes . . . Johnny Turner is my son. Ah'm the man who stole his mother's innocence all those years ago. Ah'm stepping down as the assistant pastor of the Concord Baptist Church, effective immediately. Ah only ask that yuh forgive me and continue tuh pray for me."

Johnny wrapped his arms around Reverend Oliver. "I love you, Dad."

Malcolm wrapped his arms around Johnny and his father. "Ah love both of yuh."

Tears rolled down Reverend Oliver's cheeks and he raised his head when he heard Reverend Turner's voice.

"Elizabeth is my daughter. Thirty-six years ago Ah let her down when she needed me most. Ah knew she was an innocent child, and Ah was unmerciful tuh her suffering. It was within my power to love and support her and Johnny, and even after knowing she had been raped, Ah continued tuh judge her."

The congregation was quiet. Stunned, as though everyone was in a place between, the way things were and their present reality, then the time warp snapped everyone forward and the church screamed out.

"What! Not you too, Reverend Turner?" A lady yelled out from the middle of the church.

"Oh Lord, we're all in need of prayer," another person screamed out.

The church rumbled with even louder moans and words.

"God loves yuh and will forgive yuh. That's what the Bible teaches us," a man sang out.

Elizabeth went to her father and wrapped her arms around his neck while Thea rushed to her husband's side. Malcolm and Johnny moved back while Reverend Oliver placed his arm around her waist.

Elizabeth stood to the side and held her father's hand. "For the past thirty-six years Ah've been like the unmerciful servant," Reverend Turner continued speaking, "Ah've been in the prison of my mind, tormented by my jailer, myself. Tuhday, Ah want my debt tuh be paid. Effective immediately, Ah will be stepping down as the pastor. Please forgive me and pray for me, and my family."

Loretha went to her husband and kissed him on his cheek. They gazed at each other, and smiled an understanding and supporting smile.

Sarah couldn't be left out. She left Stephen sitting on the pew and strutted down the isle to be with her father. She kissed him and stood next to her mother.

Johnny grabbed his grandfather's hand to shake it, "Thank you Grandfather. I give my honor to you, sir." Tears flooded Reverend Turner's eyes and poured down his face as they hugged. "Ah love yuh, Johnny."

The congregation was still in an uproar. "God loves yuh and we forgive yuh Reverend Turner and Reverend Oliver," a lady shouted.

"We love y'all, we forgive y'all. Please don't leave us," a man called out.

"Please, please, please," someone else screamed.

"No! No! We love and forgive yuh. Yuh taught us tuh forgive."

Deacon Jordan held his arm high waving them to the congregation to regain order. Deacon Roberts and Tatum stood on the left and right side of the church waving their arms.

"Now folks, let's settle down we got some praying tuh do. May Ah ask the family to return to their seats?" Deacon Jordan said. "Please folks, kindly return tuh yuh seats.

Finally, everyone was back at their seats. Johnny looked back at Dr. Clayton and gave him a smile. Malcolm retrieved two folding chairs from the trustee room and placed them in front of the pulpit for his father and Reverend Turner. He didn't want his father standing for a long period. Reverend Turner and Reverend Oliver sat in front of the pulpit, facing the congregation, with their heads humbly bowed. Reverend Turner beckoned and then whispered to Deacon Jordan.

The rumbling and mumbling of the congregation slowly diminished until the church was still and quiet, except for the weeping and sniffling of some of the members.

Deacon Jordan whispered to Deacon Bains and he turned to look directly at Reverend Turner. He was an elderly man and had stepped down as chairman of the Deacon Board twenty years earlier.

Reverend Turner remembered the conversation they had thirty-six years earlier about Elizabeth. *Ah just want yuh tuh know most of the deacons are uncomfortable wit' yuh fer not letting 'Lizabeth come home. 'Lizabeth is yuh daughter; she's a good girl. Yuh knew she was raped just like everyone else.* He wanted him to lead the prayer. Deacon Bains was eighty-five years old, the most worthy and knowledgeable of all the deacons.

Deacon Jordan asked Deacon Bains to lead the prayer. The other eight deacons came forward, and then the families. Next, the entire church family stood and held hands and no one broke the prayer circle that spread around the entire church.

Reverend Turner and Reverend Oliver knelt on one knee and supported themselves by leaning on the chairs. Deacon Bains placed his hands on the shoulders of the ministers. The two deacons at each end of the prayer circle rested their hands on Deacon Bains' shoulders. He spoke up as loud as he could as he began to pray.

"Dear Lord, Our Merciful Father. We come humbly askin' dat yuh hear our prayer. Yuh faithful servants have sinned against yuh, yuh church, yuh word and yuh followers. We is all sinners and we'll not pass judgment, but dese men have so named demselves as sinners and is askin' fer yuh mercy. Hear our prayer ol' Lord and grant 'em mercy. We're but mortals who love yuh, Lord. Fergive our brothers and lighten da load dat has been placed on their heart all dese years. Help those of us who be needin' consolin' tuh hear yuh word again. 'Be kind and compassionate tuh one another, fergivin' each other, just as in Christ God fergave us' . . . Merciful Lord, remove the jailer in dey mind and allow 'em tuh walk away from the prison dey done created fer demselves. Ah thank yuh Merciful Father fer yuh words tuh the faithful. Brothers and sistahs, the Father wants me tuh remind yuh as he has written in Galatians 6:1. He put it in mah head tuh tell yuh the verse; 'Brothers, if someone is caught in sin, you who are spiritual should restore him gently. But watch yuhself, or yuh also may be tempted.'."

"Oh Merciful Father, we're askin' yuh restoration of the body and mind. Fer when a mind is heavy with guilt, the body be toting a mighty weight and it's only through prayer dat healin' can take place. We thank yuh Merciful Father fer all blessin' we've asked fer and received in Jesus' name. Amen . . . Amen . . . Amen."

Through out Deacon Bains' prayer the congregation spoke out with "Amen."

"Yes Lord, hear our prayer," someone in the congregation called out.

The congregation was extremely quiet as they returned to their seats. The only sounds heard were that of people shuffling along. Men and women held tissues and handkerchiefs, but they wept quietly and dabbed at their eyes and wiped their faces. They appeared to be stunned and lost; so much to absorb for their tiny community, and church.

❋ ❋ ❋

Reverend Turner followed Loretha to the vacant seat on the pew and Reverend Oliver sat with Malcolm and Theresa on the left side of the church.

Deacon Jordan remained standing at the front of the church and used the microphone to capture the attention of the congregation as soon as they continued to return to their seats. "In light of these developments, there will be an emergency meeting tuhnight at 6:00 o'clock. We are asking all church members tuh attend. Remember church, we're all in need of prayer."

The choir returned to the choir stand, while Thea played the closing hymn. Deacon Jordan closed out the service leading the church in the Benediction.

Some of the church folk had all ready decided whom they would go to first and they sprang from the pews and crowded Reverend Oliver or Reverend Turner. Others remained standing, waiting for their turn. No one left the church and Dr. Clayton remained seated in the last pew.

Nat walked across the front of the church and weaved his way between the hordes of people. "Reverend Oliver."

Owen turned toward the sound of Nat's voice.

Nat smiled.

The men locked eyes and a bargain was struck. They shook hands, took a single head bow, and smiled before the connection was broken.

Elizabeth nervously watched Nat. Thea praised the Lord; of all men Nat Baker could and would forgive her husband. When Nat returned to Elizabeth, he kissed her on the forehead. They could relax knowing it was over.

After a while the congregation began to thin out and Dr. Clayton joined the Olivers in the front of the church. Reverend Oliver could feel the air in the sanctuary become fresher as he took several deep breaths. Some of the deacons and trustees had gathered to the side to develop a strategy for running the church without a minister. Suddenly, Mr. Davis, the head trustee asked if either one of them would reconsider, at least until they could find a replacement.

Reverend Oliver stood. "Over the years Ah had several offers to have my own church, but since that faithful day Ah've known Ah'm not worthy. Ah should've stepped down as the pastor's assistant a long time ago."

Thea squeezed his hand when he sat down. "Are we all ready tuh leave? This has been a very long day," Thea asked.

The Oliver's stood, but waited to hear Reverend Turner's response.

"Reverend Turner, won't yuh stay at least until we find a replacement?" Mr. Davis asked. He sat beside him on the pew and several of the trustees and deacons stood close by.

"Ah really hate leaving the church like this, without giving notice. This morning, when Ah came tuh church, Ah didn't come here tuh resign. In this morning's sermon Ah was trying tuh prepare the congregation tuh forgive Reverend Oliver. Then, the Lord pulled me from the pulpit and told me Ah was no longer worthy. Ah've been the minister at Concord for more than forty years. The Lord put me there and he took me away. Ah must obey the Lord. Ah'm a member of this church and Ah will always be a worker, but not in the pulpit."

All of the deacons and trustees turned to each other. They nodded and smiled. "We understand," Mr. Davis said.

The Olivers and Dr. Clayton walked from the church. Johnny and Julia followed them. "Dad, Miss Thea . . . have you ever met my wife, Julia? Miss Thea I believe you met her at Sarah's wedding reception."

"Yes we've met. It's nice seeing yuh again," Thea said and she smiled.

Julia smiled.

"Dad, this is my wife, Julia."

"It's very nice to meet you, sir." Julia held out her hand to shake his.

Reverend Oliver took hold of her hand by the tips of her fingers. "It's a pleasure meeting you."

"I think you've met everyone else. Oh, Dr. Clayton, is a friend of mine from the clinic."

"Hello Dr. Clayton," Julia said as she smiled.

"Hello, Mrs. Turner."

"Dad you look so much better. How's he doing Doc?" Johnny held Julia's hand as he spoke.

"I have to examine him as soon as he gets back to his home. Call the house in twenty minutes."

* * *

Reverend Oliver, Malcolm and Dr. Clayton walked to the den for another blood pressure check. Malcolm stood tall holding his father's suit jacket, shirt and tie and waited for the results.

"All right, that's much better, especially after a crazy day. 140 over 90, that's not great, but it's not in the danger zone. You need to have a meal, and then you need to rest. You'll continue to need the anti-anxiety medication. I'm giving you some pills. Take one at 4:00 o'clock today. Then take one pill at 8:00 tomorrow morning and one at 8:00 in the evening. I'm giving you enough pills for three days and a prescription for more. I'd like to see you in the clinic tomorrow afternoon."

"Dad, that's great." Malcolm held out his hand to Dr. Clayton. "Thanks man, how can Ah pay yuh."

"Don't worry; your brother will get the bill. I'm going to speak with your mother while I wait for him to call." Dr. Clayton left the den and walked to the kitchen.

* * *

Thea and Theresa were sitting at the dinette table sipping ice tea and waiting for the results of the examination. Thea attempted to stand when she notice Dr. Clayton.

"No, sit." He sat at the table joining them.

"Would yuh like some ice tea?" Before he could answer Thea had turned up a glass from the tray and was filling it with the refreshing drink.

"Thank you Mrs. Oliver. In case you wondering, your husband is doing much better. His pressure is in the high normal range." He took a sip of his ice tea and set the glass back on the table. "I gave him some medication and a prescription. Your son and husband will explain that. I would like to see him at the clinic tomorrow, and I also want my nurse to teach you how to take a blood pressure then you only have to come to the clinic once a week. You can buy the cuff and stethoscope at the pharmacy."

"Thank yuh. Ah would really like tuh learn how tuh do that," Thea said.

The telephone rang and Theresa answered it. "It's for you Dr. Clayton. It's Johnny."

"Please excuse me," Dr. Clayton said.

It was the call Dr. Clayton was expecting from Johnny and he gave him an update on his father's condition.

* * *

Sarah sat on the sofa and snuggled close to Stephen, while Elizabeth sat close to Nat. Johnny held tight to Julia when they left the room. He wanted her near him when he called to speak to Dr. Clayton. Loretha threw a question across the room as she served fresh lemonade to Reverend Turner then the others. "Look at Johnny and Julia. When do yuh think they'll give me great grand children?"

"Ah'd like a few grandchildren. They can make them and Ah'll raise them. Yuh know how busy they are," Elizabeth said.

" 'Lizabeth . . . yuh want them to have babies and give them tuh you?" Loretha said.

"Sure, Mama and Ah'll raise them."

"Ah think yuh both lost it," Nat said as he laughed.

Everyone began to laugh including Reverend Turner. When Johnny and Julia returned to the sofa, they wanted to know what everyone was laughing about.

"They want you and Julia to have children so they can raise them. Y'all are the last hope for this family line, but yuh so busy. So Mama and my darling sister have volunteered tuh care for yuh unborn children," Sarah announced. "Ah'm laughing, but Mama and 'Lizabeth are serious."

Johnny kissed Julia on the forehead. "Well maybe one day we'll take you up on your offer, but not yet. We just got married."

Johnny stood leaving Julia sitting on the sofa. He walked over to his grandfather. "Julia and I have to leave soon. We have a plane to catch, but I want to thank you for opening up your heart and allowing the Lord to speak to you. I never understood what it was my mother loved about you until that moment in church. I saw a light in your eyes and all of my bad feelings of the past were gone. Suddenly, I saw what my mother knew was always there. I give my honor to you, sir. I'm happy to have you in my life."

Reverend Turner stood and he and Johnny shook hands again.

"Thank yuh Johnny, Yuh are the blessing in our lives," Loretha said.

"Julia and I have to leave now if we are to catch our flight. We have to return to the cottage to pick up our things and we will continue on from there, so let's say our so longs now.

* * *

Malcolm and his father stood at the same time when Dr. Clayton returned to the den. "It was a pleasure meeting you. I'm looking forward seeing you tomorrow."

"Thank yuh Dr. Clayton. Ah would've probably died tuhday if it weren't for you. May God bless yuh," Reverend Oliver said while giving him a hearty shake.

"Now don't forget the medicine."

"Ah won't."

"I'll be seeing you Malcolm."

"Sure thing, Ah really appreciated yuh giving up yuh time tuh help my family. Thanks again."

Malcolm walked him to the front door.

"You and your brother are remarkable, take care, man." Dr. Clayton left the house.

Malcolm stood at the door and watched as he drove from the driveway. *Randy,* he thought. *Ah think Ah'll call and check on him.* He walked back to the kitchen and picked up the telephone. He turned to his family. "Ah'm calling Randy to tell him Dad's doing fine. He was worried about him. Oh, he got a promotion, too." He dialed the number and looked back at Theresa and smiled. Randy sounded sleepy when he answered the phone. "Hey man, it's Malcolm. It almost 3:00 o'clock, Ah know yuh not just waking up."

"Hey Malcolm, how's yuh father?"

"Hey man everything great. Dad's so much better. Theresa and Ah will be home this evening. Ah hope you and Gail didn't celebrate tuh much."

"Yeah man. Ah came home from church and crashed. Man Ah want tuh thank yuh for turning me around."

"Ah love yuh man. Take care of yuh family. We'll see yuh when we get home. So-long." Malcolm hung up the phone and joined his family at the table.

Owen reached across the table and took hold of Thea's hand. "May Ah sit under yuh tree?"

Thea smiled. "Yes, Mr. Owen Oliver, you may sit under our 'dancing willow tree'."

* * *

Johnny and Julia drove pass the Concord Baptist Church, and then up the road for the next two miles to the place where the willow tree danced on the current of the late summer's wind. They waved at Owen and Thea Oliver as they turned into the yard.

Malcolm met Johnny and Julia just as their car came to a stop and Theresa stepped down from the front porch to greet them.

"We came to let you all know we were leaving," Johnny said.

"Thank yuh, Johnny. This has been one difficult ride, but we made it. That wouldn't have been possible without you." Malcolm extended his hand. "You and Julia have a safe trip home."

Johnny shook Malcolm's hand. "Thanks man and you and Theresa be careful on the highway too. Thanks for not giving up on me, man."

There weren't enough words for them to say everything they wanted to say, but just one glance in each other's eyes and all was said. They smiled and Malcolm shifted his eyes away.

Thea stood and called for everyone to join them under the large draping tree. It was like walking through a curtain of ribbons that flickered between shade and the bright afternoon sunlight. There was a large clearing in the center and the trunk had grown and twisted around itself, it was larger than Johnny's hug. Johnny remembered hiding behind the tree as a young boy; a silly thought crossed his mind, that maybe the tree would remember him. He smiled and shook his head.

Julia glanced up at him. "This tree must hold many secrets," she said.

"This tree knows me. It used to be my favorite hiding place," Johnny replied.

Owen stood with his arm around Thea. "Are you and Julia leaving now?"

"Yes Dad. We need to know you'll take care of yourself." Johnny turned his attention toward Thea. "You'll call me if he gives you a hard time about his health? I love him so much."

"Ah know Johnny. Yuh've loved him since yuh've known him."

"Yes ma'am."

Johnny and Julia hugged his father. "I love you too, Miss Thea. You take care of yourself." They hugged Thea and made their way from under the dancing willow tree.

"Hey Malcolm, now that Dad is better, the four of us can get together. We have a lot of catching up to do."

"Ah'd like that," Malcolm said.

Handshakes and hugs were exchanged and Johnny and Julia drove from the circular driveway, tooting the horn as they passed the large dancing willow tree and turning right onto Rehoboth Road.

ABOUT THE AUTHOR

Anita Ballard-Jones is a native of Brooklyn, New York. In her mid-twenties, she and her family relocated to Suffolk County, Long Island, New York. She has earned an Associate Degree in Early Childhood Education at the State University of New York (SUNY) in Farmingdale, and continued her studies in Elementary and Special Education, earning a Bachelor and Master's Degree from The C.W. Post Campus of Long Island University, in Greenvale, New York. Anita is retired from New York State after working twelve years as a teacher and twenty-one years as a Treatment Team Leader with children and adults having various forms of Development Disabilities. She is married, and she and her husband have six adult children and more than twenty-five grandchildren who have been very supportive in her endeavor as a writer. She believes her reader's feedback is important and welcomes their input. Her e-mail address is aballardjo@aol.com. You are also welcome to visit her at her website at www.AnitaBallard-Jones.com.

CPSIA information can be obtained at www.ICGtesting.com
Printed in the USA
LVOW04s1059241214

420153LV00036B/703/P